Lonesome Traveler

Also by WELDON HILL:

Onionhead

Rafe

The Long Summer of George Adams

Lonesome Traveler

by

WELDON HILL

DAVID McKAY COMPANY, INC.

New York

LONESOME TRAVELER

Library of Congress Catalog Card Number: 75-114740

MANUFACTURED IN THE UNITED STATES OF AMERICA

VAN REES PRESS   •   NEW YORK

To my mother

Lonesome Traveler

ONE

MORNINGS were still shivering cold with May just begun, but nothing like the winter mornings had been. He used to wake up cold, but now he was so cozy snug in his blanket cocoon that he wished it were Saturday and he could stay there awhile. But if wishes had been chigger bites, Clem Marlow would have scratched himself to a nubbin long ago. Besides, he was hungry, and nobody was fixing to bring him breakfast in bed. Or even cook him anything to eat in the kitchen.

Lying there on the army cot in the concrete-block milkhouse making smoke signals with his vaporous breath, he thought about the old man with the burros and covered wagon and wondered whereabouts he was. Clem had first seen him a couple of years ago on his way to Route 66. Then just last month he had read an article about him in the Sunday paper, and now he thought about the old man almost every morning.

School would be ending soon. He felt excited and a little scared about what he aimed to do when school was out. And worried somebody would try to stop him. Not the Nolans, he didn't think. At least not Della, but you could never tell about old Royce, especially when he was bombed, which was most of the time now, it seemed like. It was the faceless, nameless "authorities," though, that worried Clem the most.

1

There were just too many doggone social workers and judges that got paid for sticking their noses in other people's personal affairs. Still, come May, by grabs, he was going to cut out, him and old Duke and Pedro, and any peckerwood that got in their way was begging to be slugged.

But first he had to get up and finish the seventh grade, so he started a resigned countdown. Ten, nine, eight, seven . . . When he reached zero, he peeled off the blankets and sat up, dropping his big bare feet onto the old sheepskin he used for a bedside rug because that concrete floor was plain murder.

If it had been Saturday, he would have fired up the kerosene heater and crawled back in the blankets until the room warmed up a little, but there wasn't time for that luxury on a school morning. All he could do was hurry into his clothes and do some arm-flapping exercises to get his blood circulating. That was the big advantage of sleeping in long underwear instead of pajamas; he could put on his pants and shirt without having to strip and start from blue-naked scratch. He'd outgrown the long-johns even faster than his other clothes; they hit him just below the elbows and halfway up the shins.

Trying to see the bright side of things as he pulled on his Levis and the flannel shirt that left his wrists out in the cold, he considered how lucky it was that he didn't thicken as fast as he lengthened—if he'd grown as fat as he'd grown tall this last year, most of his clothes would be skin-tight. Being tall and lanky had disadvantages, like making him seem comical to certain persons who were hard up for something to laugh about, but if he was any fatter right now he'd be in real trouble about his clothes.

The great thing about wearing tennis shoes to school, instead of low-cuts like some guys wore, was that they hid the heel holes in your socks. Another great thing about tennis shoes was that they were comfortable. Shoot, he didn't

2

care if everybody at school had engineer boots or Welling-
tons or lace-ups or ranch-style, it was a free country. It
wasn't that he didn't have other shoes, he just couldn't cram
his dang big feet in them any more. So his motto was, if
you *got* to wear sneakers, wear *clean* sneakers, scrubbed
every weekend. No mud or manure on them. Dirty shoes
were the sign of a dirty hayseed.

Dressed, he shoved his hands in his pockets and self-consciously thought of the morning prayer he had started last
Christmas, inspired by the season and his heavy-hearted
loneliness. It had never become a comfortable habit, and
probably never would. The act of praying embarrassed him,
somehow. Maybe if he tried it without kneeling . . .

Squeezing his eyes tight shut, shivering in the dank morning, he muttered stiffly, "Dear Lord, please make Mama
get well out there in New Mexico, she's been gone so long,
I don't understand how come it takes so long with all the
new medical stuff they got nowadays—and get her to write
oftener, not just picture postcards, but regular letters—and
remind her my birthday's coming soon, I don't expect a
present or anything, but she could at least send me a Happy
Birthday card." Then, feeling sheepish, like a high-school
kid writing to Santa Claus, he said *Amen* and opened his
eyes.

With no watch, and sunrise coming earlier and earlier,
he always felt uneasy about the time. But he'd never missed
the bus yet, so he took a few minutes to straighten his bed
and sweep the floor. It was depressing to come from school
to a messed-up room.

In many ways he'd gotten fond of his quarters. Some people might feel cramped, but there was plenty of room for
the cot, the kitchen-table desk with its reading lamp, the
footlocker (which, having been his father's, was considerably more than just a footlocker), and the high-stacked

3

cardboard boxes containing dishes, towels, sheets, and various other belongings of his mother's. The folded quilts he used for a cot pad and the blankets he slept under also belonged to his mother. He was looking after all of it until she got well and they had a home of their own somewhere. Anywhere, he thought, a little lumpy-throated.

The Winchester .22 pump rifle under his bed had been his dad's, but with the understanding it would be Clem's when he turned twelve, so he considered it his own personal possession now, like the kerosene heater he'd bought out of the allowance Della Nolan gave him from the money she got for his board—not child welfare or any kind of county money, but part of the Social Security checks his mother had been getting ever since his father was killed. Old Duke and Pedro were his private property, too. For a guy who didn't have *much* stuff, he had some pretty *good* stuff.

Finished sweeping, he put the broom back in a corner. He used to plan ways to fix up the milkroom, like spreading tarpaper on the floor and laying an old secondhand rug. But fixing it up was no longer important. He'd be moving out. He didn't exactly *like* the Nolans, but he didn't exactly dislike them, either, especially Della, a cousin of his mother's. If they hadn't taken him in, he would probably have been put in a foster home. And they would have been happy to give him a room in the house. It was Clem who'd insisted on the milkroom to get away from their loud quarrels, and Della had said if he were nuts enough to want to live in a barn it was okay with her. Still, he wouldn't be sorry to leave.

When he opened the door, old Duke was waiting patiently, sitting with his rump on the concrete step and his feet on the ground. He was a big dog, still winter shaggy, a mongrel of haphazard color patterns, brown and black

4

and yellow and white. Duke had a comical dignity and frequently revealed what Clem considered flashes of remarkable intelligence. Like, for instance, knowing when Royce was stoned to the belligerence point and giving the man a wide berth, but showing no fear of the used-car salesman when he was sober. Not that Clem ever believed Royce was serious those times he threatened to shoot Duke. He just wanted to see what reaction he would get out of Clem.

"I never agreed tuh support a goddamn zoo," old Royce would say, in his thick, growly whiskey voice. "You an' your animals eatin' me outa house 'n' home, highpockets, can't afford to feed a goddamn managerie. If you don't git rid of that no-good mangy cur, I'll jus' hafta shoot 'im, 'assall."

Be the *last* dog he ever shot, boy.

Sometimes he'd make threats about Pedro. "Gonna sell that jackass to the glue factory, highpockets, 'sall it's good for."

That always made Clem plenty nervous, but he had worried more about the Nolans getting a divorce, the way they hollered at each other and Della kept threatening to leave if Royce came home falling-down drunk again. If they split the blanket, what would happen to Clem? He might get put in some kind of institution where dogs weren't allowed. He wouldn't mind so much having to get along without Pedro, but Duke was his best friend, maybe his only friend, and by God he wasn't going peacefully anywhere that Duke couldn't go.

Now, hugging his dog in the chill May morning, Clem shivered and thought, Okay, Mr. Nolan—all *three* of us are fixing to cut out, boy.

"See you later, Duke," he said, and detoured a little on his way to the house to check the driveway. Only one car there. Old Royce hadn't come home last night. And that

5

was a kind of relief. One morning when Clem went in, he found old Royce passed out on the stool in the bathroom. A thing like that could spoil a guy's whole day.

Of course there wasn't any milk in the refrigerator. Neither of the Nolans ever used it, and Della seldom remembered to buy any. There was some buttermilk that had been there a couple of weeks, and Clem wondered how that would be, cornflakes with sour buttermilk. He put water on the gas range to heat for instant coffee and found some leftover stew only a few days old to warm up. Then he went on to the bathroom. He didn't bathe as often as he should, but every morning he scrubbed his face good with soap and hot water so he wouldn't get acne. The school nurse had lectured the seventh grade on personal hygiene, and she said how the way to avoid unsightly skin blemishes during puberty was to scrub the pores good and not eat too much rich food and candy and soda pop. Some of the guys claimed later she didn't know what she was talking about, that wasn't what caused boys to have hickies. Any way you looked at it, Clem didn't have much of a problem. He didn't eat a lot of rich food, and the amount of pop and candy he consumed you could stick in your ear. And that other business wasn't exactly his line of work, either.

Back in the kitchen he made some toast, and put a lot of sugar in his instant coffee because he wouldn't be eating any lunch and there was lots of energy in sugar. He was saving his lunch money for travel expenses. In fact, he was hoarding every nickel he could lay his hands on, including what he'd got for some possum hides and what he earned Saturdays working for Mrs. Whittle and the irregular allowance Della gave him in addition to his lunch money: generous or chinchy, according to her mood and finances. One week she would give him a couple of bucks, and the next week fifty cents.

6

Washing up his plates, he thought of the great breakfasts his mother used to make when his father was alive. Buckwheat cakes and sausage, oatmeal with cream, fried eggs on the side, oh man!

He went back to the bathroom to comb his shaggy light-brown hair. Needed a haircut. Nowadays everybody needed a haircut, that was the style. The longer you went without a haircut, the more stylish you were. Up to a certain point. Then the principal would say cut it or cut out.

For a minute he practiced making goofy faces in the mirror. Then he tried dignified expressions, with less success. He made an effort to look handsome, but he couldn't get the hang of that, either. What he really wished he could do was appear calm and casual, like being kidded didn't embarrass him or make him hot under the collar.

"Don't call me toothpick," he whispered gently to his reflection, "or beanpole, or sliver, or broom handle, boys. One thing I can't tolerate, it's disrespect." *Pow! Zap! Slash!* "You got the message?"

When he came out of the bathroom Della called him. "Clemmie?"

"Yes, ma'am," he said, wishing she would just call him Clem. Some of the comedians at school called him Clemmie.

"Are you all right?" she asked.

"Yep," he said, knowing she didn't mean the question literally. It was like saying, "How are you today?"

"What time is it, hon?"

"Five of seven," he said. She didn't really mean *hon*, either. He wondered sometimes if people ever said what they really meant, or meant what they said. Take Della, she was always saying, "I'm fed up to here, Royce, I've had it with you, next time you come staggering in looped to the gills I'm leaving." But she didn't mean it. And Royce was always saying, "Okay, baby, so long, goodbye, who needs

7

you?" But he probably didn't mean it, either. It was like "I'll kill your dog."

"Did you find anything to eat, Clemmie?"

"Yes, ma'am." Don't call me Clemmie.

"I forgot to buy milk and eggs, hon. You hate me, don't you?" She sounded yawny and a little remorseful. Not much, but a little.

He laughed self-consciously. "Naw," he said. He didn't hate her. Forgetting milk and eggs wasn't grounds for hate. Standing there in the hallway ten feet from her bedroom door, he could hear her stirring in bed, sighing. "You need anything before I go?" he asked politely.

She gave a drowsy laugh. "Hon, you name it and I need it." He heard the springs squeak. "What I need most, however, you can't help me with." He yawned widely at the thought of being able to sleep until noon, like Della. In a real bed with a cushiony innerspring mattress. He heard her footsteps, slippers slithering across the floor, and he got a faintly panicky urge to duck into the kitchen. Della came through the bedroom door. She wore only a flimsy nightgown that made him feel suddenly itch-hot all over. She was a tall, plump woman with a pretty, puffy face. She had a net over her blond hair, and Clem could see her big brown nipples pressing against the thin material of her gown. What scared him was the feeling that she knew he could see her big brown nipples and didn't care, even *wanted* him to see them, wanted *somebody* to see them. She gave him a lopsided smile and said, "This is a do-it-yourself sort of situation, hon."

With a nervous grin he backed against the wall. She slithered past him to the bathroom, trailing the fragrant smell of perfumed, powdered, cold-creamed woman. As the bathroom door closed behind her Clem reeled away

8

from the wall and escaped into the kitchen. My lord, he thought, How about that?

Even after he'd got his books from the milkhouse and headed out around the house toward the road, he wasn't over the astonishment of the encounter. Brown! For gosh sakes, he'd always figured pink.

All the way out to the road Duke tried in vain to get his undivided attention, growling in his throat and bumping Clem's leg with an importuning head. When they reached the gravel road and turned south, Clem blew out his breath gustily and said, "Sonofagun, Duke, you wouldn't believe it! So just forget I ever mentioned it." And he banished the picture from his mind.

It was about a mile to the bus stop. Clem enjoyed the walk, although to a boy who had spent the first dozen years of his life in the wooded hills east of Conifer, near a clear-running river, this high prairie with its sparse timber and broad open fields was hard to get used to. He still had frequent attacks of homesickness for his old stomping grounds, but there were some good things about this flat country. Mainly a lot more rabbits to hunt with Duke. Plenty of possums, too, and Duke had a great nose for tracking and treeing. (Clem had decided, after giving it a lot of study, that his dog was part German shepherd, part collie, and part bird dog.)

As he walked south inhaling the fragrance of new grass and budding shrubbery and trees, Clem searched the brushy persimmon sprout and sumac and blackberry briar-grown pasture west of the road, looking for his donkey, and after a hundred yards he saw the creamy gray shape half hidden by bushes near the fence, grazing more or less in the company of Royce Nolan's two dozen winter-gaunt cows and runty calves. Pedro was always somewhere near the road whenever Clem walked to or from the bus stop. That was

9

some kind of evidence of affection, even if the lop-eared sonofagun never showed any sign of recognition. As Clem's only link with the past, the donkey was considerably more than just a donkey to Clem. He liked to think the impassive Pedro remembered his father, who had given Clem the animal when it was a knobby-legged weanling and he himself was eight years old. But once in a while he got the frustrated feeling that the darn jackass didn't even remember *him*.

"Hey, boorow!" he called as he got closer. Petro twitched one ear but went on eating grass. "Pedro!" Clem hollered. But the big, shaggy-coated donkey went on with his breakfast, imperturbably snubbing his master. "All right, you dumb jackass," Clem yelled, "ignore me!"

Walking on with the May sun warm on the side of his face, he reflected that a guy never knew where the hell he stood with a donkey. That's what he liked about a dog. They let a guy *know* how they felt—in fact they were usually too doggone slobberin' friendly. But a dad-blamed burro wouldn't give you the time of day. Maybe old Pedro resented the fact that he had to pull the cart, while Duke never had to do any work at all. Unless you called hunting work.

One of the best things about walking to school was his daily visit with Mrs. Whittle—a plump, gray-haired, cheerful retired teacher of American history. For three years now she had lived in an attractive and comfortable brick-and-shingle cottage on a wooded five-acre tract beside the highway five miles from Conifer.

Her hobby was gardening, and she had hoed up a considerable area for cultivation. As she had remarked happily to Clem, she had bitten off more than she could chew with her vegetable garden and flowers, berries and grapes, and

10

her orchard of dwarf fruit trees. She needed help after school and Saturdays, and paid sixty cents an hour and lunch, plus between-meal snacks. She was the world's greatest employer, and Clem had an occasional pang at the thought of telling her to make arrangements for another helper. He liked the work and greatly admired her home and had made up his mind that some day he and his mother were going to have a place like that, only back over in the hills close to the river. But the house would be like Mrs. Whittle's, with a big sunny living room and a fireplace and shelves of books, and a great kitchen with all electrical appliances.

Back in September when he started catching the school bus at her corner he used to see her in her yard when he went past, working in her flower beds and looking kind of comical in striped overalls and a man's shirt and a battered straw hat. She always nodded and smiled, and sometimes commented on the weather, but he was shy and never stopped to chat or anything. Then one morning in October when he was going past, all scrooched down in his blanket-lined jumper and shivering in the cold blowing mist, she came out on her porch and called him over. "Now, see here, young man," she said in a schoolteacherish way, "there's no reason why you should stand out there catching pneumonia when you could just as well be in here by the fire. We can see the bus coming long before it arrives, so you just march yourself indoors. From now on, my living room is going to be your bus depot, understand?"

Yes, ma'am, he understood all right. And boy, did he appreciate it. He was grateful for the warmth of her fireplace, and even more to have a friend during those first miserable days in Conifer's crowded grade school that was so different from his old small country school. And he sure appreciated the hot chocolate and cinnamon toast and other delicious food she pressed upon him in spite of his half-

11

hearted refusals. Feeling beholden, he got into the habit of stopping by after school to do chores for her, filling the woodbox and carrying ashes out to the compost pile, but he never could catch up with his sense of obligation because she always forced him to eat something evenings, too. She claimed she loved to bake and had nobody to bake *for,* and the pleasure of fixing a cake or pie was in having somebody to enjoy it with. She said he was doing her a favor. Well, if you put it that way, how could a guy refuse?

Then after a couple of weeks she said she was going to pay him a dollar a week for doing the chores, and she was very firm about it, so what could he do? He certainly could use the money. Then a little later on, she said she needed somebody who was willing to work for sixty cents an hour and lunch on Saturdays, and he didn't think twice before saying yes. And man oh man, the things that constituted her idea of *lunch!* Casseroles, like hamburger and cheese and tomatoes and macaroni. Hot tamale pies or homemade chili. A delicious stew with noodles she called goulash. And smothered chicken like his mother used to make in the good old days—he had a little trouble swallowing that at first. And Mrs. Whittle was always saying, Gee whiz, it was fun having somebody to cook for who enjoyed hearty fare, as if he were doing her a big favor by eating so much.

That's how he met her truck-driver son Ken. He'd seen the big semi parked there sometimes on Sundays, and Mrs. Whittle had told him her son Ken usually came to see her at least once a month. So one Saturday afternoon Ken Whittle came driving in off the highway in the big cab-over truck and trailer, and she introduced them, and they got to be pretty good friends. Clem envied Ken, who was always fixing to take off for California or somewhere. He went through New Mexico pretty often but said he never went anywhere near the town where Clem's mother was. Usually

12

he just stayed on U.S. 66 all the way to San Bernardino.

On this Friday morning in May, Mrs. Whittle was out in the yard admiring her jonquils and checking her pink dogwood trees that were just beginning to bloom. "Clem," she smiled, "it's much too lovely a morning to waste a minute indoors, so I'll just fetch the tray out here. Okay?"

"You bet," he said, grinning.

So they sat on the front steps and he ate two crusty over-sized biscuits with strawberry jam and drank his big mug of cocoa, and she discussed the work schedule for tomorrow. They would plant sweet corn, transplant tomatoes, peppers, and eggplant and put hotcaps over them, and mulch her Irish potatoes. A layer of well-rotted manure between the rows and then a deep layer of old hay, leaves, sawdust, wood chips, whatever was available. Clem enjoyed pushing a wheelbarrow, but not that much, and he decided to bring Pedro and the cart to haul all the stuff to the spud patch. It would be less work and more fun, and besides he needed to get Pedro used to working again after letting the donkey loaf most of the winter.

Sitting there all relaxed in the green morning, luxuriously letting the sweet warm cocoa trickle down his throat, he decided that in a couple of weeks he had to tell her he was quitting. She wouldn't try to stop him, but she might talk him out of it. And if she caught him in the right mood, he just might change his mind. Sometimes his stomach kind of fluttered and shrank when he thought of it. All winter he'd looked forward to going, but now spring was here and time was running out it didn't seem quite as simple.

When he saw the orange school bus coming from the west he gathered up his books, thanked her for the snack, and told Duke to stay put. Duke was smart enough anyway to stay away from the busy highway. On his way to the bus stop, it gave him a good feeling to know Duke would be

13

waiting for him at Mrs. Whittle's gate when he came home. The sonofagun had a kind of natural clock in his head.

When he got on the bus he stumbled a little accidentally, and pretended he'd done it on purpose, just clowning to get a laugh—because he got the laugh anyhow. Wearing a deliberately silly grin, he went to the back and sat down. It didn't make life happier for him to act like a shidepoke, but it beat heck out of showing how he really felt. The first day he showed up at Conifer Elementary feeling lost and self-conscious around a mob of town kids, he'd struck some of them funny at first sight, and for a while there the giggling and guffawing had really upset him. But a guy couldn't fight a whole dang school, especially when most of the pupils who laughed at the way he looked and talked were girls. So after a few weeks he decided, What the heck, it was better to make out like he was funny on purpose, so they would be applauding instead of ridiculing him. By now it was practically second nature to exaggerate all his mannerisms.

But that wasn't the real Clem Marlow, that was just a protective disguise, a masquerade. Inside, he was a serious, dignified person who hated his ungainly physique and his idiotic mugging. Eventually he would put on some weight and develop some coordination, but he knew he would never be able to change his image around Conifer. Which was one of the main reasons he'd got such a bad case of wanderlust.

The only seventh-graders on the bus were a couple of girls and Floyd Garber, a fat kid with freckles who wore glasses and wasn't in much of a position to poke fun at anybody, and Clem always sat with him.

"Hiya, Clem," Floyd said.

"Hiya, Floyd," Clem replied.

En route to school he didn't have to goof it up.

"Got your homework?" Floyd inquired.

"Yep," Clem replied. "You?"

14

"Yep," Floyd said.

This was the easiest part of the day. No strain, no pain.

"Gotcha English theme wrote yet?"

"Yeah, practically."

"Whadja write it about?"

"I'm writin' it on horticulture."

"Hey, wow," Floyd said respectfully.

It was kind of soothing to Clem's ego to know that Floyd envied him his skinniness and perfect eyesight, and maybe his scholarship. Old Floyd was a C student. Clem made A's and B's.

"How about you?" he asked. "Wot's your topic?"

Floyd sighed. "Man, I'm tryin' to write about a trip we took last summer, where-all we went an' what-all we seen, but it ain't easy."

Nodding, Clem thought, *Next* year that's what *I'll* be writing a theme about. Travel.

When the bus reached the grade school, Clem took a deep breath, getting ready to do his funny walk routine and feeling something akin to stage fright. Most comedians get *paid* for doing that stuff, he thought.

15

TWO

THE first Saturday of June was another sunny but cold morning with a great smell of dew-wet grass and flowers. Clem didn't even bother trying to scratch up a breakfast in the Nolans' kitchen, knowing he'd get something to eat as soon as he reached Mrs. Whittle's. He was in a hurry to hitch old Pedro to the two-wheeled cart his dad had built when Clem was ten, and start earning sixty cents an hour. He'd caught the donkey the evening before, putting a halter and rope on him and staking him out where he could eat all the grass he wanted.

He skipped scrubbing his face, because Royce's car was home, and if you woke the old grouch up on a Saturday when he had a hangover he was apt to think up some jobs for you to do, out of pure-D spite, and Clem didn't want to risk getting delayed.

Lazy from a winter of loafing, Pedro balked a little at first, but Clem popped him a couple with the whip he'd braided from nylon cord and got him moving. Once they were out in the road, the donkey actually trotted briskly for a hundred yards.

Mrs. Whittle had a pan of cinnamon rolls with pecans on top, and Clem could have had more than the two he ate with his cocoa but didn't want to act like a glutton—besides, he had a hunch he'd get the others before the day was done.

16

All morning while he hauled old dry manure to the garden in the wheelbarrow and hay and sawdust in the cart, he kept waiting for a suitable opening to bring up the subject of his planned trip, but Mrs. Whittle just kept chattering like all the birds that hung around her feeders (she fed stray birds, too). She told him all kinds of stuff about her childhood days and her teaching days, and Ken's childhood days. It was interesting and educational, but he couldn't get a word in endways. Finally, when they took a break so he could have a glass of milk and another cinnamon roll, he blurted it out.

"I guess I won't be able to work for you this summer."

She blinked at him through her glasses. "Well, now. Why not?"

"I guess I won't be here."

She really looked surprised. "Oh, dear," she said. "I'm truly sorry to hear that, Clem. Where *will* you be?"

"Well, I'm planning on going to New Mexico, where Mom is."

"Oh, Clem, how nice!" she said warmly. But of course she didn't have all the facts yet. "Are you going alone, or do your uncle and aunt intend to drive out there?"

He shook his head and ate some cinnamon roll before answering. "They're not going, that I know of." But I won't be alone, he thought.

She frowned. "Clem, you're not thinking of hitchhiking to New Mexico, are you?"

He shook his head. "No, ma'am. I couldn't do that." Not and take a dog with me, he thought. Let alone a durn burro.

She watched him chew and swallow, her eyes thoughtful. "Why don't you just tell me and save us the bother of conducting an oral quiz, Clem?"

So he just laid it on the line, and her hand went to her mouth and her gray-blue eyes widened with something like

17

alarm. "Oh, my goodness!" she said when he finished. "Do you have any idea how long it would take to get there?"

"Well, I figured we might could do twenty miles a day."

She pressed a hand to her cheek. "I don't think you could possibly cover twenty miles in a day, Clem. Ten would probably be a more realistic estimate."

Clem shrugged self-consciously. "That'd still be three hundred miles a month, an' I got all summer."

"Oh, dear," she said. "How old are you, Clement?"

"Fourteen, practically. But I look older."

She nodded in agreement.

"It'd be like a camping trip," he told her. "A vacation."

"Where would you sleep?" she worried. "Not on the ground, I hope?"

"I could sleep in the cart," he said. "My donkey cart. I could put some hay or something in there and make my bed on top of it."

"What about money, Clem?"

"I got some saved up," he assured her. "Twenty-three bucks."

She pursed her lips. "That isn't much for such a long . . . camping trip. Just food alone would cost quite a bit, even if you had no other expenses."

Clem shrugged, although money had worried him sometimes. He'd need to buy dog food for Duke. Old Pedro could make out on grass, but Duke and himself would have to have bought grub. Maybe he could eat a lot of wild greens and things, but Duke couldn't. "Well, I figure to work a few days every once in a while," he said with a confidence he didn't truly feel. "Farm work or something."

She nodded absently, negating the nod with a concerned frown. "I should think your aunt and uncle might contribute some money." Her faraway gaze focused back on Clem.

18

"Incidentally, how do *they* feel about this . . . ah . . . summer jaunt of yours?"

That was a good opening for some cool lying, but he never had been good at that and always felt bad afterward. If a guy ever got a reputation for dishonesty, nobody would ever trust him. He had a mouthful of cinnamon roll, and he chewed while he debated with himself. But if he was going to tell lies to anybody, he probably ought to save them for the Nolans.

He stalled a little. "Well, I didn't mention it to Royce yet."

She picked up the false note. "Clem, don't try to fool an old schoolmarm," Mrs. Whittle said. "Did you mention your plans to *either* of them?"

Grinning sheepishly, he shook his head. "Not yet."

"You're not good at telling stories, my lad." She smiled. "How do you imagine your aunt and uncle will react when you *do* tell them your plans?"

"Why, shoot," he said, scowling a little. "They don't care if I live or die, an' anyway it's not much of their business because they're not my real aunt and uncle . . . Della's a cousin of Mom's, an' not even a *first* cousin. A *second* cousin. An' I'm only visiting at their place, so I guess I can leave whenever I take a notion."

"Don't exaggerate, Clem," she said. "I'm sure the Nolans *do* care about your welfare."

When she said *welfare* he felt a tingle of dread. Those welfare peckerwoods were the chief threat to his project. Because he was a minor, they might grab him and turn him over to a juvenile home or some awful thing like that. If anybody blabbed to the welfare department, his goose was probably cooked before he got two miles down the road. He worried that somebody might notify them in *advance,* because it had been a case-worker that had okayed his

19

living with the Nolans, back when his real uncle—or anyway his real aunt's husband—blamed Clem for something that wasn't his fault and said they couldn't keep him any more. After six months of living with the Hoggett tribe, Clem had been relieved to get shut of them, especially his cousin Melody, who had caused all the trouble. But the welfare lady had believed Melody's version of the story and had warned Clem that wicked boys usually ended up in reform school. Clem had been too worried and ashamed to argue, but he'd wanted to say, What about wicked *girls*, like Melody? But that was her business. All he cared about now was steering clear of the welfare people.

"Let's go have a look at this cart of yours," Mrs. Whittle said.

So he finished his milk and they went to examine his conveyance, which had a plywood box four feet wide, six feet long, and two feet deep, and a removable board seat. The box, reinforced around the bottom edge with angle iron, was bolted to a lightweight frame fastened to auto springs and mounted on a trailer axle with rubber-tired trailer wheels. The pulling shafts were oak and bolted securely into lengths of two-inch pipe welded to the cart's underside. All in all, it was a sturdy vehicle, and Clem had repainted it apple green during the Christmas school break, so it looked pretty good. Pedro's collar and harness were of simple, strong design and construction, and he'd kept the leather oiled and the metal free of rust.

"My dad and a welder friend of his built this cart," he told her.

"Well, it seems big enough for your journey," she said, "unless you plan to take a lot of excess baggage."

"Just camping stuff and bedding an' my footlocker," he told her. "Water can, cookin' gear, clothes, stuff like that, is all." He was watching her a bit anxiously, not sure yet

20

what her final attitude was going to be and figuring she would be a good guideline to the general adult attitude.

Mrs. Whittle leaned on the cart and gazed off into the sunny green June landscape. "I'm reminded, inevitably, of the pioneers—my own parents, for instance, came from Ohio to join the stampede during the Cherokee Strip run."

"Now there's roads and bridges anywhere a person wants to go," said Clem. "An' no Indians, either."

She smiled. "But there are other hazards now." But she didn't make a big point about it. "A boy alone," she murmured, like a question.

"There was a kid in San Diego," Clem remarked. "I don't remember how old, but not much older than me. His dad got him a boat, a sailboat with a motor, I think it was, an' let him take off on a round-the-world trip all by hisself."

"Himself," she corrected absently, a conditioned reflex. But she was nodding. "Every summer teenagers go off on trips without adult supervision—seems to me only recently I read of a quite young boy who was making a bicycle tour of the country. And kids go on hiking vacations, and follow the wheat harvest north . . ."

Clem felt a grin building up inside him, but he didn't want to be hasty about it. "New Mexico isn't very far to go," he said.

She looked at him thoughtfully. "You know something?" "Now that the initial shock has passed, well . . ." She paused. "I seem to be of two minds about your trip. It's not as if you were just wandering off aimlessly—you have a definite destination." She peered at him gravely. "How long has it been since you last saw your mother, Clem?"

"Over two years. I guess it would be three years next January."

"If only you were a bit *older*," she said. "Almost every day one reads in the newspapers . . ." Her voice trailed off.

21

"I'd have old Duke along," he pointed out. "Nobody would bother me." He didn't know what *she* had in mind, but he was thinking in terms of kidnappers, hijackers, and other traditional villains. "And I'll have my twenty-two rifle."

She beamed at him reassuringly. "I can't imagine anyone wanting to harm a nice boy like you, Clem."

"Well," he said, scowling, "they better not try anything, that's all."

"Clement," she said, "the simple truth is, I rather envy you such an opportunity for adventure."

Clem grinned, finally, and felt himself relax. She was on his side, even if she kept looking for reasons to switch.

"I guess I better get back to work, huh?" he said.

She nodded, looking briefly at the high sun. "I'd better be starting our lunch. It takes a while to smother a chicken properly. How does *that* strike you, Clement?"

"Great!" he sighed. If he had a preference among her specialties, it would have to be her famous smothered chicken. Not only was it tender and delicious, there'd be all those bones for Duke.

Driving Pedro after more spoiled hay, he felt almost happy. Now that he'd finally told somebody about the trip, and she'd practically admitted it was a great idea, his doubts faded. But she wasn't the one he had to convince. He had the feeling that Della and Royce would never okay it. They might not worry about the dangers, but they would care about the money his mother sent them every month to pay for all the great food he wasn't eating. He didn't figure they were getting rich off him, but he sure wasn't getting fat off them, either, so if anybody came out two dollars ahead on the deal it wasn't Clem.

As he loaded moldy rain-blackened hay into the cart, he decided, the heck with trying to get permission from the

22

Nolans. They might get mad and throw him back to the welfare department. What it all boiled down to, he had to take off while they were away from home. He could leave a note in the milkhouse, and maybe they wouldn't even miss him for two or three days, giving him a good head start.

At least he would have from when Della went to work around three in the afternoon until she got up the next day and found her kitchen as dirty as she'd left it.

Hey! he thought, I could leave a note saying I was just going to go visit around in our old neighborhood for a week. They wouldn't do anything about that. Then in a couple weeks I could send them a postcard saying I joined the Job Corps, and they'd probably figure well, what the hell, who *needs* him?

It would be simple, easy as falling off an oily elephant, as the town kids said.

So how come he just went right on worrying about it?

THREE

Clem's plan probably wouldn't have worked without an assist from that branch of fate which influences, and is influenced by, the vagaries of human nature. There were thunderstorms and windy nights as the next to last week of school dragged along, and considerable drunkenness and marital discord. Two nights in a row Clem lay awake tense and a little scared as thunder rent the darkness and rain drummed on the milkhouse roof. I'll never get away with it, I must be crazy, he thought. And he would try to be utterly honest with himself, wondering if maybe deep down inside he wanted to be stopped so he wouldn't have to chicken out like a coward.

But when morning dawned bright and clean, his spirits leaped again and nothing seemed impossible in the wonderful world of summertime. So he went on preparing for the summer odyssey.

I ought to put a roof over the cart, he thought. To make shade and keep out rain.

When he mentioned it to Mrs. Whittle, she got all enthusiastic and offered to help. "I'll feel much better if I know you have a proper shelter," she said. "And my son Ken gave me a set of power tools last Christmas. What materials will we need?"

We, he thought, grinning. She was cutting herself in.

But heck fire, he was glad to have a partner, particularly one who owned power tools and had a telephone so they could call the lumberyard and order the stuff they needed delivered.

That was Thursday morning, and she said she would make the phone call right away and they could do the construction Sunday afternoon. That way he could still work all day Saturday and add to his savings. What did he think they would need? She would write it down.

Oh, he said, a hunk of plywood for the roof, a couple of one-by-maybe-threes six feet long, and a couple cross-pieces four feet long, four five-foot lengths of two-by-two to hold the roof up, and some nails, finishing nails, probably.

"What about the sides?" she wanted to know, and he said he figured he could tack some cardboard on the sides, plywood was pretty expensive. And about then the bus was coming, so he let it go at that.

Then that afternoon during study period when he was drawing a cowboy on a bucking bronco, the Principal's secretary came in and said Clement Marlow was wanted in the office. Covering his drawing, he went out of the class-room, hiding his alarm by pretending to be scared to death, so the giggles and titters followed him down the hallway. I didn't do anything, he thought with consternation. That I *know* of.

But it wasn't anything he'd done, it was something old Royce had. Deputy Sheriff Red Rogers was waiting for him in the office, and at first that shook Clem even more, because when a Deputy wanted anybody it usually spelled trouble, even if the Deputy happened to be an old buddy of your father's. In fact it was Red who finally killed Billy Bob Babcock, the bank robber who had shot Clem's dad.

"Hey there, Clem," Red grinned. "How the heck are you?"

25

That didn't sound very ominous. "Okay," Clem said.

"Haven't seen you in a coon's age. How old are you now?"

"Fourteen," Clem said. "Give or take a few days."

"How about that!" Red said, scratching the thinning hair that had earned him his nickname. "How you makin' out in school, Clem?"

"Fairly good," Clem said, fidgeting. The Principal wasn't around, but his honor-student secretary was there pretending to be busy checking filing cards, but she didn't fool Clem, she was tuned in.

"Whatta you hear from your mother? How's she gettin' along?"

Clem shrugged his bony shoulders. "She's still out there."

Red nodded sympathetically. "Well, she'll be comin' home before you know it, Clem. Them miracle drugs they got now . . . sure cure for what ails people. That dry sunny climate an' all, she'll be okay, don't worry."

Red Rogers put his stetson back on. "Well, the reason I had you paged outa class, I got what you might call bad news, Clem."

Everything that had been said before evaporated from Clem's mind and he got a heavy scared lump in his guts, thinking, It's Mom, he's just been stalling, it's something terrible about Mom! His eyes began to feel hot and his throat stiffened until he could hardly swallow and he clenched his hands so his fingernails dug into his palms and waited.

"Fact is, Clem, we got your uncle in jail again on another drunk drivin' rap, an' it looks like this time he's gonna hafta lay it out."

Ohhh, Clem breathed thankfully. Ohhh. Is *that* all? It was funny, thinking about it afterward, it never for an instant even crossed his mind that Red might mean his real

26

uncle, Old Loyal Hoggett. He *knew* who Red meant, but for the benefit of the big-eared secretary he played it dumb. "What uncle?" he inquired.

"Royce Nolan," Red replied, frowning a little. "Who else?"

"He ain't no uncle of *mine,*" Clem said scornfully, for the benefit of the elaborately disinterested high-school girl. Red Rogers smiled faintly.

"Well, whatever he is, he's not gonna be doin' any drinkin' *or* drivin' for at least sixty days, Clem."

Joy leaped in Clem's mind and a vast relief, somewhat lessened at the moment by his pressing need to let the secretary know, so whoever she blabbed it to would also know, he wasn't any kin at all to the prisoner in question.

"We're not even related by marriage," he said. "What you shoulda done, you shoulda notified his wife, I guess."

Red grinned understandingly. "We would have notified Nolan's wife," he explained, "but she doesn't have a telephone out there, an' I figured maybe you'd be willin' to relay the information to Mrs. Nolan if you happen to see her, as it would save me the long drive."

"Sure, I'll give her the news."

Red winked. "Break it to her *tactful,* will you, pal? Tell her he can't be bailed out of this one, so save her money. And she can claim his car at the county garage if she wants to, it ain't impounded. I mean, if she needs it pretty bad they'll let it go."

"She's got her own," Clem said.

"Well, that's about all I had on my mind at this time, Clem—but it has been a pleasure to see you an' find out you're doin' okay. As I said before, an' told your mama on many occasions, now if there's any little thing I can do for you, anything at all, don't hesitate. Me an' your daddy was close personal friends as well as partners."

27

Clem nodded, unable to think of anything at the moment that Red could do for him, and the Deputy shook hands with him and thanked the girl and left Clem kind of stranded there in a pocket of uncertainty.

"Is that all?" he asked the girl. "I mean, I can go?"

She turned and looked at him sternly, rehearsing for a long career as a teacher, no doubt, and she was holding the file card she had apparently been searching for. She said in a voice of triumphant accusation, "It says *here* that Mr. and Mrs. Royce Nolan are your uncle and your aunt, so what have you got to say about *that?*"

Suddenly, having stripped herself of her status by her moment of malicious victory, she was just a sharp-featured girl with stringy blond hair, slightly irregular teeth, narrow shoulders and minimal bosom that clashed with her broad hips.

"That's what they call a typographical arrow," he said, and he turned and marched out with as much dignity as his long skinny legs and narrow shoulders would allow.

The rest of the class period he was aware that many of the kids were watching him curiously, wondering why he had been called to the office. He never clowned at his desk. He considered it a haven, once he reached it, where a guy could pull a curtain of concentration around himself, taking refuge in a book or in drawing pictures of real he-men riding broncos. Drawing was one of his few assets. He was good at cartoons, too, and could get crazy expressions on faces. There were a few people around school who respected his talent and envied him his gift. Like Molly Hicks, a girl with big brown eyes, not skinny like him and not tall, but slender and neat. Anyway, there were times when she looked at him soberly, with a kind of respect. The trouble was, Molly never *said* anything to him, and he didn't have the faintest idea of what to say to her. But sometimes when he was acting the fool, Molly Hicks had a kind of sad and troubled look in her big brown eyes. Not like pity, but more as if she wished he wouldn't clown all the time.

But he only did it for protection, and didn't really put himself down. He felt unfinished on the outside, but he never lost sight of the true values of a world that wouldn't always demand that he entertain it with buffoonery. He made those A's and B's, and he drew pictures, ever critical of his work and always trying to improve, and meanwhile, trapped in the long, narrow, ungainly cage of himself, he waited. With more patience than he knew, but with a great deal less insight than he supposed.

When the class period ended, some of the seventh-graders encircled him to ask why he'd been called to the office, and he saw Molly Hicks there on the fringe, looking concerned. The thing of it was, Clem had never been called to the Principal's office before, although some of his classmates had often been summoned or sent there for various infractions and fractiousness, so naturally they wondered what had finally caused him to make that nervous march.

"What did the Prince want you for?" Jug Schlosserman demanded.

Before Clem could answer, Kirby Newman said, importantly, "Wasn't the Prince wanted ol' Clem the stem, it was a cop. Deputy Red Rogers. I seen him when I went to the toilet."

"Hey! Wow!" Jug said eagerly. "What did he want with *you,* Toothpick?"

Hemmed in, Clem glanced at Molly again long enough to see a flicker of sympathy. Talking was worse than walking, because his voice wasn't trustworthy and sometimes changed in the middle of a word, especially under stress.

"Information," he said.

"Oh, yeah?" Kirby Newman jeered. "What about, stick

the hick?" Kirby was one of Clem's worst tormentors, with a mean sense of humor. Stick the hick, for example. He was always trying to think up new insulting names for Clem.

With sudden inspiration, Clem said earnestly, "Well, there's a dangerous lunatic loose around town."

"Who?" Jug said. "What's his name?"

"Kirman Newby or Noobie Koobie or something like that," Clem said, and pushed through the circle.

It took them a couple of seconds to realize he was pulling somebody's leg, and another second to figure out whose leg, and then they all started laughing hilariously. Somebody said, "Noobie Koobie! 'At's a gasser!"

He did some spading for Mrs. Whittle that afternoon, but if she noticed his gloomy preoccupation she didn't mention it.

Della had left his supper in the oven as usual, liver and onions, green beans (the frozen, tasteless kind), and some overbrowned biscuits. Still no milk, and the truth of it was, Mrs. Whittle had plain spoiled him for Della's cooking. But in fairness, Mrs. Whittle didn't have much else to do but fool around the kitchen, and Della worked the night shift at a factory making electric pump motors, and put in a lot of overtime, and was too tired around home to do much. Except mess up the kitchen. Which was her privilege, of course. Just like it was his privilege to clean it up every night.

He intended to watch television and stay awake until she got home, but he made the mistake of stretching out on the divan and fell asleep during the ten o'clock news. Next thing he knew, Della was shaking his shoulder, saying, "What in the world, Clemmie? Why didn't you go to bed?"

It took him a minute to get the fuzz out of his mind and remember why he hadn't gone to bed. Oh! Yeah. Sighing, he sat up and rubbed his face and wished he didn't have

30

to give her the message, but he had to, so he just laid it on the line. "Royce is in jail for drunk driving and Red Rogers said you can't bail him out. They're throwing the book at him and he'll be there at least sixty days."

"Oh, my God!" Della said, and flopped down in a chair, staring at him in a horrified, open-mouthed way. "How about that?" she murmured. "Sixty whole long days." Then she burst into tears.

Clem had been afraid of that. He was embarrassed and figured he'd better leave her alone. Arising wearily he went over and turned off the glaring white TV screen. "Guess I better get to bed."

Della nodded and wiped her eyes, smearing her makeup, and abruptly uttered a shaky laugh. "Why the heck am I *crying?*" she asked. "Sixty days of not having to worry where he is—and who he's with. He'll be cold sober for two whole months! Hallelujah, Clemento, imagine that." She sniffled and gave him a half-smile.

And it wasn't until then that Clem fully grasped what it meant to his summer plans. He didn't have to worry about Royce stopping him. By the time old Royce got out of the hoosegow, a guy could be in California. Which left only Della to worry about.

But not for long. The best was yet to come.

FOUR

FRIDAY when he got off the school bus and met a squirming Duke at Mrs. Whittle's gate, he smelled the doughnuts, and his lunchless stomach muttered impatiently. But not for long. She didn't make soggy doughnuts like those you bought, but firm crusty ones. And she said that since he would be coming back in the morning, there was no point in his doing any work now, it was such a lovely warm afternoon, why didn't he just go on home and enjoy it —and take these extra doughnuts along for a snack after supper.

Skimming along the road in the green and fragrant afternoon, running for the sheer joy of it and because he was anxious to get to the mailbox, he thought, Boy, I'll miss her cooking, her doughnuts and cinnamon toast and cocoa and casseroles and sandwiches and smothered chicken—you name it and I'll miss it.

Approaching the mailbox, he was, from long defensive habit, pessimistic, prepared to find nothing there for him. If you expected something and didn't get it, you felt lousy, but if you didn't expect anything and got something, you felt terrific. Yanking open the metal box he saw what he did expect to see, the daily paper, the *Tulsa World*. It was always there except on national holidays when the mail didn't come. Sighing, because even a pessimist could *hope*,

32

he snatched out the folded newspaper and slammed the cover shut on the box and whirled away. And the picture postcard slid out of the newspaper into the ditch.

He stared at the colored picture, and it was New Mexico, all right, and the happy relief swelled up in him with such pressure that it tightened his throat and made his eyes smart.

Dearest Clem, June again. Bet it's lovely there. Nice here but will soon get hot. Can see the mountain in the picture from my window. It's only that color certain days around sundown. School almost out there —anxious to see your report card. Proud of my smart son. Write me. I love you. Your Mom.

He turned it over and studied the picture again, then slid it carefully into his shirt pocket. He would read it again later, and again and again. And compare it with other cards. There were certain things that bothered him. Like she never mentioned how she was getting along any more—not for a long time now. She used to say, "I'm getting better." Then she quit saying it. She used to say she felt fine, but she hadn't given out any information like that for months. Which was one of the main reasons he had to go to New Mexico. Another thing that bothered him, she'd sent this same picture postcard before, several times, and on all of them she had written about seeing the mountain from her window. It scared Clem for her to repeat things like that, as if she didn't remember writing it before. She didn't write *that* much.

And she didn't mention my birthday, he thought. But shoot, it isn't until next week, she'll send a special card by next Thursday, a regular birthday card. She couldn't forget *that* date, boy. June fifteenth.

He took the sack of doughnuts to the kitchen and looked

33

in the oven and was pleasantly surprised. A big chunk of baked ham, a dish of mashed potatoes, broccoli with a cheese sauce. Hey, maybe *this* is my birthday! he thought. Baked ham on a Friday! What happened to the fish sticks? Who cares?

When he came back from the bathroom, he sliced off a piece of the ham and made a sandwich to keep him going until supper time. He never cheated; suppertime was any time after six o'clock, and the fact that it was ready now and he would be eating alone didn't alter anything; he'd still wait, except for a sandwich to tide him over. It was a matter of principle. A guy had to live by some kind of schedule.

Looking for mayonnaise, he opened the refrigerator and saw two cartons of homogenized milk. *Two* cartons. And a carton of supermarket cole slaw. If that's what happened to a woman when her husband had the book thrown at him . . .

He went on out into the sunshine, although he didn't like to eat in front of Duke. Sonofagun could break your heart the way he looked at you, and groaned with hunger. "What I had in mind for you, buddy, is more like raw jackrabbit," he said, and got his rifle out of the milkhouse. But he ate the sandwich rapidly, so as not to prolong Duke's agony, and gave him the final bite of it.

Because of the postcard and the ham and the doughnuts and the balmy sweet early summer afternoon, the ramble around the fields turned out to be a memorable event. A great thing happened—Pedro saw them and, instead of acting snooty, came across the pasture to meet them. He let Clem ride him bareback, without a bridle. Meadowlarks sang, blackbirds trilled around the pond, which was brimful after the good rains, and old Duke caught himself a rabbit. All in all, it was just a perfect blending of season and

34

weather and circumstances, and quietly unforgettable, with Clem and his dog and his donkey in harmony with the world and one another.

It was, Clem hoped, kind of a preview.

Usually on Saturday afternoons Della Nolan was busy catching up on her housecleaning, or off looking for Royce if he hadn't come home Friday night—and getting ready to go out with him if he was home and sober. Her idea of a Saturday night supper was like hotdogs and potato salad, something quick and simple and, to Clem's way of thinking, not very nourishing. But this Saturday was different. He came home from Mrs. Whittle's tired and hungry in spite of the splendid lunch, and Della's car was in the driveway, and she was in the kitchen wearing an apron over her stretch pants and looking (from the front) prettier than he'd ever seen her. She was putting the frosting on a chocolate layer cake. She must be expecting company, he thought.

If she was, he was it. "Hon," she said, "don't ask me why, but I'm in a mood to celebrate. I've got two of the thickest T-bones you ever saw, and potatoes baking in the oven, and a salad in the fridge, and ice cream to go with this cake."

"Wowee!" Clem said. What else could he say?

She smiled at him with something akin to genuine affection. "What can we celebrate? Washington's birthday?"

Clem grinned. "That was in February, I guess."

She puckered her face up kind of charmingly. "Lincoln's?"

Clem had to laugh. "His was February, too."

"Well, hey, you're smart to know that, hon. How many people would know that?" He shrugged modestly, and she narrowed her eyes. "Well, then, how about you, Clemmie? When is your birthday?"

"Not till July," he lied.

35

"Well, mine isn't until August," Della said, "so what the hay, we'll celebrate yours early. Okay, hon?"

He said okay, and went ahead and took a bath, and put on clean clothes, his pants and shirt that came closest to covering his ankles and wrists, and supper was really something even if he was pretty self-conscious eating alone with Della at the dining-room table with candles on it. And Della made a toast with tomato juice (his was straight, but he'd seen her put something in hers, and she referred to it as a Bloody Mary), saying, "Here's to all the happy adults in the world—if there are any. And here's to all you kids, may you never grow up." He drank with her, but wasn't buying the toast—the sooner he grew up, the better.

The broiled T-bone was out of this world. Della kept asking if it was good, and he kept saying, "Ummmm!" He meant it, but she seemed to be very pleased that he enjoyed it so much.

"This is the way to live, Clemmie," she told him. "I'd almost forgotten. I mean, there can be so many good moments. Don't expect too much of life, but try to grab the good moments. And don't always be worrying about tomorrow. You know the biggest mistake people make, hon?"

With a mouthful of sensational T-bone steak, Clem shook his head.

She had a shot of Bloody Mary. "Looking ahead," she said. "What I mean is, hon, people are so busy planning and worrying about the future that they forget how to enjoy the present."

Clem nodded. He understood that because he often thought a long way ahead, himself. But if a guy had got used to a rough time, suddenly no dad and then a little while later his mother going to New Mexico with spots on her lungs, then living with a grouchy grandmother until she had a stroke and went to a nursing home, and then living with an aunt and uncle and a dirty-minded girl cousin like Melody Hoggett who got a guy in trouble because he finally went up in the hayloft with her like she'd been asking to do for six damn months (to look at her pigeons, she said, and boy she showed her pigeon, all right), and then coming here to live with Della (who was okay—suddenly, boy, she was really okay) and old Royce. Well, after all that, a guy either learned to turn off parts of his mind and enjoy a good thing here and there, or he'd go stark raving nuts. He could now balance things out, so he could think ahead to New Mexico and still enjoy eating a T-bone steak right now. And maybe that was what she was talking about.

"Some people grate on each other's nerves," Della said. "That's why I like about you, Clemmie. You don't."

Clem grinned a little.

"I seem to be out of tomato juice," she said, getting up from the table. She was back in a minute with a full glass. "Do you know how old I am, hon?" Clem just shook his head, because his mouth was full of potato. "Thirty-seven," she said. "And what have I got to show for it?"

Well, he thought. But offhand he didn't know.

"I got married when I was about your age," she said.

Thirteen? he thought incredulously.

Della shook her head as if she couldn't believe her memory. "I was only sixteen. I developed early. But I was only sixteen."

My lord! Clem thought, and his jaws stopped moving. Did she think *he* was sixteen? Everybody said he looked old for his age, but sixteen?

"But that one didn't really count," Della said reminiscently, sipping tomato juice. She wasn't damaging her steak much, he noticed. But women were like that, picky eaters.

37

And she couldn't eat and talk both. He was lucky, he could chew and listen at the same time. "Divorced at seventeen," Della said. "Of course that's the fashion nowadays, but in my day it was a disgrace. There I was, a divorcee before I even finished high school. And all the boys really zeroed in on little Della. I guess you can imagine."

Clem looked thoughtful, but he couldn't imagine.

"I'm not proud of that last year in high school," Della said. "But could I help it if I got turned on too young?"

Well, Clem thought, trying to look intelligent. To tell the truth, I don't know.

"Of course," Della said, staring at him in the dim candlelight, "compared to the sophisticated infants of today, I was just a dumb kid."

Della Nolan sipped her Bloody Mary. "One thing I've learned," she said moodily, "being married to an alcoholic is a very lonely life. They don't need anybody, and anybody needs *them* is just s.o.l., because they're not . . . available."

He knew exactly what she meant. Royce was always gone. And now, boy, sixty days' worth of gone.

"After two months in cold storage he'll need *me*," Della said with a toss of her blond head. "But maybe little Della won't need *him*." She sipped and gave a harsh laugh. "Who am I kiddin'? When he gets out what he'll need worst is a pint of whiskey, not his wife."

The conversation was getting uncomfortable to Clem, and he was glad when she eased off for a while, letting him finish his steak. "Less have a lil music," she said, getting up and swaying over to the radio. She found some noisy rock 'n' roll music and sent him a knowing, sleepy-eyed smile. "Your kind of music, right, Clem? Your generation, I mean."

She began to move her shoulders and hips in opposite directions, with her closed hands held up like a boxer and her big breasts jiggling under the tight dress. And it just em-

38

barrassed the hell out of him. It always embarrassed him to see somebody doing something silly. Grownups shouldn't try to do the frug or the watusi or whatever the heck she was trying to do.

"Do you dance, hon?" she asked, panting from the exertion.

He shook his head, chewing food that would be hard to swallow. Not only he didn't dance, he was real glad of it right now. Boy, what started out a great supper was going sour in a hurry.

"Doesn't that rhythm get into your blood, hon?"

He shook his head. Pretty soon the record ended and she stopped.

"Whew," she said breathlessly, "that's too much for a poor workin' gal." Turning the sound down on a Coca-Cola commercial, she returned to the table, swaying and panting. "Makes a person thirsty," she said, scooping up her glass and heading for the kitchen, walking carefully.

Clem hated to leave, especially when he wasn't finished with his steak yet, but if Della was fixing to get stoned, he didn't care to watch. Maybe he could take the steak with him. Carry his plate to the sink and bootleg the T-bone out to his private pad. But just then Della asked from the kitchen if he was about ready for his cake and ice cream, and he abandoned any notion of leaving until after dessert. He said, "Yes, ma'am," and presently she returned with his dessert and her refilled tomato juice glass.

"Then I met Royce," she said, "an' the res' is hist'ry, Clemmie. I been almost one hundred percent faithful." She laughed huskily.

Whatever she meant, that was a pretty good average, he reflected.

"Whoeee," she murmured, "I feel a lil woozy—scuse me, hon. Gotta go lie down for a minute." And as she went

39

swaying out, she said, "Finish your dinner, sweetie, jus' leave the mess, I'll clear up inna mornin'."

Sighing with relief, Clem settled down to enjoy the rest of the feast alone.

About an hour later, contentedly reading in bed in the milkhouse, he heard her car start up and fade away in the night, and figured she had to go get something for whatever was the matter.

FIVE

Clem slept late Sunday morning, relishing the luxury of it. Mrs. Whittle always went to Sunday school, and he would have gone with her if he hadn't outgrown all his Sunday clothes a good year ago, but even if she didn't go to church, he would have waited until after lunch to go up the road, because he didn't want her to think he was trying to mooch a free meal. When he worked for her, okay, but when she was going to help him fix the cart, no panhandling.

After he got up he killed time rereading some of his mother's postcards and it struck him suddenly that he had no way of getting his mail after he left the Nolans. He'd have to pick out some towns along the route and have his mail forwarded. Before he left, he needed to get to the post office in Conifer. Maybe he even should go visit old Royce one time, what the heck. A guy in jail probably got lonesome, and it would be interesting to talk to Royce when he was flat sober for a change.

When he went into the house to wash, Della was snoring, and the dining-room table was just like he had left it. So he cleared it, working as silently as a burglar, and washed up. She probably had a hangover, he thought. Good old Della, she hadn't hardly touched her T-bone, so he heated it up in the oven for breakfast. How many guys had T-bone two meals in a row?

Duke appreciated the steak bones and leftover baked spud so much he let Clem harness up Pedro and hitch up the gig without strawbossing the job. First time *that* ever happened. Clem didn't need much help, anyway, now that Pedro came willingly to call, and even trotted when he wanted him to. Not that Clem would expect him to do any trotting on the trip, of course. A good fast walk would do.

When they turned south on the road Clem saw the big cab-over and semi parked at Mrs. Whittle's, and felt a little annoyed. If Ken was visiting his mother, she might not want to work on the cart. And might not let Clem use her power saw. He shrugged philosophically; there were a lot of clouds scudding across the sky, and it might be fixing to rain, anyhow.

It rained before the afternoon was over, all right, but the rest of the day turned out better than he could have possibly hoped. After the usual greetings, Ken Whittle said, "Maw told me about your summer plans, Clem, and they sound like fun. As for this fixing the cart, you amateurs stand back and let an expert show you how it's done." And he took over the job of remodeling the donkey cart. Ken Whittle was a heavy-set, amiable man with a booming laugh who both delighted and intimidated Clem. Ken always wore his dark-brown hair in a bristly burr-cut, and always had a cigar clamped in his teeth. He was loudly opinionated, deceptively slow-moving, but restless and energetic, and seemed to be an all-round carpenter, mechanic, electrician, plumber, and you name it. On this Sunday afternoon while they built a roof on the cart, Clem learned another surprising thing about the man. Ken Whittle had once been a teacher and planned to go back to teaching someday. When he could afford it, he said with irony.

42

"First year I jockeyed a bobtail rig I nearly doubled my income," he said. "Right now, after five years, I knock down close to two hundred bucks a week, Clem, plus twelve-fifty per diem on the road, and I get home with most of that, with all the free truckers' dorms along the highways and the bunk bed in the cab. It's good money, and the only thing wrong with it is not getting home as often as I'd like." He removed his cigar and looked at Clem gravely. "Actually, that's good, because my wife's hard to get along with and my kids are mean little devils."

"Kendrick, you liar!" his mother scolded. "You've got the sweetest wife and the nicest children of anybody I know."

Ken winked at Clem. "Maw don't get around much, and she's prejudiced against me because I quit teaching. Hey, this plywood is the same width as the cart bed, there won't be any side overlap, and a little overlap would help in every respect. Say, Maw, do you still have that roll of aluminum flashing around here, that four-inch stuff?"

Kendrick, Clem was thinking. That was a pretty unusual name.

Mrs. Whittle had the flashing, and Kendrick used it on both sides of the roof to form what he called drip eaves. He also said Clem needed three studs on each side to properly support the roof and avoid a sag. And he found an old tarp and cut drop curtains for the sides and back and front that could be rolled up and tied if you wanted the cart open, or let down and tied if you wanted it closed. And somewhere during the showery afternoon, when they had pushed the cart into the garage to work in the dry, Ken said, "Hey, Maw, whatever became of that old cot pad I left here for you to throw away?" And she said she hadn't got around to throwing it away yet. And he said, well, maybe Clem could use it, even if it wasn't worth a damn.

43

Clem was no authority on cot pads, but it looked like a perfectly good one to him, even if it did have a couple of small rips on one side. Then Ken said he didn't have any use for the rest of the old tarp and Clem might as well save him the trouble of throwing *that* away, too—it might come in handy for something.

Clem was suddenly reminded that he owed Mrs. Whittle for the stuff she'd ordered from the lumberyard, and he asked her how much that came to, a little worried that it was going to bite a big chunk out of his savings.

"Actually, all I had to order was the sheet of plywood, Clem," she told him, "and they gave me a very good price on that, I thought. The two-by-fours were some oddments left over from building this garage, as were the finishing nails. The plywood was only . . . uh . . . three dollars."

Three dollars! He'd figured seven or eight. He'd thought if he got off for ten bucks, he'd be lucky. Sonofagun! What a break!

And then when the job was finished, beautifully finished, and they were having some pie and coffee and milk, Kendrick Whittle suddenly said, "Say, Clem, it oughta be possible to load that cart and your donkey into an empty van, you know it? For example, if you were going today, here I am with an empty semi I have to herd back to Tulsa. When are you leaving?"

"Well, I figured about a week from Monday."

"Hmmm," Ken said. "Tell you what, pal, you keep your schedule loose and let me see what transpires between now and then. Maybe I can work out a way to give you a jump on things. This is what? The eleventh? I have a run to San Diego, five days. . . . It just might be that I can work something out."

"Right," Clem said. If he could stow away in a semi trailer while Della was at work, leaving a note saying he

44

was going back to visit his old home town and relatives, he'd be halfway where he was going before she even knew he was really gone.

Then he thought, Thursday's my birthday, the fifteenth, and I'll actually *be* fourteen, instead of just *saying* I am. And man, I don't care if I don't get a single birthday present, I figure I got all the birthday present I need right here today . . .

What he got for his birthday was a licking. All week at school the kids razzed Kirby Newman. And Thursday after school, instead of catching the bus, Clem got beat up. And would have had to walk all the way home if Della Nolan hadn't given him a ride.

"What in the world are you *walking* home for?" she demanded.

"I missed the bus," he said, keeping his head down, but she saw the dirt and bruises and the black eye.

"My God, hon!" she exclaimed. "What happened to you?"

"Koobie Noobie," he said with a wild laugh of relief because he was still alive. Boy, when all those kids made a corral around him after school, penning him up so he couldn't run out, Clem had figured, Well, this is it and all I can do is act like I'm not scared, and die like a man. But it was a heck of a way to spend your fourteenth birthday.

"Hey!" he said abruptly, looking at Della. "How come you're not at work?"

"I'm taking a leave of absence," she said. "But never mind that, Clemmie. What on earth *happened* to you?"

"Aw," he shrugged, "just a fight." He said it with something akin to happiness, because even if he'd got whipped, he hadn't *admitted* it. He hadn't begged for mercy. And he hadn't done any weeping, either. It was sort of great to know you had guts.

45

"Whatta you mean, a leave of absence?" he asked her.

"That's what I call it," she said. "I don't know what *they* call it. I'm just taking off a couple of weeks, and if they don't like it they can lump it."

She quit her job! thought Clem, and he gave her a look of alarm with his good eye. Alarm and inquiry.

"I've been in to see Royce," she said, misreading his glance.

"How is he?" Clem asked politely, thinking, she said two weeks.

Della grimaced. "Sober and repentant, naturally. Gonna turn over a new leaf. Never touch another drop. Bull!"

Two weeks. Was she just gonna lay around home for two weeks, maybe hitting the tomato juice? He couldn't make his getaway with her there.

She looked at him again. "Clemmie," she said, "do you want me to take you to the clinic?"

Clem shook his head emphatically. "Shoot, no. I'm okay."

She nodded, trusting his diagnosis, saving three dollars plus the expense of X-rays and medication. Hoddangit, even a week's delay might ruin his whole trip.

"Clemmie," she said, "do you think you could make out by yourself for a couple of weeks if I stocked up on groceries and left you some money?"

He gave her a one-eyed stare. "Huh?"

"I mean, you wouldn't be afraid to be alone for a couple of weeks, would you, hon?"

Blinking his good eye, he said, "Afraid of what?"

She smiled and patted his knee. "Spoken like a true gentleman. I'll fill the fridge with eggs and bacon and milk and frankfurters and hamburger and pork steaks and ham, things that will be simple to cook. And I'll leave you some

46

money in case you run short—you could haul groceries with your little mule, in a pinch, huh?"

"Donkey," he said, without thinking. "You mean you're fixin' to go somewhere?"

Della nodded, watching the road. "I've got friends in Kansas I haven't seen in years—you couldn't get Royce to take a vacation trip if you paid him in hundred-proof bourbon. Now all of a sudden I'm free to do as I please, and I darn well please to drive to Kansas. I've got some paychecks stashed away and I've got a good car and I don't have to worry about Royce—let him do the worrying for a change. Suddenly I feel free as a bird—except for you, Clemmie. I mean, I couldn't just run out on you, if you really needed me."

"Hey, listen," Clem said anxiously, "I'll make out fine. You think I'm a kid or something? Don't worry about me, ma'am."

"Clem," she said wryly, "you're the nicest boy I ever knew. And I'm sorry if I've seemed to neglect you, hon. I'm not the mother type, especially when it comes to big, handsome kids like you." She threw him a quick smile. "No, really, we haven't made much of a home for you. We never had any kids of our own, but I hoped that having a boy around the place might make Royce settle down. But it was too much to ask, at his age, I suppose. Still, he's never had to lay out a jail term before, and maybe that'll force him to do some serious thinking about himself and us and life in general."

"He's got the time, anyway," said Clem, thinking, Della's going away! I can just pull up stakes any time I please!

"I'm gonna be doing some serious thinking, too," she said. "I got to figure out the score between me and Royce. I guess I'm no prize, myself. Maybe this separation will do us all good, give us a fresh start."

47

A head start is all I want, he answered silently. About a week.

"That reminds me," Della said, glancing at him, "I've noticed your pants legs don't reach the tops of your shoes any more—you're growing like a weed—so if you'll dig up an old pair of jeans I can cut up I'll lengthen them. Next fall we'll buy you some new clothes for school."

"Yeah, but if you're goin' to Kansas . . ." Clem said anxiously.

"I don't plan to leave until Sunday morning."

In that case, he thought with relief, Okay. They were coming to the turn-off and he asked her to let him off at Mrs. Whittle's. When she stopped the car, she said, "I'm in a mood for pork chops and fried taters, and calories be damned—how about you, Clemmie?"

He endorsed the idea heartily, thinking that in a way he was going to miss old Della. She was a good joe when she wasn't all cluttered up with Royce. He thanked her for the ride, with Duke jumping around in his usual four o'clock frenzy. After she drove off, he got an armlock around Duke's neck and thought. Instead of notifying the post office, what I'll do is wait until I'm about three weeks gone, then write Della the truth and ask *her* to forward my mail. In the meantime I'll send a few postcards to Mama and tell her not to write me care of Nolans any more.

He'd sent his mother a fancy Mother's Day card that cost him a buck, but so far he hadn't received any birthday card from her. How could she forget June 15th? That worried him sick.

Mrs. Whittle, no stranger to schoolyard battle wounds, clucked and smiled tolerantly and asked if he had been victorious.

"I guess you could say I came in a close second." He grinned, noticing the pitcher of iced tea and thinking, I'll

48

be okay in a day or two, but old Kirby is stuck with that nickname for life.

"Will there be official repercussions tomorrow, Clem?"

"Naw, I don't think so," he said. Marble cake, too, he noted approvingly. "Last day of school an' all, I doubt it."

"Then the call of the open road," she said.

For his birthday present, Mrs. Whittle trimmed his hair, saving him a dollar and a quarter, and gave him a box of stationery and some stamped postcards and envelopes. He appreciated it.

SIX

Ken had to leave for San Diego real early Monday morning, and when Clem began his journey he still hadn't got his birthday card from his mother.

It was much easier unloading the cart than it had been to load it. But old Pedro was sore after being shut up in the dark truck for a couple of hours, and he balked about coming down the ramp and tried to kick Ken Whittle and bite Clem before he finally gave in and skidded down the tilted raft of two-by-tens in a half-sitting position. He stayed mad for a while, though, flicking his ears with annoyance and showing his long teeth.

"Well, you've got around four hours of daylight left," Ken told him. "About right for a shakedown run." He squinted into the windy west and moved the cigar around in his mouth thoughtfully. "Looks like you might get to see how rainproof your rig is, too. Remember, camp away from the highway whenever you can. I mean off the right-of-way, back in the woods or up a side road. But if you have to camp in the bar-ditch overnight, pick a straight stretch, and if anybody bothers you, you know what to do, right?"

Clem nodded, not worried about that possibility. "Shoot my rifle in the air," he said, looking around at the country-side, which already seemed somewhat alien, flatter than his homeland with scrubbier timber. Windier, too. And it

50

wasn't gravel soil any more, but a sticky mud where water had stood in the broad ditch. These shoulders and bar-ditches wouldn't be what you'd call an all-weather road. It could be tricky footing and slow going for old Pedro when it rained. "Heck, old Duke will scare off anybody comes messin' around, I guess."

"Sure he will," Ken nodded reassuringly. "Well, Clem, you're on your way—and I got to be on mine. So long, pal." He thrust out his hand and Clem shook in farewell and then stared at his palm that now contained a folded five-dollar bill. "Birthday present, Clem."

Clem protested. "I thought that icebox was."

"Aw," Ken said, "that foam plastic picnic cooler cost less than a buck." He grinned, the stub of his cigar at a jaunty angle. "Good luck, pal. Have a nice trip, huh?"

Clem nodded, swallowing. What the world needed was more people like Ken and his mother, and as he watched the big reassuring figure climb into the high cab he had a sudden moment of panic, not wanting to be abandoned in unfamiliar country. But the feeling passed quickly, and he felt instead a thump-chested eagerness to be on his way west.

One reason Ken had picked this spot to unload Clem was that he could turn around just up the road at a drive-in café, and by the time Clem had snapped Duke's leash to a ring of Pedro's collar and climbed up into the seat with the reins, the big truck was making a wide swinging turn back onto the highway and roaring east again. Ken waved and grinned as he passed, and that was that. A feeling of misgiving came over Clem again. No telling when he'd see Ken again, or Mrs. Whittle, either. Boy, just barely started and already he felt homesick. He remembered Mrs. Whittle taking off her glasses and dabbing at her eyes and saying,

"Oh, Clem, I've grown so fond of you I can hardly bear to see you go."

And her going-away presents. A box of assorted canned stuff, a three-pound coffee can full of cookies, a thirty-pound sack of Gaines Meal for Duke, and a big bag of doughnuts.

Driving a resigned Pedro up the gentle grade along the wide, flat, grassy bar-ditch toward the swift-sailing clouds in the west, Clem decided that at least he didn't have any problems about food or money. He was loaded. Over fifty bucks, with the twenty Della had left him and the five Ken just forced on him. Besides the food Mrs. Whittle had given him, and the picnic cooler full of milk, bacon, eggs, margarine, packages of frozen pork steak, cut-up chicken, stew meat, and some round steak, he had flour, sugar, cornmeal, coffee, tea, lard, salt and pepper, and a bottle of vinegar to use on the wild greens he aimed to pick on the way. All in all, he felt rich and well equipped for the journey, and as soon as he got over being sad about all the good people he'd left behind, he would be okay.

"Move out, boorow," he said to plodding Pedro. "Walk faster, boy."

But before they had covered the first half-mile of what still was almost a seven-hundred-mile journey, Pedro stumbled and started favoring his right front leg. Clem stopped him and got down from the seat and checked his hoof, but there was no visible wound, so it was probably a strained tendon. Looking for whatever the donkey had stepped on, he found a pop bottle hidden in the matted dry grass under the new green. And when he checked around a little he discovered there were beer cans and beer bottles all along the highway where passing motorists had casually tossed them out in violation of the seldom enforceable law against littering. After thinking for a minute, Clem decided that he'd

52

better walk ahead and keep an eye peeled for hoof hazards. So what he'd visualized as a fairly comfortable ride to New Mexico suddenly took on the aspects of a long and tiring hike. Still, better to walk now than wind up having to pull the cart himself.

He'd been carrying the muddy pop bottle with a finger stuck down its neck, and he started to pitch it up over the low bank, but then he thought, Hey, it's worth two cents. So he put it in the cart and made a note to watch for others. A guy could maybe earn part of his grub that way, collecting bottles and claiming the deposit value at stores or filling stations along the route.

Looking for bottles was a good distraction, taking his mind off the dismaying thought of all the endless slow miles ahead, and it was amazing how many bottles people casually discarded along the wayside.

All the cars and trucks whizzing past bothered him at first. He had the feeling all of the drivers were staring at him with amusement, but he soon realized that few of them gave him more than a brief passing glance, preoccupied by their own affairs, and after a while he was able to ignore the traffic, though he did envy the cars that were heading west at over sixty miles an hour. But it was a waste of good brains, thinking stuff like that. If wishes were grasshoppers, he could have opened a bait shop years ago. He wasn't rushed for time, and a guy didn't have to buy gas and oil for a donkey, or worry about blowouts.

That's what *he* thought. . . .

The sulphurous yellowish-gray clouds had thickened into a swelling mass of thunderheads, blocking off the sun; the wind had stiffened and grown colder; traffic had dwindled to a hurrying trickle in the threatening gloom, and Clem's spirits were very low as he squatted in the shallow bar-ditch

53

staring dismally at the flat tire. The one damn thing he hadn't even thought about happening had happened. All the years he'd had the cart, neither of the tires had ever gone flat. He must have picked up a nail or something. And it was a calamity, because he had no tools, no spare, nothing to patch a tube with. It looked as if he were going to be forced to camp right there for the night.

The premature dusk was oppressively quiet except for occasional rolls of thunder in the southwest, and the swoosh of a car rushing past oblivious to his predicament. He thought about trying to wave somebody down, but couldn't bring himself to do it, not wanting to impose on strangers and pessimistic about flagging one down, anyhow. If he was a beautiful chick some guy would stop and offer to help, but he wasn't, and wouldn't want to be one even if he could make the switch.

When he heard the explosive sputtering of a motorcycle coming from the east, its racket was unusual enough to penetrate his gloomy preoccupation. Watching it approach, he felt a stirring of hope when it began to lose speed, and then uneasiness when he saw that the face framed by a crash helmet was black. The cycle came to a stop fifteen feet away, and for a long silent moment the Negro rider impassively took in the situation, with a tongue-tied Clem eyeing him warily. Then, without a word having been exchanged, the Negro twisted the throttle into a popping roar, glanced over his shoulder, and shot away, continuing west. Clem felt more relief than disappointment. There were a few Negroes around Conifer, including three or four in high school and a couple of little ones in the first grade, but he didn't know any personally and had never talked to one—and everybody knew they all hated white people nowadays and were dangerous.

Then he tensed up again as the cycle slowed after a hundred yards and reversed its course in a U-turn to come cruising past again, the booted, leather-jacketed, crash-helmeted driver staring but continuing on east for fifty yards. Then he made another U-turn and came back, and this time he pulled onto the shoulder, his cycle backfiring and stuttering. He kicked the stand down and got off expressionlessly. To Clem there was something menacing in the gleaming black face and towering figure.

"Um-*hmm!*" the Negro said. "Look like you got a severe flat, man."

Clem nodded, feeling dry-mouthed. "An' nothin' to fix it with."

The man removed his white-and-gold helmet and, scratching his head, looked off toward the looming cloud-bank, veined now with constant streaks of lightning. "You got a jack?" he asked.

Clem stood up and leaned against the cart, wondering why Duke hadn't barked. "Nope," he said. Duke was asleep in the grass at the end of his chain. Some watchdog.

"That don't matter," the Negro said to the clouds. "Any tools?"

Clem shook his head. "Nope. Nothin' but an axe."

The Negro looked at him then, flashing a white grin. "You chop it off, man, it wouldn't fit back on so good. Got any patching?"

"You name it," Clem said, glumly, "an' I ain't got it."

The Negro laughed, stomped with his boots, slapped his leg. "Okay, baby," he said. "If my lug wrench will fit, the main pain depend whether we get done before it rain." Hanging his crash helmet on a handlebar, he got tools out of a saddlebag. Dropping them on the ground by the casing, he tested the cart for weight, lifting it easily. The man chuckled. "You got no jack but you got you a jackass. We going to need something to put under here to hold it up."

55

Clem had just the thing, the sturdy sawhorse he'd made to put under the shafts for support when Pedro wasn't hitched up. The Negro said to hold everything till he checked his lug wrench. It was a four-socket cross, and the third one he tried was a fit. Better loosen the nuts before they raised the wheel off the ground, he said. It seemed to Clem that he didn't talk like a Negro. The lugs were rust-frozen and stubborn, but the man was strong, and they finally gave, squeaking. They got the axle up on the saw-horse, causing the cart to tilt the other way for a change, and the black man turned the wheel, feeling the tire for the source of its trouble. He found a small shiny new finishing nail, and Clem sighed disgustedly. One of his own nails must have been in there all this time since they finished building the roof. "Brought that all the way from home," he said. "It must have been in there a long time. How come it didn't make it go flat before?"

"Well, it was through the side, mostly, and not much weight on it." Stepping on the deflated tire the Negro looked up at Clem quizzically. "You live 'round here?"

Clem told him he was from the eastern part of the state, a fact which immediately required clarification, and while his benefactor worked the tire free of the rim and pulled the tube, he explained about being on his way to New Mexico to see his mother.

"Baby, you got a long haul ahead of you," the Negro observed, and laughed. "But you liable to be there long befo' I reach Califo-*nyuh,* if my hog keeps actin' contrary." *Sometimes* he talked like a Negro.

"Is that where you're going?" Clem asked, as a few drops of rain spattered around them. The gusting wind made him nervous. It seemed to make the man nervous, too; he paused at his work and stared up at the spreading front of clouds.

"That's where I'm *goin',* man. Question is, does that hog

56

go with this cat, or do I sell it to the junk man an' make reservations on one them *economy* class boxcars? Or does this cat grab a high-payin' job in one them friendly, hospitable towns on ahead an' buy some organs an' repair work on that ailin' hog?" He had the tube out and had found the puncture now. "Man, that ain't nothin' but a slow leak. You could cure it with chewin' gum." He flashed that dazzling white grin again. "But I'm fresh outa Juicy Fruit, so I guess we goin' hafta use a hot patch." He rose and headed for his motorcycle, which glowed here and there in the swiftly falling darkness, as did the crash helmet. Luminous paint, Clem deduced shrewdly. Make it show up better at night.

The man wheeled his cycle down off the shoulder. "Hate for some fool to hurt my Harley," he said, digging into the saddlebag again. There was a suitcase with a bedroll lashed behind the seat.

"I'm sure not much help," Clem apologized, shivering in the wind.

"This a one-man job, Charley. But you could be a windbreak while I fire up this patch."

A few drops of cold, wind-driven rain stung Clem's back as he huddled over the wheel, shoulder to shoulder with his big benefactor, watching the stuff flare up and smelling the acrid smoke.

"Ought to wait a while for it to dry," the Negro said, "but the shades of night are fallin' fast, baby, an' I guarantee it'll hold if you don't run on it for a while." He was stuffing the tube back inside the tire, pulling the valve through the hole in the rim. Turning the wheel over, he began prying the tire back into place and then he produced a tire pump and began inflating the patched tube, and all the while big scattered raindrops splashed here and there and the thunder and lightning increased. "Hol' it, Lord," the Negro said, looking up. "We 'bout done here."

57

The rain slackened until the tire was inflated and the wheel replaced, but the lightning revealed a solid curtain of rain advancing across the fields and down the highway. Clem thought, He can't ride a motorcycle through a cloudburst. If he hadn't stopped to help me, he would have been where he could get in out of the storm by now.

Pedro was fidgeting, knowing from long experience that he ought to be facing away from the storm, and beginning to edge sideways. So Clem got hold of his bridle and turned the cart around. Then he unsnapped Duke's chain and fastened it around the shaft where he could get under the cart. When he finished the Negro had put his crash helmet on again and zippered up his leather jacket and was sitting astride the motorcycle.

"Hey, wait a minute!" Clem said. "Where you goin'?"

The white teeth flashed. "I don' know *where,* but I know *how—wet,* man. Soaked an' saturated."

For an ungrateful split second Clem was tempted to just let it go at that. Then he said, "Heck, you don't need to do that! Get inside the cart an' wait till it lets up."

The Negro hesitated for a moment, grinning up at the flashing violence as if tempted to accept the challenge of the storm, but he got off the cycle and quickly unstrapped his suitcase and bedroll, and climbed into the cart behind Clem just as the deluge struck.

"I got some candles here," Clem said, shivering with apprehension as the heavy rain drummed on the plywood roof. He got a candle lit and set it on the seat and told the big Negro—bigger than ever now in the cramped confines of the small cart—how to lash down the rear curtain so it hung outside and kept out the rain. Then the man sat on his bedroll with his small suitcase behind his back, and Clem sat on his own rolled-up bed, and they grinned at each other in the candlelight as the thwarted storm raged outside.

58

"Man, that's what I call cuttin' it close," the Negro sighed.

Clem nodded, and said hospitably, "You hungry? I got some homemade doughnuts an' cookies, an' milk to drink. Or how about a sandwich first an' then a couple doughnuts?" His generosity was slightly suspect, because he hated to finish his doughnut supply too soon. He had plenty of canned meat and sardines and could always buy more if he ran out, but there wouldn't be any more of Mrs. Whittle's doughnuts after these.

"You bet," the Negro said with enthusiasm. "If there's two things I like to do, the other one is eat."

Clem had never been host before, but it struck him that when you had a guest for dinner you ought to know who he was. "Reckon I oughta introduce myself," he said gruffly. "I'm Clem Marlow."

The incredibly white grin reflected candlelight again, and the Negro stuck out a hand that engulfed Clem's with gentle strength. "Would you believe Abdulla Akbar?"

Clem was surprised, but said, "Pleased to meet you."

Abdulla chuckled. "Make that Gaylord Jackson, okay? I shucked Abdulla when I left Chicago. Any religion that says cut out the chicks an' pork chops ain't my road to heaven, baby."

Clem had no idea what he was talking about, but as a gracious host he just said, "You come all the way from Chicago?"

"By way of St. Louis," Gaylord Jackson said, arranging himself more comfortably in the cramped space. "Things brewin' in both those towns I want no part of. Don't like cities nohow, but even if I did I wouldn't crave to join any of them burn-baby-burn sessions all them young ghetto cats hummin' up a storm about. When they preach guerrilla war, I got Uncle Tom ears. That don't buy nothing but more of the same." All the while he was speaking his gaze was

59

upward, as if he might be a trifle nervous about the storm. Clem was nervous about the storm, too, and glad not to be alone in it. The wind rocked the cart now and then, and he appreciated Gaylord's considerable extra weight to help hold things down. "No," the Negro went on, "the militants aren't for me."

If Clem understood him correctly, Gaylord didn't endorse violence. The box of canned stuff was between them, and he opened the top and held the candle over it and said, "Pick out whatever you want to eat." Gaylord Jackson checked the stock and looked impressed, but hesitated to make a choice. Anything would suit him, he said, listening with frowning concentration.

"Clem, you ever been in a tornado?"

"Not yet," Clem said, deciding to open some Spam. "Have you?"

"Uh-uh, but I have seen the *results,* and they are something."

Clem nodded and began making up sandwiches. Then he got a carton of milk out of the picnic cooler and filled a couple of the plastic glasses Mrs. Whittle had given him, and they ate and drank in silence. They had two sandwiches apiece, and a doughnut apiece, and several of the raisiny oatmeal cookies, and by the time they had finished eating, the main fury of the storm had passed, the thunder rolling away east as the wind subsided and the rain gradually slackened and quit.

"I'm mighty obliged for the supper, but if my hog ain't drowned I best be on my way, Clem."

"How far you figure on goin' tonight?" Clem wondered.

"I got gal cousins in Drumright," Gaylord said, grinning. "They the best kind." He had the back curtain unfastened now, and when he raised it, Clem saw that inky night had arrived during the storm. Opening the footlocker under the seat, he got out the three-cell flashlight that had belonged to his father, shining it on the motorcycle so his departing guest could see to lash on the suitcase and bedroll. "Hol' yo' breath," Gaylord said, and began trying to start the cycle. "Better cross yo' fingers, too." Clem crossed his fingers and the motorcycle started. "Okay, baby, exhale," Gaylord hollered. "Good luck, Clem." He turned on his headlamp, fastened his chinstrap, and waved.

"The same to you, Gaylord!" Clem yelled after him, and then he was alone in the black, dripping silence. Except for Duke and Pedro, of course, but at the moment they were not very much company. It wasn't that he was afraid of the darkness, it was just that he had a sense of having permanently cut himself off from everything familiar. Duke emerged from under the cart and shook himself, wagging his tail and showing his teeth as if to say, well, now that it's *over,* that wasn't so bad, was it?

"I'll feed you extra in the mornin'," Clem told him. "We'll get an early start, ol' buddy. Hey, how come you never barked at that big mean-lookin' guy?"

Duke stopped wagging his tail and eyed him solemnly, as if to say, What the heck, I assumed you knew what you were doing.

"Okay, but in the future, boy, watch it," Clem said. He got out in the sloppy grass, waited for a couple of cars to pass, and relieved himself. Then he patted Duke's hard head, climbed back inside, and tied the curtain down. He unfastened the front curtain and checked on Pedro, using the flashlight. The donkey flicked a wet ear irritably and half turned his head. "Well, I'm sorry," Clem said. "It isn't *my* fault we had a flat an' got caught in a storm."

Closing the front curtain, he unrolled the mattress and blankets, took off his sneakers, got a comic book out of the

61

locker, and stretched out to read in bed awhile. He'd been sleeping in the cart almost every night since he'd got it enclosed, and was by now used to it. He fell asleep almost immediately.

Sometime during the night he was awakened by Duke's furious barking and the sound of a man's voice calling his name against the background of an idling truck engine.

"Hey, Clem!" the voice shouted again, and he recognized Ken Whittle. "Are you in there, Clem?"

"Ken?" Clem said, yawning.

"Are you all right, pal?"

"Sure, I'm fine," Clem said thickly. "Hey, what are *you* doin' here?"

"On our way to San Diego with a load of airplane parts," Ken said. "Hey, you didn't get very far."

Clem remembered Ken saying they always took the turn-pike as far as Oklahoma City, going to California. "I had a flat tire," he said.

"You're headed back the way you came—don't tell me you changed your mind." Ken sounded like he was probably kidding.

Clem yawned and shivered. "We hit a storm, hard rain an' the wind blew like the dickens, so I turned Pedro facin' away from it, is all. By the time it slacked off it was too dark to go any farther, so I'm spendin' the night here." He felt it necessary to add, "I left Pedro hitched up so we can get an early start in the mornin'."

"So you're all right? No problems, Clem?"

"Everything's okay," Clem assured him.

"Well, excuse me for waking you, Clem. Good night, and if I didn't say it before, good luck. Be seeing you, pal."

Boy, I hope so, Clem thought. He listened as the diesel engine's throbbing changed into a powerful thunder. As the friendly sound of the truck faded, he pulled the blanket over him, thinking, Man, the best place to be this time of night is in the old sack, snoozing away. Or up in the curtained bunk of a big diesel truck, like Ken's partner Jasper Hicks. Probably no kin to big-eyed Molly Hicks who had said, that last day of school, "I guess I'll see you next year in junior high." Not wanting to make her feel bad, he'd let it go at that, not telling her he was planning to attend school in a town called Carrizozo next year. Then Molly had spoiled things by saying shyly, "I just want to say I think you are one of the nicest boys I know, Clement—and the *funniest* person I ever met, I really mean it."

That soured the whole thing, as far as he was concerned.

But maybe someday when he filled out he'd go back to Conifer and look her up and say, "Okay, Molly, who's funny *now?*" And he'd tell her . . . he'd say . . . well . . .

He was awakened in the chilly pre-dawn grayness by Pedro sneezing and stirring around. He got up thinking nervously of where he was and how far he had to go. After feeding Duke a generous ration of Gaines Meal he punished himself by only eating one doughnut and some milk for breakfast, thinking, How would *you* like to stand up all night in water and mud, boy? Then he got an even earlier start than he'd planned, walking ahead in the wet grass and slick mud, kicking beer cans out of the donkey's path and picking up pop bottles to convert into cash. It was a beautiful morning after the rain, and he didn't mind his soggy sneakers so much when the sun came up and warmed the rest of him. Things sure seemed more cheerful on a sunny morning than they did on a stormy night.

He was unconsciously counting steps, thinking how each step brought him that much closer to his mother, and then

63

the idea hit him; he would keep track of how many steps he took each day. Then when he got there he could add up the total and he would know something that probably nobody else in the world knew—how many steps it was to Carrizozo, New Mexico, from any given point along his route.

When the sun was high and hot in the sky he came to a stretch of lush grass that Pedro could eat for lunch, near a small creek where he could build a fire. Walking in soggy sneakers made a guy's feet sore and tired. As soon as he stopped he took the shoes off and hung them in the sun to dry. It felt pretty good to go barefooted, and he decided to walk that way a lot of the time, but of course he didn't know about sand burrs and bullhead nettles and cactus and stinging weeds then.

Along about noon that day the first big cross-country truck blasted its horn at him, the driver waving. It was an eastbound Sundown Trucking, Inc., big semi trailer on a cab-over bobtail diesel tractor. A little while later, a big Blue Zephyr Van Lines eastbound also trumpeted a greeting. But it wasn't until the fourth or fifth truck passed that the driver yelled something over the roar and rumble of his swift passage that caused Clem to break stride and lose count of his steps.

It had sounded as if he driver had yelled, "Hello, *Clem!*"

But the significance of it eluded him. Doggone, he thought, feeling suddenly less alone in the world, that must have been somebody that *knows* me.

He picked up the count again and walked on. A couple of other eastbound truckers honked and waved during the hot afternoon, and whatever their motives, it made Clem feel like a recognizable member of the human race and not just a pair of sore, burning feet. And then he got a real

64

break. He came to one of those marked speedometer-check measured miles, and it came out just a little over nineteen hundred steps. So he didn't have to count anymore. The miles were marked on his map and all he needed to do was multiply by nineteen hundred. That would be close enough. Who would ever check up on him?

SEVEN

B Y late afternoon, when he came to the country gas station and general store, he was tired, thirsty, and painfully sunburned. That was something he hadn't somehow expected, the hot, stinging misery of his face, the back of his neck, and even the backs of his hands. It was simply one more thing he hadn't foreseen and would just have to get used to. If he'd never needed a hat before, he needed one now. And he needed to get shut of the forty-odd bottles rattling around in the cart, making it heavier for Pedro to pull.

Several cars were parked around the highway store, and a group of men were loafing on the shady side, waiting for some diversion to take their minds off the heat and monotony of their day. A gangling, sunburned boy with an unusual donkey cart was just what the doctor ordered. There were several old men, mild-mannered and harmless enough under ordinary conditions, and several rowdy boys.

"Well, looky heah, now!" somebody said.

"Howdy do if it ain't a mule train for certain, boys!"

One of the young rowdies hee-hawed like a jackass. Clem didn't know whether to ignore the peanut gallery, or grin like a fool, or what. There was something about them, something familiar in those bawly, guffawish voices that put him on his guard. Later he realized that they reminded him of

66

Royce Nolan when he'd been drinking. Maybe these guys had been drinking a little, or wished they had. All he wanted was for them to leave him alone. He wasn't in any mood for horsing around.

"Hey there, where did you get that Texas jackrabbit?"

"Hee-haw, heeyawww, heeyawww!"

The audience snorted and guffawed. "By God, Carl, if your ears was a mite longer you'd do to farm a cotton patch with," one of the men remarked, provoking a laugh not at Clem's expense. Unfortunately, it must have stung Carl into the action that later caused all the trouble.

"What'll ya take for that there burro?" an old man called out.

"Ain't for sale," Clem said, embarrassed.

"Trade you a good pocketknife for that pot-licker," a man said.

"Already got a knife," Clem said, resenting the insult to Duke. If his initial instinct had been to clown the way he did at school, he was no longer in a mood for entertaining. He just wanted to sell his bottles and buy a hat and a drink and move on.

"Where'd ya git that chicken coop on wheels, feller?"

Clem shrugged, too weary to think up answers. He stopped Pedro by the gas pumps, where the cart wouldn't block anybody's way. "Stay here, boy," he told Duke, and went limping into the cluttered grocery store. A sharp-eyed woman and a fat girl were chatting behind the checkout counter, and he figured the woman was the boss. "I've got about four dozen empty pop bottles, ma'am," he told her.

The fat girl giggled. "You drink all that yourself?"

He gave her a patient smile. "I picked 'em up along the highway," he said. "I heard they're worth two cents apiece."

"Who told you that?" the woman demanded.

He blinked at her. "They're *not?* Worth two cents apiece?"

She shrugged. "Depends on whether anybody wants to buy them or not, kiddo."

He had spotted a rack of straw hats and billed caps, quite a selection. "Well," he said, "do you want to?"

She shook her head. "Not at that price, if you picked them up along the highway. They'll be dirty, some of them chipped. No thank you."

Nodding glumly, he turned to leave. He had money to buy a hat with, but he didn't want to buy any hats from *her*.

"I might give you a cent apiece for the good ones, kiddo."

He shook his head and kept going. Back in the hot sun, Carl was sitting astride Pedro, rocking back and forth, grinning.

"Hey, doggone it!" Clem hollered. "Get off, mister!"

"Take it easy, boy, nobody hurtin' your jackass none."

"Well, get off of him, that's all."

"Why, boy, *he* don't mind, why should you? It ain't your back."

One of the men said, "Come on, now, Carl."

"Just taking me a little donkey ride, no harm in that."

"Get off, damn it!" Clem said hopelessly.

Carl was an oversized lout, probably shiftless and mean and wanting attention. "You shore ain't friendly, boy," he scowled.

Clem took a ragged, deep breath. "Get *off!*" he yelled.

"Why, boy, you too damn bossy, you know it? You givin' orders, an' I never was built right for takin' orders from punk kids. You gone hafta change your style. Ast me nice, maybe I'll get off, if I happen to feel like it. Otherwise you'll hafta git me off, boy."

"He's liable to sic his dog on you, Carl," somebody said, and that drew some strained laughter, because Duke was

68

just lying there at the end of his chain, panting and ignoring the whole thing.

"Good way to git his dog kilt," Carl said harshly.

Clem had moved to within reach of the donkey, and was wishing he had a club or a knife. In desperation he finally leaped forward and tried to shove Carl off. But the brawny hooligan grabbed him by an arm and the seat of his britches and just pulled him on up over Pedro's back and dumped him head first onto the gravel. Breaking the fall with his hands helped, but Clem got the wind pretty well knocked out of him, and skinned a hand on the sharp gravel.

"Come on now, Carl," someone protested mildly, and a cracked old voice scolded, "No call for that, dadgum it." But none of them moved out of the shade. Nobody came to help Clem. His skinned hand smarted, and he felt bruised from the tumble, but mostly his *pride* was hurt. Scrambling awkwardly to his feet, embarrassed and furious, he saw that Pedro was bucking and kicking now, and Duke had got up and begun to bark. Some fool laughingly hollered, "Ride 'im, cowboy!" Clem brushed gravel from his cheek and went back for more.

"Wah-hooo!" Carl bellowed, yanking off his dirty straw hat and whacking the donkey with it like a rodeo bronc rider.

Clem grabbed his thick left leg and levered it upward, trying to unseat him, as Duke belatedly went into action, running under the donkey and stupidly wrapping the chain around one of Clem's ankles, barking and growling and generally getting in the way. "You lousy guy!" Clem was yelling. "Get off 'im!"

Carl lifted his burly leg and put a mud-caked shoe against Clem's chest and straightened his leg in a violent push-kick which, because of the tangled chain, sent Clem backward in a skidding dive onto the gravel.

69

As he lay there blinking up at the hot blue sky, getting ready to get up and try again, he heard the loud explosive hissing of airbrakes and the throbbing thunder of a big engine being double-clutched down the gear range. A truck was stopping, thought Clem, that was all. It had nothing to do with him.

Sitting up slowly, he discovered that he had gravel in his hair and down the back of his shirt, and the sunburned nape of his neck was scratched. He was getting up, looking around for a rock to kill somebody with, hearing brisk footsteps in the gravel behind him, and beginning to twist around to see if it was some other guy coming to enjoy the show, when a pair of big hard hands plucked him up and set him on his feet, and a deep, tough voice said, "Would you be Clem?"

Not if I had any choice about it, Clem thought dizzily, blinking up into a hard brown face. "Yessir," he said. "I'm Clem."

"Hold the fort, partner," the tall newcomer said, and stalked on toward the no longer grinning Carl.

"We're jist funnin' a little," he began in a self-righteous tone.

The truck driver drove a big fist savagely into Carl's ribs. He grunted and fell off the donkey, whereupon Duke, having finally figured out whose team he was on, grabbed the bully by the pants leg and started shredding the cloth savagely. Dragging the dog, Carl frantically crawled and hopped beyond the reach of the leash, his mouth slackly ajar and a hand pressed against his ribs. He should have run then, but he didn't, and the tall trucker caught up with him there by the corner of the store and, in a sudden shocked silence, dug a casual left hook into Carl's stomach, followed by a chopping overhand right to the jaw. Everybody just sat and watched Carl crumple like a punctured sack of water, falling into the shade with just his feet out in the sunshine.

Which was about the only intelligent thing he'd done all day.

"Any comments?" asked the truck driver.

Not meeting his stare, the men shrugged and shook their heads.

"Well, I'll make one, then," the deep-voiced knight of the road said with contempt. "You're a sorry chicken-livered bunch to sit there while that fellow bullied a boy half his size." He turned his back on them and stalked over to the outdoor pop machine, and that's when Clem, hugging Pedro's neck and soothing him, noticed that the woman and the fat girl had come out of the store to watch the fun. And never opened their mouths to stop it. I didn't know there were people like that, he thought dully, watching them gape at Carl, who was either out cold or afraid to let on he wasn't.

The truck driver walked back to Clem, smiling calmly and giving him a conspiratorial wink. "That was dry work." He handed the boy a frosty bottle. "You all right, Clem?"

Clem nodded shyly. "Yeah, but how did you know my name?" he asked.

"Your friend Ken Whittle told me about you this morning in Amarillo. I'm Sam Sorrenti. Put 'er there, Clem."

A little overwhelmed, Clem shook hands with Sam Sorrenti, one of seven brothers who owned the Sorrenti Trucking Company, Newark, New Jersey. Sam was a heck of a lot farther from home than Clem, and had come along at a most opportune moment.

"Ken's spreading the word about your trip, Clem," said Sam. "He seems to think you're quite a guy, and he's asking all the truck jockeys to be watching out for you." He smiled again. "Told me I'd probably see you along here somewhere, but he didn't warn me you'd be having a war on your hands." He was about to say something more when the storekeeper interrupted.

71

"Say, kiddo," she called pleasantly, "maybe I'll buy your bottles after all, two cents apiece, okay?"

Clem stared at her, surprised but not feeling very friendly. "How come you changed your mind?" he asked her.

"Oh, to make up for your trouble, let's say—and because someone finally knocked the stuffing out of loud-mouthed Carl Kinster, which I've been waiting to see for a long time."

Clem sloshed the Coke around in the bottle and looked at her, and finally shook his head. There was something wrong with her reasons. If she hadn't wanted the bottles before, she shouldn't want them now, either. Besides, he didn't like her looks.

"No, ma'am, I guess I'll keep 'em awhile longer," he told her.

She made a sour grimace. "Well, don't say I didn't offer, kiddo." Shrugging with cold indifference, she went back inside the store.

"Maybe you ought to hit the road, partner," Sam Sorrenti suggested mildly. "I've got to shove off in a minute, but I'll hang around until you're clear of these characters. And remember, Clem, you're not alone, you've got friends all up and down the road. You get in a jam, just flag a truck and tell the driver—wait a minute." He took out his billfold and extracted a card. "Show him this," he said. "Tell him we won a fight together." He winked and gave Clem a push toward the cart—not knowing, of course, that Clem didn't ride, but walked—and tossed his empty pop bottle toward Carl, who was sitting up groggily now, tenderly feeling his jaw.

The card just said Sam Sorrenti, with an address and phone number and Newark, N.J., but Clem tucked it carefully away in his billfold, which used to belong to his father. Then he got hold of Pedro's bridle and led him past the pumps, anxious to get away.

When he was about a hundred yards off, he looked back, and Sam Sorrenti was standing by the cab of his truck, watching, and waved a big hand in farewell. Waving in return, Clem remembered with awe, *Thud ... whack ... pow!* Boy, that's real class. That's how to do it. Don't waste time arguing, just zap.

A mile or so later, with the sun a red ball sinking behind a far green blackjack ridge, he came to another small and shabby country gas station with a neat, shabby house behind it. An old couple were working in a garden beside the station. Clem turned in and asked if they would care to buy about fifty-some empty pop bottles, and the old man said, "Don't see why not, sonny." And paid two cents without any quibbling. A dollar and fourteen cents wasn't a bad day's wages for a guy that walked about eleven miles at the same time. Boy, if he could earn a dollar a day picking up bottles, he wouldn't have any problems about buying food.

The old couple were lonely for company, as old couples usually are, and asked so many questions they pried Clem's story out of him before he knew it. They seemed to think he was very brave for undertaking such a long journey, but they thought it was a wonderful thing to do, and wouldn't his mother be happy to have him out there with her after such a long time?

They were so friendly he hated to leave, but he explained he had to find a place to camp for the night. Well, now, my goodness, why didn't he just drive around into their yard and camp for the night? He could turn his burro into their small pasture, just the milk cow with all that grass to keep down. And say, now, would he mind doing them a great favor? Would he take supper with them?"

"I wouldn't want to be any bother," he said.

"Bother, my foot!" the woman said. "You'll bother me if you refuse."

73

So he grinned and said, Well, okay then.

"You menfolks go catch me a chicken to fry," the woman said bossily. "We'll have peas and new potatoes. And I just happen to have a loaf of homemade bread left— do you fancy homemade bread, young man?"

He felt a lump in his throat for a second, because his mother used to bake big fat loaves back in the good old days. He nodded.

"We churn our own butter," she boasted. "You'll see, you just wait. Now go catch me a fat fryer, you two."

At dinner they stuffed him full of not one, but two, chickens and wrapped up the leftover pieces for him to make a lunch on the next day, and they talked his arm off, not asking questions any more but telling him about themselves, their children who were scattered all over—Houston, San Francisco, Indiana, and a daughter in Denver—and their grandchildren. They stuffed old Duke, too, with scraps and clabber milk until he got glassy-eyed. They stayed up late for them, ten o'clock; usually they went to bed with the chickens, they assured him. My goodness, didn't the time fly when you were enjoying yourselves? Ten o'clock, for heaven sakes!

Clem went to bed finally and lay awake for a while thinking, People sure are different. You run into a bunch of creeps like old rotten Carl and all those people about a mile east, and just when you're starting to think everybody is mean and nobody cares whether you live or die, along comes a guy like Sam Sorrenti. Then you meet a couple like the Milfords and they make you stay for supper and treat you like a special guest. So how can you ever know?

Sure a lot of nice people in the world . . .

Naturally, they made him eat breakfast. Fried eggs and biscuits and gravy and coffee with pure cream, and strawberry preserves. They gave him a half-gallon fruit jar of

74

milk and a big pat of country butter, the leftover biscuits and the last of the homemade bread, and they wrote down their name and address and begged him to drop them a postcard once in a while, so they would know he was all right.

When he went out onto the highway and headed west again, Mrs. Milford dabbed at her eyes and blew her nose, just like Mrs. Whittle had done. Women were funny that way. But shoot, what would he do with all that milk? He still had some store-bought milk in the picnic cooler, and the ice was mostly melted. If he didn't get some ice pretty soon, not only the milk would spoil, but some of the meat, too. That was something he hadn't figured, how far it would be between places that sold ice.

Pedro seemed to be in a good mood and full of pep, as if he'd enjoyed being with a cow again. He had a thing about cows. But he'd never been around anything else, and probably wouldn't know a donkey if he met one.

Along about ten o'clock he came around a bend and saw a beat-up old car beside the highway, with a lot of boxes tied on top and people sitting around. A thin, homely girl was sitting on the bank holding a dirty little crying kid, and talking to another as dirty but a little bigger who sat beside her looking sad. Beyond them two worn-looking women were watching an unshaven, overalled man sitting on the ground with the pieces of a dismembered carburetor in his lap.

"Oh, looky, kids, looky at the donkey," the girl on the bank said. The bigger one looked, but the littlest one kept on crying.

"Hi," Clem said self-consciously, because he had to pass right by them and it would have been pretty rude not to speak.

75

"Hi," the girl said. She looked about his age, maybe younger.

Clem stopped, because the women and the car had him pretty well blocked and he hesitated to go out on the road on a curve like that.

"See the pretty donkey, Lily Lou," the girl said, but it only seemed to make the crying kid mad, and she cried louder.

"What's she bawlin' for?" Clem inquired politely.

The girl sighed. "Hungry an' tired, is all."

The other little kid said, "I'm hungry, too, but I ain't cryin'."

The man and two women were looking at him, and Clem scraped around for something to say, and said, "You folks got car trouble?"

"Nothin' but," one of the women said. "Ever since we left Memphis."

He noticed the car had a Tennessee license plate.

"Where you headed?" he asked the girl. She was sort of pretty in an unkempt way, but she looked so tired and sad.

"Fur as we can git," the man answered without looking up. "Which may not be much further."

"California," the girl said, jiggling the crying kid.

Clem didn't know just how to say it without offending somebody, but he couldn't stand to hear the kid crying like that. Cars kept whizzing around the curve, and here these people were broke down beside a highway and the little kids hungry, and him with his belly full of a free breakfast.

"Where you goin'?" the girl asked him.

"New Mexico," he told her.

She looked flabbergasted, the way he knew she would. "In that donkey cart?" she said incredulously, and the other little kid puckered up and began whimpering. Clem nodded, thinking ruefully, Not *in* it, in *front* of it, walking. The girl

76

was hugging both little kids and saying, "Don't do no good to fuss, honey pie, soon as Daddy fixes the ol' car we'll get on to the town an' buy some breakfast."

My lord, Clem thought. They haven't had any breakfast.

"Listen," he said, "could you use some plain unpasteurized milk? I got half a gallon that's fixin' to go blinky on me because I got no ice to cool it. I'd hafta throw it away."

The girl started to say something, then caught herself and looked toward the women, like she'd been warned time and again about accepting gifts from strange men. "Mama?" she said.

"I heard," the lanky woman said, still watching her husband scraping something with his knife. "Tell the young man we'd be most beholden for the loan of some milk for them youngins, Sis."

The girl looked at Clem. "We'd be most beholden, sir."

Sir! Clem thought, feeling a grin working up inside him. "Stay put," he told Pedro, and went around to the side of the cart and reached in under the partially raised curtain. He brought the fruit jar to the girl, and she took it in a rather embarrassed way, not looking at him. "Ma'am," Clem said, addressing himself to the woman, waiting for her to turn and look at him. "Ma'am, would it be all right if I offered these little kids some cold biscuits to go with the milk?"

She nodded and said simply, "They're terrible hungry."

He got the biscuits. And mumbled to the girl, "What about *them*? Your parents? I mean . . . well . . . ?"

She put it succinctly. "We're *all* hungry. Been a long time since yesterday." She looked at him squarely when she said it, unblinking.

"Well," he said, low-voiced, "would it make them mad if I offered to sort of loan you all some stuff?"

77

She turned her head and called out, "Would it make you-all mad if he offered you-all something to eat?"

It seemed like five minutes went past while they just stayed the way they were, the man intent on his repair job and the woman watching him. Then the man looked up at his wife for a while, and finally nodded, and she turned her head and said, "We'd be mighty obliged."

Clem was a generous man, but not a fool about it. He got out the rest of the bakery bread, saving the homemade for himself. And he took out a couple of cans of the lunch meat, and a stick of oleo. Then he got six big oatmeal cookies, thinking remorsefully, Boy, when they're gone, they're just gone, that's all. As for the doughnuts, he just pretended he'd forgotten them. Some things a guy had to be stingy about.

He carried all of the food to the woman, and she looked at him curiously and smiled warmly as she took it, and the man sitting cross-legged on the ground said, "We'll pay you for the grub, mister."

Mister? Clem thought. He always had looked old for his age. "Well, listen," he said earnestly, "this stuff was given to me, I didn't buy it." Suddenly he felt an unusual self-assurance. "Some people gave me a good supper last night, an' breakfast this morning, an' that milk an' biscuits. So I'm just passing it on. I couldn't take anything for it, that's all."

He wheeled around and went back to Pedro and took hold of the bridle. "Nice to meet you," he told the girl, who so far hadn't touched the milk or biscuits, being too busy stuffing it into the little kids.

"Nice to meet you, too, sir," she said.

Ducking his head, he covered his confusion by gruffly ordering Duke to get up. Then he led Pedro around the car, worriedly watching the blind curve behind and breath-

78

ing with relief when he had the cart safely back in the bar-ditch.

Looking over his shoulder he saw that they were all watching him. When he had gone about a hundred feet, the woman called after him, "What's your name?"

He walked backward a few steps. "Clement Marlow," he said.

"Thank you, Clement Marlow," she said. "The Lord bless you."

Were you supposed to answer anything to that? In a way he wished she hadn't said it, for it made him feel that he should have given up a few of the doughnuts, even if they did have sentimental value. Those people didn't know he had them, but the Lord probably did.

It was around noon when he came to the outskirts of the town, and the people from Memphis still hadn't passed him. Clem wished he'd left them stuff for lunch.

EIGHT

He'd been dreading the towns. Highways went right through the middle of towns, usually right on Main Street, and there'd be blocks and blocks of people staring at him and maybe grinning, not necessarily unfriendly, but curious—how often did a guy come marching through town leading a donkey cart? But if he didn't stick to the highway, he might reach the other end of town away off course. He just had to follow the signs.

As he entered the first town he saw a sign reading ICE and he needed some. So he pulled in past a Dairy Queen and stopped beside the service station where a coin-operated machine dispensed bags of cubed ice. A quarter in the slot unlocked the lid, and he leaned in and got a frosted sack frozen so the cubes were stuck together. He left it in the bag, figuring the plastic would insulate it and make it last longer.

A jolly fat man in greasy green coveralls looked around the corner. "Hey, bub, what'll you take for that desert nightingale you got there?"

"Five hundred dollars," Clem grinned, putting the ice in his cooler.

"Too steep for me," the station attendant laughed. Seeing as how he seemed so friendly, Clem asked if he could water Pedro, and the man said, "Betcha a nickel we can, feller." And he got a bucket out of the Men's. "If he ain't too par-

80

ticular," he said. "this here's my mop bucket, but we can rinse her out clean in no time." He did, too, and filled it with clean water from the hose. Clem was filling his two canvas water bags when the truck pulled in at the Dairy Queen, a big sleeper cab dragging a long open-top trailer loaded with something under a tarp.

Two men got down from the high cab, and one of them nudged the other and they looked at Clem, grinning.

"Hey, is that you, Clem?" one of them called.

It was the first westbound truckers to wave at him. They walked across the asphalt parking area, looking at Clem with friendly interest. "How'd you know my name?" he asked, because the truckers' grapevine ran west with Ken Whittle, not east.

"Ran into a friend of yours in Little Rock last night, Clem."

Little Rock! Then it hit him. "Sam Sorrenti?" he asked, grinning.

The trucker nodded. "Said you an' him whupped a whole covey of mean stubble-jumpers yesterday afternoon." They all grinned. "Say, Clem, we were thinking about tying into a couple jumbo-burgers an' malteds—how about joining us for lunch? My swamper's feeling generous."

The other man said indignantly, "The hell I am—the *company's* feeling generous, you mean, and anyway who you calling a swamper, swamper?"

Clem mulled the proposition over for half a second. He couldn't think of any polite way to refuse, or any sensible reason for wanting to. The men were called Pete and Shrimp. Pete gave the order and they sat under the striped awning, with Pedro tied to one of the steel pipe supports. The truckers jawed at each other good-naturedly. When they found out the donkey's name, big Shrimp hoorawed his smaller partner. "That's Spanish for Pete," he said. "That

81

there is your long-lost twin brother, Pedro." And somewhere during the eating and joshing Clem mentioned how much he hated the thought of parading through the heart of town in order not to stray from the highway.

"No problem at all," Pete assured him. "Take the truck route. Every town has a truck route, Clem. All you gotta do is veer left at the next corner, an' follow the signs."

The more Clem saw of truckers, the more he felt like being a truck driver himself some day. His art could be a hobby.

Neither Pete nor Shrimp ate all of his burger, and Duke got the scraps, causing him to brighten up some and wag his tail hopefully.

"Well, boys, it's been delightful, but we gotta roll, Shrimp," Pete said. "Nice to meet you, Clem. We'll be seein' you." He grinned. "By the time you reach New Mexico we'll probably see you four, five times going and coming—we always get stuck with this hot run during the summer months, don't we, Shrimp?"

Shrimp nodded. "Yeah, but we ain't always unlucky, Clem. In the wintertime we get the nice northern runs, Wisconsin, Montana, the Dakotas. Sometimes even New England, if Pete behaves himself, which he usually don't."

Clem tried to thank them for the lunch, but Pete said, shucks, the company was picking up the tab, forget it. And they climbed up into their high cab, Pete on the driver's side, and roared out into the street. When they made the left turn onto the truck route, Pete honked four short quick times, and Clem, leading Pedro up the street, knew they were showing him where to take a left.

The truck route started off on a wide smooth street, and he decided to see if Pedro would allow him the foot-easing pleasure of riding the cart. Climbing onto the seat, he untied the reins and shook them, and said, "Now doggonit, boorow,

82

move!" Pedro moved. So Clem sat there in the cool shade of the cart and they clip-clopped through the detour. A few men and women smiled as he passed, and all the little kids gaped and grinned, but it didn't make him feel self-conscious, except in a proud way. They weren't laughing at him, but at Pedro and the cart. That was the big difference. In the driver's seat he had dignity.

After the truck route turned west again, he came to a neighborhood grocery store and stopped to see if they had any straw hats. They did, but none his size in the wide-brimmed style he had in mind. In fact the only hat of any kind that fitted him was a chocolate-brown straw, narrow-brimmed, with a rainbow band and a little plastic palm tree with pea-sized coconuts. It was streaky faded, and the blurred tag said it was worth two dollars—a lie in any language. The only thing good about it was that it was his size, and none of the others were.

"A perfect fit," commented the gray-haired woman behind the counter. "On you it looks real nice—you know? Jaunty."

Reluctantly, he removed the hat, not because he liked it, but because he needed one badly. Besides, there probably weren't any others around just like this one. It might not be jaunty, but it sure was unusual. He put it on again.

"On you the hat looks sharp," said the woman.

There was no mirror to gauge her honesty by, but he was flattered. Sharp. Nobody had ever called him sharp.

"Yeah . . . well," he said, "I don't know if I can afford it."

"Oh, yes, you can!" she said. "That hat was created especially for you. It brings out your personality." She reached for the hat and looked at the price tag. "Two dollars? That was the price originally. What'll you give?"

Clem shrugged indifferently. "Two bits?" He wasn't really serious.

"Don't be insulting," she said. "Six bits?"

He was surprised. Shoot, he hadn't expected her to knock off more than maybe fifty cents, and even then he couldn't afford it. But six bits! How could you pass it up? Even if he didn't want it to wear, he could buy it as an investment, maybe sell it for a dollar and make a quick quarter profit. "Four bits," he said, just testing.

She clapped the hat back on his head. "Three years that hat waited for you to come along. Who am I to quibble with fate? Sixty cents, you got a hat."

Clem reached in his pocket for some pop bottle money. "Looks like I got a hat, then," he said, counting out sixty cents.

"Plus two cents tax," she said sternly.

There goes another pop bottle, he thought, adding two pennies.

"You come back now," she said as Clem left.

Clem nodded, although he doubted he ever would. He got back in the cart feeling jaunty because she said that's how he looked.

"You like my new hat, boy?" he asked Duke, who was lying down staring glumly into space. Duke looked at him reproachfully. The heck with hats. He didn't like his chain. Always before he had had freedom, now suddenly through no fault of his own, his freedom had a radius of eight feet. If he stopped to scratch a flea the chain snapped taut and yanked at his collar. If he forgot and tried to run on ahead it jerked him up short. And he had to wear it night and day. What did he care about new hats?

Clem was still waiting, not sure if Pedro would let him ride on through town, when the woman came to the door, beaming and waving. She stood there smiling as Pedro went clip-clopping away.

84

Clem touched his hat. He wouldn't sell it, he decided. Not even for two bucks.

That afternoon a couple of trucks from the east honked greetings at him, the drivers waving recognition. The grapevine was spreading the word in all the places where truckers stopped to eat—Watch out for a kid with a donkey cart. He's a friend of Ken Whittle's and Sam Sorrenti's. An honorary member of the gear-jammer's fraternity, now, so look for him along the road, help him if he's in trouble, let him know he's not alone in the world.

As soon as they were through the town and back in the bar-ditch, Pedro had stopped, flicking his ears and shaking his head. Clem dismounted and to break the monotony of walking he unsnapped the chain from Pedro's collar ring and took off at a fast lope along the flat, level roadside, with delighted Duke racing alongside and then taking the lead, tugging Clem along on the leash. After fifty or sixty yards, Clem drew in and stopped, panting, not wanting to get too far ahead of plodding Pedro—and the donkey almost ran over him, because when he saw his two companions apparently running away and deserting him, Pedro frantically raced after them.

"You sonofagun," Clem laughed. "I didn't know you had it in you, boy. I'll be doggone—you were actually *running!*"

After a while he tried it again, sprinting ahead with Duke and this time watching over his shoulder. Pedro laid his ears back and lunged in pursuit, not trotting but galloping.

"Okay, okay, take it easy," Clem said. "Remember your blood pressure, boorow. You still got a long way to go yet today, boy."

Giving the donkey and himself a breather, he fastened Duke's leash again and retrieved a pop bottle in the grass, putting it in the cart with the others. They were fewer today,

85

mostly because of the long detour through the town. He wiped sweat from his sunburned brow and was gingerly replacing his new hat when the black-and-white highway patrol car came around the bend up ahead, giving him a sudden attack of anxiety. The authorities.

The cruiser seemed to slow a little as it neared, and the trooper eyed Clem thoughtfully, giving the briefest of curt waves. Clem experienced a twinge of worry. This same trooper had passed him a couple of times yesterday without stopping, but he must be wondering a little now, thinking, I saw that kid east of town yesterday and here he is west of town today, so what's the story? Must not be a local kid, after all. I better check him out.

Clem started on, with Pedro plodding at his heels. Presently he glanced over his shoulder and saw that the patrol car had gone over a distant crest. He breathed a sigh of relief and started thinking about what kind of a story he would tell if the trooper ever stopped him and started asking questions. If he already looked older than fourteen, his new hat probably made him look sixteen. Possibly even seventeen. Anyway, if the trooper asked how old he was—well, he could say, Would you believe seventeen? It wouldn't be actually lying. And if asked where he'd come from, he could just shrug and say, over east of Tulsa. He didn't have to say ninety-some miles east. Just a little vacation trip, officer. Going to visit some kinfolks up the road apiece and camp out a few days here and there.

This was a rolling stretch of country with low hills covered with scrubby blackjack timber, mostly pasture land and hay meadows and once in a while a field of foot-high corn. It sure wasn't like the country back around Conifer, all high ridges and tall timber with gravelly creeks and clear blue lakes. But this strange country wouldn't be so bad if the creeks weren't so muddy, the dirt so reddish.

86

Some instinct made him look over his shoulder again, and there was the black-and-white cruiser again. Clem sighed heavily. He crossed his fingers, praying the trooper wouldn't stop. He looked straight ahead and tried to act casual, natural. But a tingle crawled up his backbone and made his scalp quiver when the patrol car slid past and slowed and stopped on the shoulder ahead. If they send me back, I'll just start out again on a different route, he thought desperately. Next time I'll stay off the main highways.

The tall trooper walked around the front of his cruiser and waited for Clem to approach, leaning against the patrol car with his arms crossed in a very official way.

"Hello," Clem said, his voice not too steady.

"Afternoon," the trooper replied. He was a very business-like-looking man with a weathered face, a sprinkling of gray at the temples, and a certain bleakness around the eyes that may have resulted from seeing too much death, too many accident victims.

"Sure is hot," Clem observed, trying to make his voice deeper.

The trooper nodded, scrutinizing the cart. "Did you build that yourself?" he inquired.

"I had a lot of help," Clem said.

The trooper's mouth smiled, but his eyes didn't. "When I was a boy, ten or eleven, my dad bought me a goat and goat wagon. I don't know if they still build those things or not. Used to be able to order them out of the catalogs, Sears and Roebuck, Monkey Ward." A flicker of smile, and the eyes a little less flinty, a trifle less vigilant.

Clem smiled uneasily, waiting for the officer to get through with the preliminaries and start earning his salary.

"Where do you come from, youngster?" the patrolman asked quietly.

Well, you're either a born liar, or you acquire the knack,

or else you go through life blurting out the truth. Sighing, Clem said, "Conifer."

The trooper nodded. "I've been there. Pretty country. Good fishing and deer hunting." He studied Pedro awhile and pursed his lips. "That's a long ways to drive a donkey cart, isn't it?"

Clem explained about hauling the donkey and cart the first hundred miles, and the trooper listened, looking at Clem's hat.

"How far are you planning to go, son?"

"Over west of Oklahoma City a ways," Clem said. "I'm going to visit relatives, and camp out and all."

The trooper plucked at his ear and looked at the scrub oak timber, then pushed away from the cruiser. "Mind if I look at your cart?" he asked, and Clem said, "Shoot, no," and the highway patrolman went to the side of the cart and leaned in under the rolled-up curtain. "Say, it looks like you're fixed up fine for traveling. Plenty of room for one man, plenty of grub." He reached up and tapped the top with his knuckles. "Sheds water okay?"

He withdrew his head and took out a pack of cigarettes. "Most young fellas nowadays think they've got to have a souped-up automobile to drive. They have no place in particular to go, but they're in one hell of a hurry to get there. I'm glad to find a member of your generation who doesn't have to go at eighty-five miles an hour to enjoy himself."

Clem gave him a weary grin. "Yeah, but a guy can get awfully tired of walking. My feet are pretty sore."

The trooper smiled. "They'll toughen up, and once you get used to it, I'll bet you'll like it—by the way, what's your name?"

"Clement Marlow," Clem said. My dad was a deputy sheriff, he added silently, wanting to say it out loud. "Everybody calls me just Clem."

88

"Trooper Walters," the patrolman said. "Well, the reason I turned around and came back, Clem—there's a narrow bridge around the next bend, and I thought I'd better see that you get across safely. I'll park on ahead a short distance and turn on my roof flasher to slow down the westbound traffic, so nobody will barrel around the curve and demolish your cart."

And that's what he did. Drove on ahead a hundred feet, and when Clem passed the patrol car, said cordially, "Have a nice trip, Clem."

When Clem reached the bridge itself he got a sudden inspiration. Waiting until an eastbound car cleared the narrow span, with no westbound cars in sight behind, he unsnapped Duke's chain and said, "Let's go!" And went running across the bridge with Pedro in frantic pursuit, going on until the guardrails fanned out and the shoulder widened enough so he could veer off the asphalt. Then he slowed and led Pedro down into the weedy bar-ditch and looked back to see the patrol car coming off the bridge. Trooper Walters must have seen them racing across, because as he passed he grinned and held up his hand with two fingers making a circle.

After that Clem didn't worry much about the bridges ahead. Or the highway patrolmen, either.

NINE

FRIDAY, the fifth day of his journey, a scorching afternoon sun beat down upon the scrub oaks and red-gullied pastures and the shimmering asphalt-patched concrete. Clem limped gingerly in the old weeds and thickening new grass of the bar-ditch because he was barefoot. He kept his eyes cast down, concentrating on the ground immediately ahead, watching for dead weed spikes, broken glass, and rock fragments. His blisters had broken, leaving raw-skinned places on his feet so he couldn't stand his tennis shoes. One thing, though, his feet were cool for a change, and the new grass felt lush and smooth. But all the same he was fixing to camp as soon as he found a good place.

Suddenly over the *ballup-ballup-ballup* of hard rubber on concrete joinings he heard the hissing of airbrakes, lifted his weary head, and suddenly forgot his aches and pains when he recognized Ken Whittle's big red-and-yellow trailer, coming back from San Diego. Ken eased the truck off onto the sloping shoulder across the hot pavement and braked to a stop.

Climbing down from the cab, Ken checked to be sure his pass signals were blinking and came on across, chewing on the ever-present half-smoked cigar.

"Hello, Clem—howdy, Pedro and Duke," he said. "Figured I'd be seeing you fellers along here somewhere." Then he frowned. "How come you're barefooted, somebody steal your shoes?"

Happy at the unexpected meeting, Clem said, "Aw, heck, I like to go barefooted. Sneakers get pretty hot."

Squatting abruptly in the ditch, Ken reached for an ankle and said, "Let's see those feet, Clem." And whistled in concern.

"It ain't as bad as it looks," Clem said deprecatingly. "It's just the blisters busted finally and sorta peeled off."

Ken sat back on his heels. "How come you got blisters on your feet? Why didn't you get blisters on your rump?"

Clem explained sheepishly about Pedro not allowing him to ride the cart in bar-ditches, just on streets going through towns. "But heck, I don't mind." He shrugged. "My feet'll toughen up in a few more days. Anyway, I need to walk so I can pick up pop bottles without having to stop and get off and on again every time."

"You're in the secondhand bottle business, are you, pal?"

Clem nodded, beaming. "I already made over seven dollars, turning 'em in for two cents apiece, Ken. A guy can earn expenses that way."

"How about that?" Ken said with wonder. "That's what you'd call living off the land, isn't it? But listen, Clem, you better doctor up those feet. Do you have any iodine or Mercurochrome?"

That was something Clem had overlooked, a first aid kit. "I'll lay in some medical supplies at the next town," he assured Ken.

Rising to his feet, Ken said, "Otherwise, how goes it?"

"Okay," Clem reported. "I guess I'm making pretty good time, huh?"

Ken thought for a moment. "Yeah, I'd say you're racking up fair mileage, Clem. I calculate you've averaged right at ten miles a day so far, and you'll probably increase it when

91

you get used to the daily grind." He puffed on the cold cigar and did some more calculating. "You've only got about sixty-six more walking days ahead of you, at ten miles an hour."

Clem nodded vague agreement, never having thought that far ahead. He'd just figured he had all summer, and the best thing to do was take it a day at a whack.

"It'll be hot and dry by the time you hit the panhandle," Ken said. "For your donkey's sake you'll need to start laying up a couple of hours during the heat of the day—take a siesta. Start early and travel in the cool of morning, then stay with it until dark, and a recess in the early afternoon won't mess you up." He removed the cigar stub, examined it reflectively, and put it back. "Well, gotta get on into Tulsa and unload. You need anything, Clem?"

"Oh, I could use a spare set of feet," Clem said wryly.

Ken laughed. "Well, ol' buddy, I'll see you about Monday morning, real early—unless we get routed to Seattle, which is a possibility. In that case I may not see you until a week from Monday, somewhere out in western Oklahoma. Incidentally, Maw is due in Tulsa this weekend. I'll tell her you said hello, right?" Clem nodded, feeling a stab of sadness because Ken was already leaving. That was the trouble with truck drivers, they were always in a hurry. "So long, Clem," said Ken. "Hey, I'd like to steal that hat. Certainly lends you an air of insouciance, pal."

Watching the big truck pull back onto the highway and pick up speed, Clem sighed and thought, Hello and good-bye. That's how it would be whenever he saw Ken or Sam, or Pete and Shrimp, along the road west. My lord, he thought, they went clean to San Diego and back while I was peeling off about fifty-some miles. Talk about slow, boy. And it struck him he'd not yet ever seen Ken's sleepy partner, Jasper.

Duke was chewing on the chain again, wasting his time and ruining his teeth. Clem scolded him and he quit, acting sulky. Duke wasn't ever going to get used to that chain, but Clem figured he was learning the reason for it, and maybe in a few more days he could start letting old Duke run loose part of the time.

When it was still a couple hours before sundown, he came to a valley with a creek winding down the middle and a short wide bridge. As he loped across with Pedro trotting behind, he took time to look and saw that it was a fairly clear creek with a sandy bed and an inviting grove of big cottonwoods a little farther upstream. Man, that's it, if I can find how to get in there, Clem said to himself. But the fences were unbroken along both sides of the highway, and the road began its ascent up the west slope of the valley where scrub oaks spread along the rim. He was about to give up when he saw the faint tracks leading out of the pasture through a wired-up gap gate. He didn't like to go in without getting permission, but there were no houses in sight, and no Keep Out signs anywhere . . .

He was wiring the gap-gate back in place when a motorcycle came roaring over the crest to the east and zoomed down the long hill toward the bridge. When it got closer, Clem recognized Gaylord Jackson. (Who else had multicolored luminous paint on his Harley and helmet?) As soon as Gaylord spotted the donkey cart he throttled down and coasted to a stop on the pavement, looking at Clem impassively. He wasn't wearing his leather jacket. Just a tight, wide-striped, short-sleeved shirt.

Another swift glance along his backtrail, and then he flashed his incredibly white grin and said, "Howdy do, Clem. Good to see you still well an' happy. How you makin' out?" He didn't give Clem a chance to answer. "Can't linger longer, baby. I'm bein' pursued. You gonna make camp yonder?"

93

Clem nodded. "Who's chasin' you?"

"Some young white gen'lemen." Gaylord uttered a wild, rich laugh. "Jus' can't seem to speak impolite of any Mister Charley." He looked east again. "Sho' hope them nice white cats have give up the pursuit. My hog don't like goin' so fast."

"How come they're chasin' you?" Clem asked him.

Gaylord stared at him for a moment. "Why, baby, if they got to have a reason, maybe they got a grudge on motor-cycles. Or maybe jus' 'cause they had a few drinks and are feelin' so good. Man, it surely ain't due to race, religion, or color." He laughed.

Clem didn't know what to say, and abruptly it became unnecessary to say anything, because Gaylord Jackson had spotted a car coming over the hump to the east.

"Uh-oh, baby, we gotta move fast! Come on, hog, le's go!"

He went roaring away up the western slope of the valley as the red-and-silver sedan came down the eastern slope, horn blaring with exuberant menace. Clem watched the car come down the center stripe and onto the bridge, a howling souped-up engine in a dented and dirty ten-year-old Ford body. As the carload of yelling whites was about to pass, the driver and the passenger directly behind him added a little extra competitive fun to the chase by trying to hit Clem with pop bottles thrown left-handed over the top of the speeding car. They were so short that Clem had to crawl through the barbed-wire fence to gather up the four cents' worth of merchandise. He sniffed the Coke bottles and made a face, recognizing the whang of rotgut moonshine.

Stashing the bottles in the cart, he removed the chain from Duke's collar, praying that if he jumped a rabbit it wouldn't head for the highway, and led Pedro down across the pasture toward the cottonwood grove. He got a sand burr in his right big toe, and after yanking it free he decided it was time to put his sneakers on again.

There was sand, but no sand burrs, under the cottonwoods, and the shallow creek pooled there deep enough for bathing and clean enough for doing some laundry. First thing he did was unhitch Pedro and prop up the cart. Then he removed the harness so Pedro could roll in the sand, which he immediately proceeded to do. Meanwhile, Duke had been prowling eagerly around with his nose an inch from the ground and now barked at the base of a cottonwood, staring up into the tree. Clem thought, Squirrel! The next thing he did was get his rifle out of the cart.

They were fat red squirrels, bigger than the ones back home, and they were eating the oily rich cottonwood buds. When he looked again, he saw three—no, by gosh, four! Hold it, five! *Five* fat young red fox squirrels in *one* cottonwood tree—but don't count your chickens before they hatch, just draw a bead on the closest one and squeeze that trigger slowly.

The first one folded and fell. He missed the second one. The third one hung for heart-stopping seconds, finally came down end over end. Oh, baby, one more—two for supper and one for breakfast, two stewed and one fried. He missed again. They were hiding up there now, freezing behind limbs. Gray squirrels would run; red squirrels just hid. But these were still young and foolish. One of them eased around the thick trunk ten feet up, watching Duke instead of the sharpshooter. Old juicy number three, Clem hoped, taking careful aim. Crack! Number three slithered down onto the sandy ground. Fair shooting, Clem modestly admitted. Right through the head. Three was enough for now. Maybe in the morning he'd bag a brace to take along.

Skinning and cleaning the game in running water downstream from where he aimed to bathe, he gave the entrails to Duke, organs included. After putting two of the squirrels in his stewpot and the third in the cooler, he ate one of his few remaining oatmeal cookies to stall off starvation while he did some washing. Lying on his back half floating with his heels dug into the yielding sand, he gazed peacefully up at the blue sky, listening to the chatter of birds and muted highway noises. Would there be squirrel hunting in New Mexico? "You dope," he said to himself. "In the desert?"

Sometimes the idea of living in New Mexico hit him with dismay. It would be so different from the Ozark country. But maybe in a few more months his mother would be well enough to come back to eastern Oklahoma. She couldn't go on staying sick forever.

After hanging his laundry on the cart shafts to dry, he went about his camp shores buck naked, figuring he'd hit the water again before dressing. Digging a firehole in the sand, he made a green-stick tripod to hang the kettle on. He turned some flour, salt, and water into dough for stick bread, which he'd learned to make once when he'd been a Boy Scout for a couple of months, before his grandmother had her stroke and he had to go live with the Hoggetts. Wished he could have stayed in the Scouts, learning all that camping lore: how to start fires without matches. How to do it *with* matches, too, he reflected, spiraling the snake of dough around a green willow stick.

By the time he got supper started, the sun was sliding down behind the blackjack ridge. A couple of mosquitos pronged him pretty good, so he took a final dip in his private pool and dressed. It was nice in the grove in a slightly spooky way, secluded and quiet but close enough to the highway so that when an occasional truck rumbled past, it was reassuring. No sign or sound of farmhouses anywhere near, just the cottonwood oasis in the valley and wild scrub oak timber on the ridges . . .

Gaylord Jackson arrived in plenty of time for supper, coming down across the pasture in low gear, headlamp glowing. Clem thought at first it might be the landowner coming to chase trespassers out of the valley, but it was his friend— well, not friend, exactly. Fellow traveler, call it.

Gaylord stopped under the trees, killing the engine and dowsing his light, sitting there with his feet braced on the ground at the edge of the firelight, not taking his welcome for granted. In the campfire glow he looked kind of sinister, with his dark face framed by the big luminous crash helmet. Until he smiled, anyway.

"Well," Clem said, "it looks like you got away."

Gaylord hung his helmet on a handlebar and approached the fire. "Right," he said amiably. "Reckon there's elbow room enough for all us travelin' men here?"

"Sure," Clem said. "This is a swell place to camp."

Gaylord nodded. "Something sho' smell good, Clem."

"I'm makin' squirrel stew and stick bread."

"*Soul* food," Gaylord said. "You lucky, man. All I got to eat is some bakery goods."

"What kind of bakery stuff?" Clem asked interestedly.

"Aw, just an ol' cherry pie, some jelly doughnuts, an' a few cinnamon rolls," Gaylord said with a sly smile.

"Wow!" Clem said enviously. "Say, listen, there's plenty squirrel stew for both of us."

"I'll accept yo' invitation to dinner," Gaylord said gravely, "if you will allow me to furnish the dessert." He didn't even wait for Clem's answer, but went to get his sack of bakery goods from the motorcycle. Must have known he had a deal all along, Clem thought.

It was a delicious supper, very filling, and afterward they

97

stretched out on the clean soft sand, Clem content to gaze drowsily at the bed of glowing embers and let his companion do most of the talking. Gaylord was from Chicago, although born in the South. He didn't like Chicago.

"All that long hot summer jive disturbed me," he drawled, "but so did those long cold winters. That wind come in off Lake Michigan whistlin' an' moanin' through the ghetto, hoo-weee! It ain't no place for a thin-blooded Alabama boy."

Won't be cold in New Mexico where Mama is, Clem thought. Not that he minded a little snow and ice. Wintertime was okay, if you didn't live in a concrete-block dairy barn.

"California's supposed to have the kind of climate a cat wants all year," Gaylord mused. "An' free colleges anyone can go to. But first I got to get there, right. Then locate me a job so I can eat good an' keep outa trouble."

I'll get me a job in New Mexico, Clem thought. I'll do anything.

"I have quit all that lootin' an' shootin' Chicago scene, 'cause them Afro-cats are formin' gangs an' keepin' the people uptight, an' you got to be either with 'em or against 'em. Guys like me ain't scared of the white folks any more," Gaylord said, "but we're scared of our soul brothers, our own takin'-over cats that say loud an' frequent, you *with* us or you *agin* us. I dunno, man, seem like people in cities don't know what's goin' on other places an' don't much care, but I care an' I'm gonna go see. Was a time if you say education to me I'd say who you kiddin'. But things openin' up. And no cat can make it without education." He rolled his head and peered at Clem in the dim rosy fireglow. "That applies to everybody."

"I'm fixin' to go to college if I can," Clem said.

"Right!" Gaylord told him. "Do that." He stretched luxuriously on the cushioning sand. "You want some mo' good advice?"

Clem said he guessed he did, but he was actually wondering if he ought to go see about Pedro, out there grazing in the dark.

"Don't ever waste a single minute of yo' time *hatin'* folks, 'specially those you don't even *know*," Gaylord said softly. "A man start hatin' people in bunches, it poisons his whole system an' ends up bein' a full-time job with no wages."

"I don't hate anybody," Clem said, "but I do have to go take a look at my donkey."

Gaylord offered to help, but Clem said that wouldn't be necessary. He put on his sneakers and got the flashlight and halter, and Duke uncurled from the sand, shaking himself, ready to go. They went out of the trees and presently the flashlight's beam found two bright eyes in the darkness. Clem turned off the light and relieved himself while waiting to see if Pedro would come to him. It was quiet on the highway now, and he heard a whippoorwill up in the scrub oaks, and for a moment he imagined he was back in Conifer. Summertime the valleys and hills had echoed the plaintive call of whippoorwills at night, and he used to fall asleep with that monotonous lullaby in his ears. Now this solitary night bird made him homesick and for a moment he was appalled at the thought of walking for another sixty-some days—and the uncertainty of what he'd discover when he got there.

She might not *ever* get out of that place, he thought. They might not even let him go in to see her. Kids under sixteen weren't allowed to visit patients in the hospital at Conifer, and a TB hospital might be even stricter. But shoot, they would let him see her through a window or *something*, wouldn't they?

He heard two sounds mingled in the stillness, the soft tread of Pedro's hooves and the explosive roar of a

99

souped-up automobile growing louder as it came east on the highway.

Clem snapped on the flashlight. "Hiya, baby," he said softly, and slipped the halter on unresisting Pedro. "That sounds like that same group that chased Gaylord today." He patted the donkey. "I won't tether you, but you be here close by in the mornin', you hear me?"

Starting back to the grove, he listened to the straining howl of the hot-rod approaching the valley. Now he could hear the rebel yells and hooting of the car's occupants, and he said, "Yep, Duke, that sounds like the same nuts."

The racing hot-rod reached the top of the long grade and began its frenzied descent toward the bridge, and Clem stopped at the edge of the grove to watch. Boy, they're really traveling! he thought. Then it happened. First there were several short squeals of rubber on concrete as if the driver were recklessly jiggling the wheel left and right to thrill his passengers. Then Clem heard a protesting yell of "Watch it, you jerk!" But instead of ending, the rubber-screech suddenly intensified into the frantic and desperate sound of a car going out of control. Clem stood frozen in his tracks, watching the headlights swing around directly toward him as the nightmare squealing of tires became a sustained scream of treads sliding on pavement. Then the headlights went into an erratic pinwheeling blur and the night was filled with the sound of ripping metal and shattering glass as the hot-rod flipped and became a rolling projectile spraying the darkness with showers of sparks, shedding bumpers, window glass, and people. To Clem it seemed to go on and on forever before the din or hurtling disaster climaxed in a final thumping impact well beyond the east end of the bridge.

Then there was total silence except for the thudding of his heart, the continuing cry of the forlorn whippoorwill.

100

Shivering in the eerie silence, Clem's mind tried to reject the whole thing, and he moved on into the trees thinking, It's none of my business.

Gaylord Jackson was on his feet, silhouetted against the firelight. "There's people hurt bad, Clem," he said in a shaken voice.

None of our business, Clem wanted to protest. We don't have to do anything. Cars will stop when they see the wreck and do something about it.

Gaylord sighed. "Nobody 'round here but us, Clem."

"Cars will come along," Clem said in a quiet voice.

"Maybe somebody will have to flag 'em down," Gaylord said. "Seems like I got no choice if I'm a man. You coming?"

The idea terrified Clem; still, if he didn't go, he would probably forever regret it. He sucked a deep breath into his tight lungs. "I better chain Duke up so he won't follow me," he said. I won't go close to it, he thought, I'll stay back on this side of the fence.

When they were in the open, south of the trees, a car came over the eastern ridge and down the long hill, but it didn't stop. It slowed, but then it sped on across the bridge and up the long west grade. None of *his* business either, Clem thought shakily, jogging along behind Gaylord, following the small creek toward the bridge. People didn't want to get involved.

"That cat will notify someone," Gaylord panted. "I hope."

Clem hoped so, too. He was holding the flashlight so Gaylord could see where to go and he kept wanting to give it to the Negro and dawdle behind.

"Can't see where it is," Gaylord said. "You see where the car went?"

"East of the bridge somewhere," Clem said, having trouble breathing.

Another car came from the east, swiftly, its headlights

101

cutting a white tunnel out of the darkness, and the driver began pumping his brakes, but then he too reconsidered, lost his nerve, and hurried on across the bridge. Nobody wanted to be the first arrival where death sprawled beside a lonely stretch of highway. I'll bet Ken would stop, or Sam Sorrenti, Clem thought.

"Give me the light," Gaylord said, reaching. Clem relinquished it gladly. "Good place to cross," Gaylord said, cutting down the sandy bank and splashing through the shallow creek. Clem had to follow or be left in the blind night, stumbling into no telling what. He had to hurry now to keep up with the big Negro, who had quickened his stride once he was managing the light. When the barbed-wire fence rose suddenly before them, Gaylord Jackson put one hand on top of a post and vaulted over. Clem crawled between the middle and top strands, forgetting that he had planned not to go any closer to the wreck. He caught up to Gaylord on the steep shoulder where the Negro had paused, shining the light out onto the wide concrete-balustered bridge and then back along the highway.

"She sure slid," he panted, and sent the beam east along the surface of the highway where the hurtling car had left a scarred, oil-streaked, rubber-smeared, glass-littered trail. "Wish some cars would pass," he said walking along the clear trail, with Clem following so close behind that he bumped into Gaylord Jackson when he suddenly stopped to sweep the beam out into the south side ditch. "Uh-oh!" he muttered, and Clem saw the boy face down in the grass. "We'll check him in a second," Gaylord said. Up ahead in the ditch Clem saw the battered car on its side, with one front wheel still rotating slowly and a thin haze of smoke issuing from the front end.

They both heard the car coming from the west and turned to look. Gaylord began signaling with the flashlight and

102

the car slowed, but just when they thought it would stop, it swung over to the left lane and speeded up. As it passed they could see the two women, scared white faces staring in panic at the big Negro trying to make them stop on this lonely road. Gaylord sighed. "Next time you better try," he said bitterly. "Nobody going to stop out here at night for no nigger!" He accented the word harshly, as he turned on his heel and strode on toward the wrecked automobile.

Clem followed, not wanting to look inside the overturned car, but not wanting to miss seeing whatever might be inside it. He hung back when Gaylord leaned over and shined the light down through the rear left window, but he couldn't avoid hearing the moaning.

"Hold it," Gaylord said, handing him the flashlight. "Shine it in so I can see what I'm doing."

Clem held the light pointed down inside the car, but didn't look. There was a hot scorching smell in the air and the moaning went on, and Gaylord said in a hoarse whisper, "My God!" He was reaching deep inside and he came up with blood all over his hand. "Got to get the door open," he said, and climbed up on the side of the car. But both doors were jammed tight. "Go see if you can flag that car" —there was a car coming from the east—Gaylord told Clem. "Tell them we need a couple of ambulances right away."

Clem stopped the car. There was a young couple inside. The man said he would phone at the first booth he passed. The girl said, "Are they dead? Do you know them?" They won't be fast enough, thought Clem. We're going to have to do it ourselves.

That's what he'd been afraid of doing all along—having to *touch* them. When he got back to the car, Gaylord Jackson had a bleeding unconscious boy half out of the rear window, but he needed help and made Clem crawl up and take hold

103

of the boy. Clem fumbled for a grip on the sticky body, and they heaved the boy up through the narrow opening and slid him over the edge of the tilted car. Another car was coming from the west.

"Try flagging that one from here," Gaylord said.

This car stopped right there fifteen feet away, and the two older men got out. "Anybody go call an ambulance yet?" the nearest one asked. Clem said yes. "Which way?" the man asked. "West," Clem said. "How many people hurt?" the man inquired. Clem didn't know, and Gaylord Jackson said, "At least five, counting the three still inside the car." The man said, "Well, you'll need extra ambulances. We'll go on to the next town east of here and send some out, fellas."

They took off at top speed, but it still left Gaylord Jackson and Clem with three people to get out of the car.

"I smell gasoline," Clem said nervously, and Gaylord Jackson said, "Yeah, so le's move fast."

They got another boy out, the one who was moaning, and his face was a bloody mess. When Clem got hold of an arm, he felt the crunching of broken bone and suddenly felt very sick. But he didn't have time to stop because some tentative blue flames had started licking along the oil-caked motor.

Two more cars came from the east. The first one slowed and stared out, and drove slowly on, as if maybe the man and woman inside were arguing whether or not they should stop. The other car pulled off the road. A girl got out and said, "Can I do anything to help?"

"Drag those boys on *away* from here," Gaylord said. "This car is going to explode pretty soon."

That really scared Clem, but he fought down his panic and stayed up on the car. Gaylord crouched down inside the car and lifted another victim up through the window,

104

this one a long-haired blond. Clem pushed her toward the girl who was helping and crawled painfully back onto the sticky slippery side of the wreck.

Another car stopped and a man got out and said, "I'm a doctor." And the girl, "Over here, doctor."

Inside the wreck Gaylord shouted, "Jesus, this one's got his arm pinned under the car." He came out squeezing his big frame up through the window. "I'll get back here against the bank and see kin I lift it some, Clem. You get in and pull his arm loose the minute you can." He sniffed and said, "I sure wish the fire department would come." Then he was wriggling down between the car roof and the high bank, and Clem reluctantly lowered himself into the overturned car, noting that the small flames by the engine seemed to be going down. While he was crouching inside, he heard another automobile stop and a woman say, "You kids stay in the car, you hear me?" And he thought numbly, Where are all the *men* at, tonight? Then he felt the car shift, and tugged at the mangled arm and got it loose. "Okay," he shouted and gagged convulsively because the arm seemed to have two elbows, one of them a jagged sticky bone.

Through the car roof Gaylord Jackson said, "Can you get him out by yourself, Clem?" But he didn't wait for an answer, shouting at the doctor and two women, "Help him get that boy out. There's another one down here mashed between the car and the bank."

One of the women with kids reached in and got hold of the boy. With her heaving and Clem boosting from below, they got the limp body out just as the welcome scream of sirens sounded in the distance.

In a hoarse voice, Gaylord said, "When I push at the car, Clem, see if you can move this last one. Okay, boy?"

Gaylord had his hands and knees braced against the bank and his back against the car top. The boy was pinned full-

105

length along the base of the bank, too mangled to have a chance to live, but Gaylord still wouldn't leave him. He groaned with the agony of making himself into a human jack. Clem reluctantly squeezed into the space and tugged at the dead boy. "Now, baby! Pull!" said Gaylord through gritted teeth. It wasn't that he didn't move the car, it was just that Clem wasn't strong enough to drag the dead boy out of the confining space. He was still grunting and straining when the gasoline fumes finally reached the igniting flames in the engine. There was a blinding flash as the fumes were consumed, then a column of fire where the ruptured gas tank had spilled gasoline on the ground. Clem was protected by the roof of the car, and so was Gaylord except for the back of his neck, which got pretty well singed. But after the moment of shock he said, "See if you can go the other way, man." Because Clem had been trying to drag the dead boy toward the rear end of the car, where the hot flames now were. Obediently, Clem squeezed forward over the body and under Gaylor's taut rump and turned around enough to pull at the body, but it was no use. "I can't," he said.

Gaylord sighed. "Where is everybody?" he complained. "Clem, we'll try one last thing. Get in alongside me and let's see if we can tip this baby over on its wheels."

Clem got in beside him. They grunted and strained in unison, and the wrecked car moved, lifting, tilting, balancing on two wheels, hesitating—then finally lurching over onto its four wheels. Clem fell sprawling down on top of the dead boy.

Gaylord helped him up, and they dragged the body away from the growing heat and stench of burning paint and rubber. Now all of a sudden, when all the gory work was finished, the place was filled with sirens and blinking red lights, ambulance drivers ran to collect the wounded, and

106

cars stopped on both sides of the highway filled with people anxious to help where help was no longer needed. Men threw handfuls of dirt on the burning wreck, and women tried to get Clem to lie down, mistaking him for one of the casualties because of all the bright-red blood on his hands and clothes. A couple of white-shirted orderlies tried to put him on a stretcher, and he had to fight them off, hollering, "I'm not hurt, darn it! This isn't my blood!"

But some of the blood on Gaylord was his own; he'd gashed his arm on broken window glass. The doctor put on a bandage, but said it needed sewing and he'd better go on in to the hospital in one of the ambulances.

"I be in latuh," Gaylord said. "Doc, how many of 'em . . . ?"

He was interrupted by an agitated woman calling from the west side of the bridge, "There's a girl over here—I guess she's dead!"

"I'll go see," said the doctor, finishing the bandage and looking up at Gaylord. "She'll make three certain; one other probably won't survive the ride to town. Worst single-car accident I've seen—and all just kids."

Gaylord Jackson nodded. "For nothing. Just for kicks." Turning around, he found Clem waiting for instructions, sticking close like he wasn't acquainted with another soul in the world. "You ready to go on back?" Gaylord asked, and Clem nodded, his teeth clenched tight against a terrible need to vomit.

They pushed through a crowd of curious onlookers who were asking each other what had happened. Holding the flashlight, Clem followed Gaylord back across the fence, hearing the ambulance sirens fading in the distance. Unable to hold back any longer, Clem bent over, convulsively emptying his stomach, continuing to gag and retch when there was nothing left to vomit. When they came to a pool

107

that was deep enough, he washed the flashlight and handed it to Gaylord and then threw himself in, trying to scrub away the smell of blood and death. He stayed in the stream afterward, staggering upstream while Gaylord silently followed along the low bank, lighting his way.

At the camp he got his soap and lathered himself, clothes and all, and went into the water again. Presently he peeled off his clothes and scrubbed his naked body, racked with shivers that had nothing to do with the night air. Dry pants and a shirt made him feel better. Gaylord Jackson built up the fire and sat staring into it impassively.

"It wasn't the car that was chasing you?" Clem said dully.

Gaylord shook his head. After a moment he said, "Same breed of cats, though. Everybody's crazy some way, these days. None them kids wanted to die, but maybe they didn't want to live, either." Bending his head, he gingerly felt his singed neck and gave an abrupt, angry laugh. "Show you how us human cats mix ourselves up, I'm sitting here talking about dying and all the time my brain is fretting about something else, worrying how much that doctor is fixing to charge me for stitching me up—how much it's going to cost me for not mindin' my own business. Ten bucks, maybe. Depend on how much sewing he has to do, I suppose. What I know is, it ain't ever free."

"I could loan you some," Clem offered.

"I thank you, but keep your money. I was going to have to stop and earn some cash, anyway. This will just make it sooner. But I appreciate your offer, baby." Gaylord cocked his head and listened for a minute. "Sounds quiet. All the ghouls went home." He rose to his feet. "Hate to leave you, but you heard what the man said, I better get it stitched."

Clem nodded, wanting Gaylord to stay but knowing he had to go. "Maybe you could come back," he said hopefully.

Gaylord gazed into the darkness. "Might, if it ain't too

108

far." But they both knew he wouldn't. "One thing, Clem, we got no reason to be ashamed. If we hadn't helped, none of those kids would have had a chance."

Clem sighed. "I guess so."

"You'll be glad later, anyway." Gaylord looked down expressionlessly for a moment, then offered his hand. When Clem took it, he grinned. "Been good to know you, man."

Clem nodded, thinking, I don't want to be here all by myself, thinking about those dead people.

Gaylord Jackson mounted his motorcycle. "Cross your fingers and hold your breath," he said, kicking down on the starter. Clem was almost hoping it wouldn't start, but it did, and Gaylord put on his leather jacket and crash helmet and gave Clem a parting salute.

Alone, Clem took refuge from the crouching shadows of the grove by getting into the cart, but he had no way of closing out his ugly memories of the wreck. He lowered the curtains except that next to the fire and lay down under his blanket. He tried to think of other things, but his mind kept returning to the car and the cut and broken kids and when he finally fell asleep, his dreams kept shocking him awake, nightmares full of bone fragments, gore, and screeching automobiles hurtling and disintegrating.

When daybreak came, he gave up and got out of bed. Early-rising squirrels were already busy in the cottonwoods, barking and chattering, breakfasting on buds, but hunting was the farthest thing from his mind. He just wanted to get away. After a quick breakfast of jelly doughnuts and milk, he went after Pedro and hitched up. For a while there he was going to abandon the pants and T-shirt he'd worn the night before, but frugality won over queasiness, and he hung the clothes over the tailgate to finish drying in the sun.

All the way up across the pasture he managed not to glance toward the bridge and the burned wreck he supposed

109

was still just beyond, but when he was out on the highway he couldn't resist one quick look. The charred wreck was gone, removed by a tow truck during the night, and in an odd way he was disappointed. At the top of the hill he took one final look backward. The bridge seemed peaceful in the quiet dawn, and he wouldn't have spotted the scorched earth where the car had burned if he hadn't known exactly where to look.

By the time the sun was fully up in the sky, he was a mile away and thinking more about his feet than the accident. There was nothing like a bright June morning to cheer one up. Meadow larks sang from fence posts, and quail called in the fields and timber. Half a dozen noisy crows bickered over a squashed rabbit on the highway, and a line of black-and-white cattle moved in leisurely fashion behind a neat white house in a yard full of flowers. As he passed, Clem heard a woman singing. He embraced the golden morning passionately, knowing that it was his salvation, and that each morning hereafter would push the horror of the wreck a little farther back in his mind.

TEN

THE doughnut deliveries began on Monday, when he was still northeast of Oklahoma City. Practically all the big trucks saluted him now, but none of them stopped until this westbound red-and-yellow Ora-Noko pulled off onto the shoulder behind him. It wasn't a bedroom rig, just a short-haul job with one driver, a large, heavy-set Indian, who stepped down to the ground holding a grease-spotted brown paper bag.

"You Clinton Marland?" he inquired.

Clem straightened him out on the name, and the big Indian grinned.

"I was pretty close," he said. "Ken Whittle asked me to deliver this, from his mama. He had to go to Seattle."

Clem accepted the sack and looked inside. Doughnuts! Oh, boy!

"Said to tell you she'll send more if she can catch another rig comin' west. I'm Coonie Burris. How you doin'?"

"Okay," Clem said shortly, because he could tell from the grease marks there had been more doughnuts in the sack when it started its trip.

"Well, I got to get them wheels turnin' round," Coonie Burris said, and Clem thanked him anyway and watched him drive on west. You couldn't really blame the guy, he thought as he trudged on munching a delicious doughnut.

111

She should have put them in a box and sealed the top. Thinking of Mrs. Whittle made him think of Della, who was due home this week. Maybe when she found his note she'd just think he'd gone to visit in his old home and wouldn't bother about him for a while, maybe not at all.

One thing that worried him, though, was Royce Nolan's cattle. They had grass and the pond and salt, but someone ought to count them once in a while. He had to write to Mrs. Whittle anyway, so he could ask her to check. When he came to some big shade trees, he got out one of the stamped addressed postcards and his ballpoint pen.

So far so good, he thought. Now comes the hard part.

"Dear Mrs. Whittle," he wrote. "We're fine, making pretty fair time but quite a ways to go yet. Saw Ken last Friday." He was tempted to mention the awful wreck, but he didn't want to worry her. Anyway, he didn't want to relive it in his mind, so he wrote, "Would you please count Nolan's cattle when they're where you can see them, should be about twenty-three not counting new calves. Say, don't let Coonie Burris deliver any more doughnuts. I think he ate half the shipment. I sure thank you for the ones that got here, though." He signed it "Your friend Clem."

When he came to a farm with a mailbox near the road, he put the card in it and raised the flag. It was handier to mail stuff that way than in a town.

One thing continued to bother him as he walked along the bar-ditch. If Ken didn't come west next Monday, she would have to find somebody else to bring the doughnuts, and who could you trust?

He was used to the hot sun now, and without socks the sneakers didn't rub blisters on his feet any more, but he liked to stop a couple of times a day anyway and let Pedro rest and graze. There was grass all along the route, but he

112

tried to wait until he found some shade, preferably as far from the pavement as he could get. Ever since Friday night he mistrusted all fast-driving automobiles, figuring any one of them might suddenly have a blowout and come hurtling off the road. This morning around ten o'clock he'd found a big culvert with a lush growth of grass where he and Duke could relax while Pedro ate.

Now at three in the afternoon a wall of black locust and osage orange trees stretched interminably along the north side of the road without any openings and the safety zone strip between the cars and the trees was too narrow for Clem's peace of mind. He was thinking, tiredly, no telling how far they'd have to go before Pedro could rest, when he saw a perfect small clearing practically enclosed by trees, furnishing more privacy than he'd had in a long time. As soon as he sat down, though, he began thinking about the wreck. Saturday, passing through the next town, he had bought a *Daily Oklahoman* and learned that there were three dead. One boy was on the critical list; the other three had multiple fractures and internal injuries. The paper said passing motorists had pulled the victims from the wrecked car before it burned.

Sitting there with his back to the elm, hat in one hand and a doughnut in the other, one gloomy thought led to another, and he found himself brooding about not getting a birthday card from his mother. She must be awful ill to have forgotten. But maybe she sent it late and it was in the Nolans' mailbox now, and Della would mail it on when he finally got around to writing her. Which was another good reason for not writing Della. If there was no birthday card, he was in no hurry to find out.

He didn't hear the Shetland pony until it was almost on top of him. The rider was about ten, with sun-bleached yellow hair in pigtails and a freckled nose. She wore a sleeve-

113

less blouse and shorts and cowgirl boots. And a stern frown.

"You are not supposed to be here, boy," she told him.

Well, he'd figured that. "Okay," he sighed, getting up.

"This is my grandfather's land and you are a trespasser."

"Just restin' my donkey," he said, putting on his hat.

"Oh, well, I guess it's okay," she relented, wrinkling her freckled nose amiably. Maybe his jaunty hat had influenced her. He removed it and slumped down against the tree again gratefully.

"Thanks," he said. "I'm pooped. Care if I take off my durn shoes?"

"I guess that would be okay, boy. What's your name?"

"Clem Marlow," he said, admiring her horse. Okay for a kid to ride, but it wouldn't be as good as Pedro for pulling a cart.

"My name is Trisha Vanders." She giggled suddenly. "Some of my best friends call me Trashy. Do you have a nickname?"

"Well," he said, feeling obliged to match honesty with honesty, "some people call me Clammy." And wished to hell he hadn't told her.

She laughed, a real cool little kid. Abruptly changing the subject, she said, "Will you sell me your donkey cart? My grandfather is very wealthy. If I ask him to, he'll buy it for me."

"Couldn't stand to part with it," Clem told her. "I'm on my way to New Mexico and need it to sleep in."

"Oh, wow!" she said, widening her blue eyes. "Lucky you!"

Clem grinned ruefully. "Oh, yeah? Listen, I have to walk so my donkey won't wear out, an' it's still sixty-some days of hoofing it ahead. Sure wish I could soak my feet in a tub of water."

"I know where there's a whole pond of water," she said,

114

twisting in the saddle to point into the woods. "It isn't very far, Clem."

"Well, lead the way," he said. Because never mind his hot feet, old Duke and Pedro could use a refreshing drink about now. Replacing the sneaker he'd taken off, he got up and said, "Come on, burro, they're givin' away free water."

The little girl trotted her pony on ahead, and when Clem took out after her with Duke, old Pedro followed briskly. Fifty yards into the woods a spring trickled down a mossy rock ledge in a hollow, and a concrete dam converted the hollow into a shallow pond maybe thirty feet long and half as wide. It was crystal clear with a sandy bottom and looked very inviting. He asked Trisha how deep it was and she drew an imaginary line across her chest and said up to here was all, but she swam in it all the time, anyway. "You have to dive shallow," she said.

That was a pretty good rule any time, he reflected, watching Duke and Pedro drinking thirstily. Burros might not need much water, but Pedro usually drank whenever he got the chance. Motes of sunlight lanced down through the trees to make shimmering spots of bright gold on the sandy bottom, and there were little perch swimming just under the surface.

"Wish I had my swim trunks on," he said wistfully.

"It's more fun to swim *without* anything on," Trisha said, with that bubbling unself-conscious laugh.

Well, sure. Anybody knew it was more fun to swim buck naked, but there happened to be a lady present. He could change into his trunks in the cart, but it wouldn't seem right with her there. Why not just wear his jeans, they needed washing—and he could sure use a bath, after going since Friday night without one.

"Okay if I go in?" he asked, and Trisha said "Go ahead," so he peeled off his sweaty shirt—he would launder it separately—but left on his sneakers. "Here goes," he said, and jumped in. The water was colder than he expected, but after the initial shock it just felt good and refreshing.

"I guess I'll swim, too," Trisha Vanders said.

He glanced around, and she was removing her boots. Well, it was her pool. Or her grandfather's, which amounted to the same thing. He grinned and ducked his face down in the water, opening his eyes to look at the bottom. Man, talk about clear water. He could almost count the grains of sand. Show her how long I can hold my breath, he thought, and set a new personal record before he emerged and looked toward her. And whatever breath he had left was jarred out of him.

Trisha Vanders was stark naked. Not a stitch, and not the least bit embarrassed.

"Hey, my gosh!" Clem protested.

"Didn't you ever see a nude person before?" she demanded scornfully, standing there in a kind of look-at-me attitude. "Don't be such a prude."

He couldn't look at her—but couldn't look away either. For all his dismay he was fascinated, never having seen the complete female figure so unadorned before. He'd *wondered* about it, naturally. Who didn't? But holy police commissioner! He'd never expected to ever see a girl stark naked right out in broad damn daylight, not even a kid like Trisha.

Having posed long enough to make whatever point she had in mind, she made a flat dive into the water and came up blinking and laughing beside him. Inching away, he felt she had put him in a dangerous predicament. He remembered how the welfare lady had acted about Melody, and he figured if anyone came along he could be arrested.

"Okay, you had your swim," he said nervously. "Now you better put your clothes back on, huh?"

"But I haven't even started yet," she said.

116

"Hey, what would your mother say if she knew you went in swimming with a guy without wearing a bathing suit?"

"She wouldn't care—my goodness, we *all* go nude around home whenever we feel like it. Even Corby and Monkey."

"Who's that?" said Clem distractedly.

"Daddy and Mommy—Corbin and Monica. We all have nicknames. My two younger brothers are Iggy and Iddy. For Ego and Id, but those are not their real names, of course."

"You mean the whole family just parades around stark naked?"

"Wow, are *you* old-fashioned!" she said, pityingly. "But it isn't your fault, I guess. Corby says most people are still living in the dark ages, with Puritanical moral standards that make them neurotic prudes. People who are ashamed of their bodies are salaciously inhibited, Corby says."

What the hell does Corby know about it? Clem thought defiantly. "You mean you all belong to, like, a nudist colony or something?"

She splashed some water on his back and helped him bathe, and her cold hands felt pretty good, rubbing around on his skin like that. It had been a long time since anybody washed his back for him. But how would he explain that to the sheriff? He ought to get the hell out of here before it was too late. A guy could get in serious trouble just being in the same pond with a naked girl her age.

"We don't belong to any group," she said. "I mean not an organized group. Some of the other professors' families feel the same way—mostly the humanities people, though Benjy Roberan's father is a physics instructor—but my goodness, it isn't like a nudist colony. We're just enlightened, Corby said."

Clem had got thrown off on the first curve. "Professors?"

"Corby is a professor at Fenster-Sabine University, in fine

117

arts. He is a sculptor. This summer they're in Europe on a fellowship, Corby and Monkey, and us kids are staying with Grampy and Grandma."

Grampy and Grandma weren't keeping a very close watch on Trisha, he thought. Or maybe they were coming right now, fast.

"Well, how do your grandparents feel about you runnin' around naked?"

She gave him that bubbling laugh again. "Grampy said he didn't mind, but Grandma said he is a dirty old man and she doesn't want me traipsing around her house without clothes on."

Clem kind of leaned toward Grandma's point of view on the subject. "You mean to tell me all them college professors go around at the college bare naked?" he demanded.

"Not on the campus, stupid. At *home*. But the important thing is they all encourage their children to have a wholesome attitude about their *bodies,* and not to be *obsessed* with furtive thoughts about themselves and everything. Corby says if nobody wore clothes there would be a lot less crime and fewer divorces and maybe no mental illness at all."

Yeah, Clem thought, but they'd sure freeze their butts off in the wintertime.

"I mean," Trisha Vanders said earnestly, gazing up at him with her clear blue eyes, "my parents, and the other parents who are good friends of theirs, they *want* us to experiment and learn about everything. About ourselves and about *other* people, too. The trouble is, all of the boys are younger than me."

Clem threw himself over backward in the stinging cold water. He came up a safe distance away from her and looked around nervously for the authorities.

"Monkey says it's all right to experiment until I reach
118

the age of puberty," Trisha said in what may have been a reassuring tone. "I'm eleven, but I haven't started developing my secondaries yet." She saw his blank look and added helpfully, "Manifestations." It was no help.

"Oh," Clem said, washing his face again.

Suddenly Trisha Vanders burst out laughing. "You're *scared*," she said. "You're scared of *girls*."

He was only scared of the authorities, but he didn't argue the point. The thing to do was to get out and get out fast.

"I'll bet you've never even *seen* a girl before," she taunted.

"Well, not as young as you are," he said, splashing ashore and gathering up his shirt. Putting it on, he took a final regretful look at her out of the corner of his eye. It was a terrible temptation, maybe the chance of a lifetime to satisfy his curiosity about the female anatomy. One thing for sure, he'd be even more curious from now on. He put on his hat and tilted it over one eye and looked at Trisha to say goodbye, but she had slipped on her clothes and now just looked like any ordinary little girl.

Back on the highway, walking uncomfortably in wet jeans and sneakers, he could think about Trisha more calmly. But she sure was going to get some tourist in a mess of trouble.

ELEVEN

Detouring around north of Oklahoma City on unpaved outlying streets and dirt roads took three days, during which time he lost contact with the friendly truckers. Nobody knew him along the detour and he got to feeling pretty lonely before he found the highway again. But it was worth it. From the start, he'd dreaded walking through the city, knowing that it would take him more than one day and that he would surely be caught at dark with nowhere to stop. He'd also feared the heavy traffic, mobs of motorists impatient to reach their jobs and go home in the evening—they would hate a slowpoke like Clem.

So he skirted the northern fringe of the seemingly end-less city, staying on narrow dirt roads and graveled streets. The third day, which was the thirteenth day of his journey, it rained during the afternoon and the red dirt road he was following south turned to slick, gummy mud that stuck to his sneakers in increasingly heavy lumps. Finally he took his shoes off and cleaned them as best he could and hung them on the sulky shafts.

He just didn't have time to wait out each rainstorm, and a little water wouldn't hurt a guy. Soaked clothing was un-comfortable, but heck, nobody ever died of discomfort. It would be stupid to put on dry stuff before the weather cleared up, or he stopped for the night.

120

The countryside had flattened out, mostly pasture and wheatfields, with oil derricks everywhere. There were no trees except along the small muddy branches or in people's yards. The scrub oaks were behind him now, with sprawling prairie ahead. He wondered if he would have trouble finding firewood. Maybe, he thought with a grin, there'd still be a few buffalo chips lying around, but the grin was a feeble one. It was hard to remain cheerful on such a wet and cold day, and without meaning to, he found himself thinking back to the wreck. One good thing about a dirt road on a rainy day, there wasn't much traffic. Nobody drove on it unless he had to, and then much slower than usual.

When an early dusk began to shroud the soggy prairie and Oklahoma City became a misty glow off to the left that stretched as far as he could see from north to south, Clem spotted the gray wreckage of an abandoned farmhouse and figured it might be his only choice of a place to get off the road for the night. There was a muddy overgrown driveway full of puddles, with the skeletal dead trees of an ancient orchard on one side and a weed-matted garden plot on the other. Somewhere nearby he heard the spooky chugging of another oilwell pump. The old house had caved in from neglect and age, but it hid the cart from anyone passing on the road and furnished plenty of half-dry rotten boards for a fire. It was a desolate place, and he had the feeling all of the people who'd ever lived in the decaying old house were probably dead now, but he didn't really believe in haunted houses, and once he had a crackling fire going and put on dry clothes he began to feel a lot better. The rain stopped, and night blacked out the ugly landscape as he scrambled eggs and corned beef hash together in the skillet.

Supper tasted great after the long wet walk. Sitting on dry boards with old Duke curled companionably beside him,

121

he ate bread and butter and hash and felt temporarily at peace with the world. For dessert he had two doughnuts and was inevitably reminded of Mrs. Whittle, thinking with alarm, Hey, what if she sent some more stuff and I missed the truck while I was off the highway? No one could haul the world's greatest cinnamon rolls or pie clear out to California and back without eating it. He wouldn't even trust Ken.

While scowling at the thought of losing any of Mrs. Whittle's baked goods, he had another idea so obvious that he felt like kicking himself. If she could deliver doughnuts by truck drivers coming west, she could forward his mail the same way, if he *had* any. Unless Della was home already, in which case it was too late. If only she didn't go to the welfare people. Clem was sure he could satisfy any curious highway police, but if Della reported him as a runaway, he was sunk.

Out in the prairie darkness a chorus of coyotes had begun yipping, and Duke raised his head and growled deep in his throat. Clem had never heard coyotes before, only foxes, but what the heck *else* could it be? The eerie serenade made him a little uneasy. Anyway, it was bedtime, so he chained Duke lest he get a sudden urge to fraternize with his wild cousins, and crawled into the cart, grateful for its snug dry comfort. As he drifted off to sleep he thought, a week ago right now, me and Gaylord Jackson were just relaxing by the campfire . . .

The nightmares were inevitable, and the abrupt, breathless, frightened awakenings. Each time he was shocked out of sleep his tired body relaxed, relieved that it had only been a dream. Even if a guy looked sixteen, when he was alone in the dark he got every bit as scared as any little kid of twelve.

But morning came, as always. This one dawned bright

122

and clean and summery, full of hope and promise, full of bird songs and the smell of breakfast cooking. They were back on the road before the sun cleared the blue-hazed skyline and the thirsty land had leached most of the moisture from the muddy road so that, although the footing was still somewhat slippery, it was much less gummy. And it still beat eating dust. Then, before Clem had gone a quarter of a mile between the green fields, he saw the highway and he just hoped none of the westbound trucks were carrying any doughnuts or cinnamon rolls or oatmeal cookies that belonged to him.

There was a cluster of mailboxes where the dirt road intersected the highway, and while he was writing a postcard to Mrs. Whittle, an eastbound Mack cab-over blared a good morning. It was great to be back among friends.

There were a lot of cars and pickups going into the city, but not much traffic coming out, and he guessed the in-bound people were on their way to jobs.

He was almost to the next north-south section line when a big GMC with a flatbed trailer loaded with lumber wheezed and rumbled to a stop on the shoulder beside him. There was just the driver, a stranger to Clem, and he got out and walked around in front of the truck, beckoning, so Clem stopped Pedro and went over to him.

"You must be the kid I've heard about," the trucker said. Clem nodded.

"A special buddy of all truck drivers, right, pal?"

Clem nodded again. "I guess so."

"You'd want to do them all a favor, I reckon," the man suggested.

Clem allowed as how he would if he could. "Doing what?" he asked.

The trucker told him. The Size and Weights boys had set up a portable weighing station on the route into the city,

123

and the eastbound truckers needed to be tipped off, so they'd know to stay on the bypass and not use the old route.

"How come?" Clem inquired, puzzled.

"Well, some of 'em may be haulin' a little more than the legal max, we all do it sometimes." The trucker grinned and winked. "Most of the time, in fact. It isn't a crime, but it can be expensive, and anyhow weight inspection causes delays when a man's in a hurry. Whenever we spot a sneak check station we signal all the other trucks so they can detour around it if they want to. That's where you come in, pal. I got to turn south, and someone needs to tip off the rest of the trucks coming east. Eventually the drivers coming out of the city will give the warning, but meanwhile if you'd take over . . ." He interrupted himself. "Here comes one now, pal, watch how I do it." As the big truck came roaring east he began making an up-and-down gesture with his extended left arm, as if pushing down on an invisible set of scales. The oncoming trucker answered by making a circle with his thumb and forefinger. He also hollered, "Hello, Clem!" So Clem waved and grinned, feeling good. It sure made a guy proud being known by name to a whole mess of important truck drivers.

"Clem!" the trucker said. "That's it. You're the feller I heard about, all right. You see my signal?" Clem nodded. "Try it out," the man said. Self-consciously, Clem held out his arm and made the warning signal. "You got it, Clem," the driver said approvingly. "Just do that when a truck comes from the west, they'll be your buddies for life."

"How long should I keep it up, all day?" Clem wanted to know.

"Couple hours, just to be safe, Clem. Westbound trucks will be passing the word. If the inspectors haven't loaded their portable scales and moved to a new location, due to

124

lack of business." He winked again, said "So long," and got back in his truck.

Clem watched him drive away and was stricken again with envy. That guy could drive clear to the Pacific Ocean and back a dozen times while he was hoofing it to Carrizozo.

Watching for trucks interfered with his bottle hunting, but he was glad to be of service to the truck-driving fraternity. He had warned eight or nine trucks and collected seven empty bottles when the lady in the bucket-seat Chrysler had her blowout about fifty yards behind him and passed, slowing, with the tire making a flapping sound, to pull off onto the shoulder fifty yards ahead of him.

She was probably the most beautiful woman he'd ever seen. He would have helped her anyway, but boy, she was really something. Blue-black hair piled up on top of her head, Oriental eyes with the longest lashes he'd ever seen, a truly beautiful mouth made more exotic by a kind of pearl-pink lipstick. She wore a velvety-looking sleeveless black blouse with a silver belt and black stretch pants with flat silver slippers.

"Damn my luck!" the woman said in a startlingly high voice. "I knew I shouldn't have bought those bargain tires."

"I'll change it for you," Clem told her eagerly.

"Would you, sweetie?" she said thankfully. "I'm not dressed for it." She got the keys and held them out. "The jack and spare are in the trunk, sweetie. And you're a real doll for helping me."

Unlocking the trunk, Clem was puzzled; her voice and her manner of speech didn't go with the way she looked. When he got the bumper jack out, she was yawning. "Nothing personal, sweetie," she said in that surprisingly immature voice. "I'm just not used to being alive this time of day. Me and my early start! I should have stayed in bed until

125

noon, the way I'm accustomed." She narrowed her eyes. "I don't suppose you'd have a benny on you, sweetie?"

"What's a benny?" he asked. She told him: a pep pill. He shook his head. If she usually slept until noon she must work nights, like Della Nolan. But not in a factory, boy.

A big diesel sleeper-cab was roaring out of the west, and he had to leave the jack and move from behind the car so he could give the signal. The trucker tootled acknowledgment, and when Clem started jacking up the sleek sedan (the first Chrysler he'd ever touched), the woman raised her eyebrows at him and said, "Why did you do that, sweetie?"

As modestly as possible he explained that he was a special friend of the nomad truckers and that he was giving them a secret warning. She was impressed and uttered a brief, throaty laugh.

"If they're all your friends, sweetie, maybe you could flag one down and borrow a benny for me. It is a well-known fact that truck jockeys practically live on pep pills."

That fact wasn't well known to Clem Marlow, and he wondered where she had heard it. Why would a guy need any special pep to just sit up there driving a truck?

When the next eastbound truck came roaring along, the woman laughingly helped Clem give the signal, and the bemused driver continued tootling his horn for half a mile before he got control of himself. "I think we shook him up, sweetie," she said and yawned again.

He started worrying about her. She shouldn't be driving if she was as sleepy as that. "How far you goin'?" he asked, as he loosened lugs.

"Amarillo, Texas," she said. That was a long trip for a sleepy person all right. "I open for two weeks at the Longhorn Club tonight," she said.

126

He blinked up at her for a second, then went on with his work. "You a singer?" he asked.

She laughed. "Not exactly, sweetie. I belt a couple of novelty numbers in my act, but I'm essentially a dancer." She laughed again. "Basically, I'm a dancer, you might say."

He nodded, dropping lugs in the hubcap. Well, she sure had the legs of a dancer.

"Here comes another truck, sweetie."

She let him do a solo job on this one.

"Actually, sweetie, I'm a stripper," she said when he squatted by the raised wheel again. "An exotic dancer, according to the ads, but we're strippers to the customers."

He couldn't look at her. His ears felt hot, and his heart was pounding. A beautiful lady like her, taking off her clothes in front of a lot of evil-minded old men. He had read about strip-teasers in one of Della's paperback murder mysteries—a burlesque queen got murdered and one of the strippers helped the young detective solve it and they fell in love and were fixing to get married but she wouldn't leave the stage to be a housewife. Now Clem could feel a genuine sympathy for the sleuth, if his stripper was anything like *this* stripper.

Clem suddenly remembered Trisha Vanders. She would probably grow up to be a stripper, if she had the looks. She already had the urge. Boy, you sure met some unusual people along the highway.

"You know about strippers, sweetie?"

Clem nodded, but couldn't meet her sleepy gaze.

"Well, it's a living," she said. "A damn good living, sweetie. But the hours are murder. So this is what they call morning, huh? Give it back to the Indians. Do you suppose a broad like me could ever live a normal life?"

He sensed that she wasn't asking him, but just talking to herself.

127

"I haven't done so bad for an ignorant carnie kid," she said. "Would you believe I can barely read and write, sweetie?"

Clem gave her an uncertain grin. "I guess you're kidding me."

"I wish I was," she sighed. "Traveling with a carnival a kid seldom sees the inside of a schoolhouse. But you learn things they don't teach in schools. How to look out for yourself. I've been driving all over the United States by myself since I was sixteen, hardly able to make sense out of a road map, and I've been knocking down a couple hundred a week since I wore my first pasties. How much would I be earning if I'd finished high school?"

Clem didn't know how to answer. He carried the wheel around, put it in the trunk, and got out the spare. It wouldn't be so bad if you couldn't write, but not being able to read would be awful—especially if you liked to read the way he did.

"The trouble is," said the stripper, "there's not much future in my racket. I'm twenty-three, I never made the big time, and at the clubs where I work I'm competing with teenagers on their way up. But it's all I know how to do. And as long as I keep my looks and my figure . . ."

She was talking way over his head, and without realizing he was speaking out loud, he said, "How much do you take off?"

"Aha!" she said with a practiced smile. "You're *thinking,* sweetie. You're imagining, aren't you?"

Hotly embarrassed, Clem shrugged. "I just wondered, is all."

"It's all right, sweetie, I'm used to the male reaction— my gosh, without it I'd be nothing. And I'm kind of glad you asked. Talking keeps me awake." She yawned, as if to show how sleepy she was. "Well, sir, it depends on the local

128

laws, and on the club, and in particular it depends on the money Candy gets—that's my stage name, Candy Labra; candelabra, get it? I do a fire dance, I have these tassels I dip in a mixture of lighter fluid and water, and I light them and they black out the joint and I make them go like this." With her forefingers she described opposing circles in front of her chest. "Anyway—here comes a truck, sweetie."

Clem stopped replacing lugs and went to signal another unknown buddy, all the while picturing the fire dance this beautiful lady performed. It sounded kind of dangerous.

Back at the wheel, he said, "You ever burn yourself?"

"Oh God, yes!" she said. "Blisters are practically part of the act, but without a gimmick a stripper is just a stripper. And whenever I do burn myself, I always get a real ovation like they figure I ain't got talent but I'm a real little trouper."

Clem nodded, tightening lugs.

"So it's a living. I breathe foul smoky air and fend off drunks." She yawned again. "Are you positive you don't have a benny stashed somewhere, sweetie?"

He shook his head. "But I wish I did," he said, reaching for the hubcap. "If it would help you stay awake. I mean, it's none of my business, but if you went to sleep driving . . ."

"You're so right," she said. "Even if I don't care about my own thrilling life, I might kill someone else."

Clem began to unjack the Chrysler. Boy, if she'd seen that wreck . . .

She had her purse open in her hands. "How much do I owe you, sweetie?"

He looked at her, offended and hurt. He sighed and shook his head sadly. She sure had *him* figured wrong.

"No money?" she said, snapping her purse shut and smiling. "You really are a sweet guy. What's your name?"

129

"Clem Marlow," he said, embarrassed by what she'd called him.

"Well, Clem, real gentlemen are very rare these days," she said. Hanging her purse in the crook of her elbow, she took his face between her hands and kissed him in a way he'd never been kissed before, a way that made him suddenly dizzy. Still cupping his feverish face in her hands, she said, "How did you get to be friends with all the truck drivers? Do you work at a truck-stop service station or something?" She took her hands away when he tried to shake his head, but left her right hand resting lightly but electrically on his shoulder.

He told her about Ken Whittle and going to New Mexico, and her eyes widened with sympathy as he talked.

"Ah, sweetie, I know how you feel," she said earnestly. "My own dear mama died from tuberculosis." He must have reacted visibly; she said instantly, "Oh, I'm sorry, Clem. That happened years ago, before they had all these fabulous new drugs—anyway, she didn't get in a hospital until it was too late. Now don't you worry, your mother is going to be okay, you'll see."

"Sure, I know it," Clem nodded, reassuring both of them.

She narrowed her long-lashed eyes, thoughtfully. "Hey, look, sweetie, it shouldn't be far to the next town . . ."

He had to interrupt her to signal a couple of trucks. When he turned back, she was finishing a shuddery yawn.

"I'll check into a motel and sleep like crazy," she told him. "If it's very far, I'll pick a motel on this side of town. If it's only five or six miles, I'll go on through and find a place the other side of town, do you see?"

Clem nodded, although he didn't quite see what she was getting at.

"Then," she said, drawing a circle on his chest with a forefinger, "when you get there, watch for my car. Wake me up. We'll eat an early dinner together, okay? You'll be my guest, handsome. Okay?"

"I don't have any dress-up clothes," he said.

"So what? We won't go to a fancy place, Clem. We'll find a drive-in and eat in my car. I usually do that, anyway." She studied her expensive-looking wristwatch. "If I get back on the road by four-thirty or five, I'll have plenty of time. I drive like a maniac on good highways. So let's see, now . . . that gives you seven hours to reach wherever I'll be, and gives me at least six hours of sleep, oh joy, six lovely hours. Right?"

"Right," Clem said.

She gave him another quick kiss before he realized she was going to, and then she said "So long" and got in her Chrysler and took off. Very fast. Leaving him a trifle stunned and hopelessly in love, but thinking with astonishment, Eighty miles an hour! Holy police commissioner! She can go as far in one hour as I make in a damn week!

Ten minutes later Clem saw another truck and prepared to do his duty. But when he gave the signal, the driver began braking to a stop. It was just the one man in a rather dirty truck pulling an open trailer. He stopped just across the highway from Clem, and when a couple of cars had passed, hollered, "Come here, kid."

Clem tied Pedro to a fencepost, so he wouldn't try to follow, and loped across.

"Who told you to do that—flash the high-sign, kid?" the trucker inquired gruffly, staring at Clem with red-rimmed eyes. He looked like he hadn't shaved in three or four days. Or slept much, either.

Clem explained about the signaling.

The driver pointed a finger at Clem like a pistol, his red-rimmed eyes widening to reveal bloodshot pupils. "Hey,

131

you're the kid I heard somebody say was walking to New Mexico, right?"

"Yeah," Clem said ruefully. "But if I'd known I'd have to walk all the way, I guess I wouldn't have started."

The man didn't smile; he hadn't been listening, but staring ahead through the bug-spattered windshield, rubbing his bristly chin. Abruptly he turned back to Clem and said, "You're gonna stay on this highway, kid? I mean, you're gonna be right alongside it the next three, four days? In plain sight?"

"Sure, except maybe at night. I don't like to camp in the ditch if I can find some place back off the road a little."

The trucker massaged his bristles some more, then he blew out his breath in a kind of sigh. "Listen, kid, how'd you like to earn yourself a buck? For doin' nothin'?"

"Sure," Clem said. That was fifty pop bottles.

"I got a package here," said the man, "that belongs to another guy. He left it in my cab. So I need to get it back to him—seems like he said it's a birthday present for his wife, somethin' like that. I don't know when he'll be comin' through here, or which way he'll be goin', but in the next three, four days he's due back, an' no tellin' where I'll be." He looked at Clem intently.

"If I could leave it with you, I can get word to this guy to pick it up. That wouldn't be a problem. Listen, kid, you got a safe place to stash it in that covered wagon of yours? I wouldn't want anything to happen to it—I don't know how much of a beatin' it could take, it might be glass. You think you could stow it where it would ride without jarrin' much, an' wouldn't get stolen or anything?"

"Well," Clem said, losing whatever eagerness he'd had. He didn't want responsibility for something delicate or expensive. He shook his head uncertainly, hating to lose the

132

dollar. "I couldn't take the responsibility, I guess," he said. "How do I know it isn't already busted?"

The trucker smiled for the first time, and it wasn't a good smile. He had a broken-off tooth, and the others were stained. "I made too much of it, kid, it ain't all that important. But I'll be turnin' south here to skip that party up ahead. I oughta just toss it out in the ditch, only he's a friend of mine, so I'll give you two dollars if you put the thing in your buggy an' just hang onto it until he comes along an' claims it. Just do the best you can, an' if it gets busted it just gets busted, okay?"

Two dollars, Clem was thinking. A *hundred* pop bottles! He shrugged. "Okay, I guess."

The trucker handed him the money first, then reached for the package. But before he passed it down to Clem he looked in the rear-view mirror and waited for a couple of cars to pass. "Okay, kid, here you go—beat it on back across while it's clear."

Clem took the package, which was somehow smaller than he'd expected. On the other side of the highway he turned. "Hey," he shouted, "how will I know him, mister?"

"He'll know *you,* kid," the trucker hollered back. "Don't worry." He shifted gears, roared his engine, looking in the mirror, and pulled out onto the highway. Clem leaned into the cart to stow the package. It was about the size of a shoe box and not very heavy, but he wrapped his blanket around it and shoved it up under the seat where it wouldn't get accidentally stepped on. Two dollars just for keeping something until a guy asked you for it. Man, that sure beat collecting bottles.

"Let's go, boorow," he said, untying Pedro. "Get up, dog," he ordered Duke, who was lying in the grass snapping at gnats. "We're runnin' late an' I got a date. With a beau-

133

tiful girl, wowee! If kids back in Conifer could see ol'
Clement now, they wouldn't laugh."

About ten minutes later he signaled an eastbound truck,
thinking he could probably quit after this one. He turned
to wave and there behind him was a black-and-white patrol
car, pulling off the road. The car stopped on the shoulder,
and the trooper, a young guy wearing glasses, pointed a
stern finger at Clem and then crooked it in the unmistakable
command: *Come here!* Sighing, Clem approached the right-
hand window.

"Yessir?" he said, trying to look sixteen or older.

"What was that signal you just gave that truck driver?"

"They got the highway tore up back there a few miles,"
Clem said. "I was warning him about it."

The young trooper stared at him through his thick-
rimmed glasses. "Who told you that?"

"A westbound trucker. He would of warned the eastbound trucks himself, but he had to turn south up ahead."

"Why did he turn the job over to you, chum?"

Watch out! an inner voice warned Clem. Watch your
big fat mouth, boy. He shrugged innocently. "I don't know,
I guess because he saw I'd be around here all morning. But
he said I could quit after an hour or so, and I guess the
hour must be up by now."

The trooper nodded impassively. "You can quit, all right.
The Size and Weights boys moved to a new location about
fifteen minutes ago, chum."

Clem blinked at him. "Sir?"

"Okay, fella," said the trooper, "nobody could act that
innocent unless he was pure in heart or a born con man.
What you've been doing is warning the eastbound truckers
that a Size and Weights unit had set up a spot check down
the road. In case you didn't know, all trucks are rated for
maximum weight loads, and it's amazing how often they

134

exceed this figure. The only way to catch them is to set up portable scales here and there and check. That's what was going on this morning. Unfortunately, the usefulness of such a check station is limited because the truckers always spread the word in both directions. You must have done a good job today. All the trucks that were weighed were within their specified maximum. Any violators must have circled around the trap."

Clem couldn't think of anything to say.

"How did you happen to be here at such an opportune time for the trucking industry?" the trooper inquired.

Clem figured he meant where was he headed, and was well prepared for the question, having studied his road map.

"I'm just taking a vacation trip," he said. "Visiting historical spots an' state parks."

"You headed for any particular place at the moment?"

"Well, I want to see the Washita National Wildlife Refuge at Lake Foss," Clem said blandly, because he *would* like to see it if he had the time. "Then I'd like to swing back up to Roman Nose State Park," he said, because if he had the time he'd like to do that, too.

The trooper regarded him steadily. There was an amused twitching at a corner of his mouth. Like he wasn't buying the story. "If you took all those side trips," he said, "you'd never get to New Mexico." When Clem looked flabbergasted, he grinned and added, "You'd almost *have* to be Clem Marlow, since we don't get that many donkey carts through here."

Okay, Clem thought. He knows about me.

"Believe it or not, truck drivers speak the same language I do," the patrolman said. "And waitresses like to gossip. I heard about you days ago, Clem. You must have a good press agent."

135

Okay, Clem thought with relief. So far no one back home was after him.

"They say you're going out to see your mom," said the trooper, "that you haven't seen her for a couple of years, right?"

Clem nodded, the lump of worry stirring in his chest, wishing to hell he could hear from her some way. Distractedly, he wondered if Della was home yet, looking in the mailbox.

"I believe you met a friend of mine last week, over east of the city," said the trooper. "Sergeant Walters. He was at headquarters Saturday and mentioned you." He smiled. "Told us how fast you get across bridges, with your donkey galloping after you."

Clem grinned. "He's scared I'll run off an' leave him, I guess."

Very friendly now, the trooper said, "I expect Walters wishes he had more donkey carts and fewer hot-rods in his district. There was a bad accident east of Latham last Friday night. Carload of teenagers traveling at high speed, lost control—the driver said it was a blowout—" The trooper saw Clem's automatic shake of the head, but decided it was just a gesture of sympathy. "No way to be sure, since the tires burned up and the only possible witnesses disappeared before Sergeant Walters arrived. Three kids killed and the other four pretty badly smashed up. Maybe you read about it."

Clem nodded, wanting to tell of his part in that grim business, but hesitated. The mention of witnesses made him uneasy. Witnesses had to appear in court and testify about things.

The trooper was in no hurry. "Walters said a woman who got there right after it happened—she was the first motorist to stop and help—says a Negro and a kid were

136

pulling the teenagers out of the car. They must have lived nearby, but she swears there were no other cars at the scene. Anyway, whoever the good Samaritans were, they can't be located." He got out some chewing gum and gave Clem a stick and went on talking. "One of the doctors sewed up a glass cut on the Negro's arm, but didn't get his name. It's a tough case for Walters."

"Is it important?" Clem asked. "I mean, about the witnesses?"

The trooper shrugged, chewing his gum. "If they could throw any light on the situation, yes. In case someone wants to sue the driver."

He stopped then because the radio in his patrol car crackled and a voice said, "We have a one-car accident report, sedan ran off the road just east of Kanook, no other details at present."

The trooper reached in, picked up his speaker, and said he would take the case. He listened for a minute and hung up. "Some idiot fell asleep at the wheel, I expect. That's usually the case when only one car's involved. Listen, chum, no more aiding and abetting. Don't help law violators, you hear?"

Clem nodded sheepishly, feeling a little guilty but not much. What difference did it make if Ken Whittle, for example, hauled a few extra pounds or not? Then as the trooper got in his patrol car Clem felt a sudden stab of fear. Asleep at the wheel. Kanook was where Candy Labra was going to stop and rest, only maybe she didn't quite make it and dozed off. Maybe he'd put her spare on wrong and it came off or blew out . . .

For a minute, watching the patrol car speed out of sight, he didn't want to go on and find out whether his premonition was right or wrong. He thought of taking a side road, but then he decided that even if it was her, maybe she wasn't badly hurt and he could help her. He set a brisk pace along the roadside, ignoring all the traffic and not even looking for pop bottles. His eyes were fixed intently on the distance, straining for first sight of the accident ahead, the flashing red light of the black-and-white cruiser, even while realizing it must be a couple hours away, at his speed.

When he was finally in sight of the town, he spotted the area where the wreck had taken place. The car had been towed away, and only broken glass and the plowed-up shoulder remained as testimony. Clem gave the scene a brief looking over, thinking at least the car hadn't burned. And he saw no shining red trails of blood. Nobody hurt real bad here, he thought.

He had been in such a hurry to reach the accident that he got to the town much sooner than he had anticipated, and he decided that Candy Labra must have gone on to a motel on the far side of town—if she was okay. He wasn't really looking for her car as he plodded past the first motel, but there it was, sleek and gleaming and totally undamaged. His relief was so overwhelming that he suddenly didn't want to see her and went past pretending that he hadn't seen the Chrysler with the Illinois license plate.

"Okay, boorow," he said gruffly, "time for the boss to ride, like I'm supposed to." He climbed onto the seat and untied the reins, and Pedro obeyed, his unshod hooves clip-clopping delicately on the concrete. Clem hadn't realized how tired his feet and legs were until he sat down. Riding was sheer pleasure. He'd got so he really looked forward to the towns.

Shoot, it's way too early to wake her up, anyway, he thought. She wanted to sleep till three-thirty or four, and it's only about two. What she expect me to do, hang around her motel for a couple hours? I just can't afford to stop. She probably didn't mean it about having an early dinner, any-

138

how. And if you're never going to see someone again, what's the point of getting too friendly?

People smiled as he passed, and on one long shady street a couple of small boys on bicycles cruised alongside him. One of them finally said "Hi!" Clem returned the greeting, thinking that kid sure took a long time making up his mind. Encouraged, the boy got off and pushed his biked alongside for a while and finally spoke again. "Hey, listen. You a Mennonite?"

"Heck no!" Clem said. "Where'd you get that idea, for Pete's sake?"

The boy was about nine or ten. "Oh," he said, "they use horses an' buggies. I *told* Jody you wasn't one. Mennonites always wear black clothes. An' their buggies don't have rubber tires, neither."

"Except this don't happen to be a buggy," Clem observed mildly.

"Well, whatta ya call it, then?"

"Well," Clem said, feeling inventive, "with the curtains rolled up it's a sulky. With 'em down, it's a gig. If it didn't have a top, it'd be a trap."

The boy was visibly impressed. "Then it must be a sulky at the moment, ain't it? Seein' the curtains is up."

"That's about the size of it," Clem agreed.

"Looks like you got a bed an' everything in there," the boy said, craning to take inventory. "You on a campin' trip?"

The other boy, Jody, had joined them now, riding his bike slowly with wiggling unsteadiness. "You a gypsy?" he asked, before Clem could answer the other question. He fielded the last one first.

"You could call me that," he said, rather liking the idea of being a gypsy. He cleared his throat. "I'm taking a little summer trip out west, fixing to poke around in the desert

139

some, and the mountains of New Mexico. Might do some gold prospecting while I'm at it."

They were speechless with admiration, and Clem felt no compunction about his story—after all, he wasn't really lying. He had all sorts of plans for the future. Maybe not gold hunting, though. Uranium. That's where the big money was, nowadays. Maybe if he struck it rich he'd find out where Candy Labra was performing and give her a lot of money so she wouldn't have to stay up all night scorching her stomach for a living. It suddenly struck him funny— not counting the family from Tennessee, he'd only met two girls so far on his trip, and both of them were strippers. One too young and the other just a shade too old for him.

"Hey, where you gonna camp tonight?" the boy on the bike asked.

Clem shrugged. "Wherever I am around sundown."

"Well, there's a roadside park a few miles west of town."

"That's probably where I'll stop, then."

"Hey, gee, I jus' hadda terrific idea, Jody. You an' me could ride our bikes out there, takin' quilts an' some chow, an' spend the night campin' out with ... *him!*" He looked at Clem eagerly.

"Name is Clem," he said, "Clem Marlow."

"Mine is Artie Adler. His is Jody Bell. Would it be okay with you?"

Clem shrugged. It was a free country. Maybe overnight company would put a halt to his nightmares. "If it's okay with your folks."

"Hey, wow! Le's go get ready, Jody. We'll be seein' you, Clem." And grinning happily, they took off at high speed on their bikes. Clem sighed and grinned a little himself, remembering what it was like to be a kid. Except he never'd had a bike. But he'd lived in the country and couldn't have used one, anyway. You needed paved streets and sidewalks

140

for riding a bike, but if he had to choose between a bike and living in the country, they knew what they could do with the bike. He kind of pitied town kids. But then he envied them a little, too.

He found a place to buy ice, and turned in thirty-two pop bottles. Using the trucker's two dollars, he bought some milk and bread and eggs and chewing gum. It was a great feeling to have come this far without having had to dip into his emergency money. If he continued to avoid tapping his capital, he could buy his mother a nice present when he got to New Mexico.

He was out of sight of the town except for the sun-gilded concrete towers of the mills and storage elevators when Candy Labra overtook him, honking wildly and pulling onto the shoulder just ahead of him. She got out, wearing skimpy shorts and a sort of jacket that left her midriff exposed. She had beautiful tawny skin, and although Clem had never paid too much attention to female legs, he could appreciate truly great ones when he saw them.

With a ferocious scowl, Candy said, "You dirty dog, you stood me up! Nobody stands me up, see?"

He had to grin, although he was kind of embarrassed.

"Thought you could run out on me, huh?"

"Well, listen," he said uncomfortably, "I got to town a lot sooner'n I figured, it was only about two, an' it seemed like to me you needed the sleep . . ."

She smiled suddenly. "Sweetie, don't apologize; the fact you're so far up the road is explanation enough. But I was worried. I drove back east to see if you'd had an accident or something. When I didn't find you, I added two and two and got seven." She laughed, and he had to laugh. "I took the chance that you hadn't stopped in town. And sure enough, here you are."

141

"Well," Clem admitted sheepishly, "I been kind of expecting you."

"But sweetie, what I'll bet you *didn't* expect is that when I invite a handsome gent to dinner, he's stuck with me. So fasten your horse and get in the car. I've got yay hamburghers and beaucoup French fries, and a couple of chocolate malteds."

So they had dinner together, after all, and it would have been great except for the fact that Clem was so dazzled by her beauty that he hardly knew what he was eating. He'd never been in love before, but a guy recognized it when it hit him. If she said leave old Pedro and old Duke there beside the highway and come go with her forever, he wouldn't even ask which way she was headed. But he knew it wouldn't work. He wouldn't want any wife of his taking her clothes off for money, not even two hundred a week, and he wasn't in any position to keep her in hamburgers and gas for her Chrysler.

"Listen, sweetie, if you reach Amarillo while I'm still there, I'll be there two weeks, you call the Longhorn Club and we'll *really* go out on the town. Okay? Will you do that, sweetie?"

"Sure," he said. But he knew he wouldn't make it in two weeks. He'd reach Amarillo, at best, a couple of days after she'd gone on.

She got some music on the car radio and chattered away while they ate a little too fast for pleasure, both of them aware that she still had a long drive ahead of her.

"You can tell I don't have a boyfriend waiting in Amarillo," she said, "eating all these onions. The guy I marry, if I ever do, has got to love onions, that's all. That might even be the main qualification for the job."

Clem Marlow qualified for the job. He was hooked on onions. And he kept wanting to say, Wait for me, give me

142

a chance to locate some uranium out there—and maybe finish high school.

"My ideal man," Candy said, "would own a big lovely ranch along the California coast, because I love horseback riding and surfing—and maybe I could break into the movies. Not stripping, of course, although, my God, they get away with murder in the movies today."

I'll buy a ranch in California, and a couple of surfboards, Clem thought. When I'm rich enough.

"California is beautiful in the late wintertime—have you ever been there?" No, he hadn't, but give him time. "Kind of purple-green hills with golden poppies all over them," she said. "The sad part is, though, by this time of year the hills start turning brown. If they had rains the year round, it would be just too beautiful to put up with, I guess. Along in March and April it's so lovely it makes you want to cry, Clem."

So are you, he thought, swallowing with difficulty.

Too soon, they were finished eating.

"Clem," she said earnestly, "it's the story of my life, always moving on and leaving my friends behind. It gets awful lonely sometimes, sweetie. I envy people who live in one town all their lives, instead of living *everywhere*, like me. I got to go, sweetie. You ever kiss a girl with onion breath? Well, you're going to now."

And he did. It was just a friendly kiss, but how would he know that? How many times had he been kissed these past few years? To him it was all a guy could ask, and he got out in a daze and shut the door and looked in at her smiling perfection and couldn't think of anything at all to say.

"Sweetie," she said, blinking her long-lashed eyes, "stay *nice,* please. Just be nice, that's enough. There's not much

143

of that going around now." She paused and then turned the key in the ignition. " 'Bye now."

He nodded, drawing a deep breath, and managed a grin. All the things he wanted to say, and he couldn't say anything at all. Just stand there and watch her drive out of his life. By the time she was half a mile away she was doing eighty or better. In an hour she'd be about as far as he'd get in the next week. There weren't many guys who already met and lost the one perfect woman of their lives at fourteen. It probably didn't happen to most guys until they were seventeen or eighteen. If it ever happened at all.

"Let's go, you slow sonofagun," he growled at Pedro, and they resumed their turtle-paced journey.

Arrived at the roadside park before sundown, he stopped, hoping to see the two kids. Only they never came. He wasn't surprised, though, because what parents in their right minds would let their boys ride bikes that far on a highway and camp out overnight with a guy they'd never seen before? As he was drifting along the edge of sleep, he wondered about the hungry family from Tennessee. They'd probably passed him in the night, and were already in California picking grapes or working in an aircraft factory for three dollars an hour. As for old Gaylord, he could be anywhere on ahead. Texas, New Mexico, Arizona. Well, probably not that far. Say, Amarillo. Be funny if he had a job washing dishes or waiting tables in the Longhorn Club, and got to watch Candy Labra do her death-defying strip-tease . . .

In his dream she set her clothes on fire while eating an onion and he was running around with an empty bucket looking for water but none of the faucets worked and he kept yelling at passing motorists on the highway—"Help! Help! Somebody help. I need some help"—and they stuck their heads out and said, "We'll notify the fire department

144

at the next town . . ." and after that it got pretty confused and he woke up feeling confused and wondering what time it was.

He finally got back to sleep, thinking, Maybe only fifty-nine walking days left.

TWELVE

MONDAY found him safely beyond the Federal reformatory; he'd felt uneasy about it ever since noticing it on the map, even though he doubted anyone there knew about his disappearance. But Della was home now, and she might have reported him as a runaway. Sometimes when he was plodding along the open highway he wished he'd taken the back roads instead of having so many people know who he was and where he was going. Even the highway patrol kept in touch with him, and they had car radios that picked up those all-points bulletins. The cruiser passed him several times a day, and he always held his breath, but the trooper never stopped, just waved amiably and kept going.

According to the map it was a long way to the next real town, nearly four days of walking. Monday a strong wind blew out of the southwest over the rolling prairie land, driving heavy clouds across the milky sky. This was a country of cattle and wheat, with few farmhouses along the road, and Clem's homesickness deepened, especially after Ken Whittle stopped for a brief chat and to deliver some oatmeal cookies and an apple pie from his mother. Ken had been over there Sunday, he said, and she'd asked him to convey her fond greetings to Clem. "I hereby do so," he said.

"Ma got your card," Ken added. "She says don't worry,

146

Coonie Burris will never deliver another doughnut for her, the rascal."

Clem smiled, thinking she'd be getting his other card today, probably. The one asking her to forward his mail. He said, "I don't guess anybody's been around asking her about me, have they?"

"She didn't mention it, Clem. Well, buddy, time is money, I gotta shove off. How's it going—anything happen along the way, or is it just a routine run so far?"

Well, Ken was in hurry, so there just wasn't time to tell him about the wreck, or anything else. "Nothing much." He shrugged.

Ken nodded, eyeing him closely. "You seem to be thriving, pardner. You look fit as a fiddle. I'll see you Friday, the good Lord willing. So long, pal."

And he was gone again. San Pedro, this time, he'd said. The seaport named after Clem's donkey. So now, watching the truck dwindling in the distance, Clem said, "Come on, San Pedro, let's go."

That was around eight in the morning, and it turned out it was Clem's bad luck that Ken hadn't had another ten minutes to chat. If he had, he would have still been there when the cops arrived. First he saw the highway patrol car, with several men in it besides the trooper with the horn-rimmed glasses. They kept going, fast, but behind them was a police car that stopped just in front of Clem. Two policemen looked out grimly.

Well, Clem thought, Della finally notified the cops.

The policeman on his side got out. "You see anybody on foot out here, boy?" he asked harshly. "A red-headed man, wearing gray pants and shirt. Big, heavy-set."

Clem was so relieved he started trembling. "No, sir," he said.

The policeman stared at him for a moment, then looked

147

at the cart again. He glanced back at his partner and gave a jerk of his head. The other policeman got out, and they both drew their short-barreled pistols from the holsters on their belts. The driver had his around back so it stuck down in his hip pocket. Clem, completely unnerved, stood holding Pedro's bridle and watched them approach the cart from opposite sides, guns ready. They yanked back the side curtains and looked in. When they saw the cart was empty, they holstered their pistols, and the first cop looked at Clem again.

"Why are you so nervous, boy?" he demanded.

"Well, jeez," Clem said, "who wouldn't be?"

"Where you from?"

"East of Oklahoma City."

"Where you going?"

"Well, I'm on a camping trip."

"Headed where, at the moment?" the driver asked curtly.

"I thought of stopping at Foss Reservoir, sir." He wasn't lying. According to the map the highway ran directly toward the Foss Reservoir and if he'd had the time, Clem would have liked to camp there.

"Good fishing lake," the cop said. "Let's go, Yancey."

The other cop nodded, still looking at Clem suspiciously, or so it seemed to Clem. "Look, boy, if you see anybody fitting the description, you report it to the first patrol car you see, understand?"

Clem nodded. "Okay. Who is the guy, anyway?"

"Escaped convict," grunted the policeman, already hurrying back to the car. They wheeled out onto the concrete and roared away.

Whew! Clem thought. That was too close for comfort! What if they'd given me the old third degree? Asked me questions over and over for seventy-two hours without sleep? I'd have probably confessed all about running away.

148

The wind made him worry about reaching the next town before a storm broke, but he sure wasn't worried about any escaped con. You think he would be stupid enough to walk or hitchhike on a main highway like this? Maybe he stole a car, or kidnapped a carload of people and was forcing them to help him escape.

He heard a dull roar overhead and looked back to see a low-flying airplane coming from the east, and it was zigzagging back and forth over the area. It was a Piper Cub, and Clem guessed it was searching for the escaped con—who was probably fifty miles away by now in a stolen car, or terrorizing a captive family of tourists.

Clem was watching the Piper Cub grow small in the west when he came to the concrete slab in the ditch. He'd encountered these things before, and appreciated them because they carried water from the highway out of the ditch, making his way easier. Each time he came to one he would pause and peer inside, not expecting to discover anything but simply checking to see if they were open all the way through.

This time as he crossed the spillway he looked into the slab as usual. But to his horror, instead of seeing daylight at the other end, he found himself face to face with a ferocious-looking man who said, "Okay, hold it right there!"

Duke bristled and began growling as Clem stopped the donkey.

"Cool it with the mutt or I'll slit his throat." Clem saw that the man had a shiv! He cleared his throat and said, "Shut up, Duke! Knock it off."

Duke subsided obediently, and the man squirmed forward until his head was out of the pipe. He had red hair—of course. And pale blue eyes and a ruddy complexion. "Don't look at *me*, buddy, look straight ahead." Out of the corner of his eye, Clem watched the knife-wielding con emerge from the pipe, his mind reeling with various horrible possibilities. The guy would kill him and stuff him into the pipe and assume his identity. Or . . . the guy would merely punch him unconscious, steal a bunch of stuff out of the cart, and flee. Or . . . the guy would take him captive and use him as a hostage to trade for his freedom—except the cops wouldn't swap and Clem would probably be caught in a deadly crossfire and riddled with bullets.

"Have you seen any fuzz, boy?"

"Y-yes, sir," Clem quavered. "Th-they checked my cart."

"They looked in your cart?"

"Y-yessir. About half a mile back."

"They already *checked* the portable doghouse, boy?"

"Yessir—my n-name's Clem." He wished, somehow, that he hadn't said the cops had already checked him.

"Hmmm," the convict said thoughtfully. "Anything coming, kid?"

"Clem," Clem corrected him tensely, looking east and west. "A bus and a couple of cars coming west. And a truck coming east."

"Okay, freeze. No funny movements. Just act natural."

Yeah. Sure, act natural.

The truck driver, nobody Clem remembered seeing before, saluted him with short blasts of his horn, but Clem didn't wave back or grin. He just gave the trucker a stricken gaze as he passed. If it had been Sam Sorrenti, or Pete and Shrimp, or Ken Whittle, they would have stopped, but no such luck.

"What was all that honking about?" the con asked suspiciously.

"Aw," Clem said, "they always do it. I guess they're m-makin' fun of me and my d-donkey."

"Yeah, the stinking world is full of smart alecks. Tell me when it's clear—and no tricks, Charley."

150

Watching both ways for a lull in traffic, Clem tried to think calmly, praying that the traffic would get thicker instead of thinning out—only in that case he'd have to stand there forever, unless a police car came along and wondered why he was just standing still looking scared. He could run, if he wasn't so paralyzed—but if he ran, the con might run faster and catch him and stab him to death. Clem thought irresolutely of making a dive for his rifle in the cart, but remembered that the gun was empty and that even if it weren't, he wouldn't have the nerve to use it on a man.

"It's cl-clear," he said, finally, scared to wait too long, in case the con flew into a homicidal rage and slashed him to ribbons. "N-nothing coming right now."

The con squirmed out of the tight-fitting pipe and made a lunge for the cart, yanking the curtain up and scrambling inside. "Okay, Charley," he snarled. "Keep in mind I'm watching you every second—one false move and you'll be wearing your guts like Christmas decorations, not to mention carrying your head under your arm. Now move out."

Up to now Pedro had been bored by the proceedings, but as soon as he felt all that two-hundred-plus pounds of added freight back there, he threw his head back and balked. "Come *on*, dammit!" Clem hissed in frantic anger. You dumb jackass, you wanta get us all killed? Twitching his long ears with obvious indignation, Pedro advanced under protest, slowly. Clem got the lead rope over his shoulder and dug in grimly, half-dragging the balky animal.

"Well!" the unwelcome passenger exclaimed. "A rifle, blankets, grub—everything I need but a change of clothes! Who said there ain't no Santy Claus?"

Clem would say it. No Santa Claus and no justice. But now he was glad the rifle wasn't loaded. He had kept it empty in case a trooper found it in the cart and checked it.

He didn't know the law about carrying concealed weapons, but figured if it was unloaded they wouldn't have much of a case against him.

"You thought of everything, Charley," the convict mumbled, like he had his mouth stuffed with Clem's food. "You just keep playing it smart and we'll get along fine, kid."

The Piper Cub was coming back on the south side of the highway.

"What's that?" the con demanded.

"Airplane," Clem said, adding soothingly, "Coyote hunters, probably."

The con snorted. "A two-legged coyote. Don't you look at it. Like I said, one false move—you dig me, Charley?"

"Yes, sir," Clem said earnestly, panting on the taut lead rope.

"Hey, you got anything to drink with this pie besides milk?"

"There's waterbags hangin' on the outside." But suddenly he lost his fear in fury. That guy was eating his apple pie!

Furthermore, he couldn't keep dragging Pedro like this all day. In fact, not much farther. That lousy guy! Who did he think he was, anyway?

"You treat your guests well, kid," said the con.

Clem saw the black-and-white sedan coming out of the west, just cruising normally, and he knew he had to do *something* to get that rotten crook out of the cart before he ate up all of Mrs. Whittle's stuff and no telling what all else. If he just waved at the patrol car, it might not stop, and then he'd be at the mercy of the knife-welding thug. Whatever he did had better not fail.

Then as the patrol car drew closer, not waiting for him to figure out a plan, he had a sudden inspiration. Hanging onto the taut lead rope with his right hand, he extended his left arm at his side and began making the warning signal for the Weights and Measures ambush. He saw the horn-rimmed glasses as the trooper leaned out of his window staring at him, and he changed the signal, pointing back at the gig with a jabbing thumb concealed in front of him, in case the con happened to be peeking out past the front curtain.

The patrolman was either very perceptive or extremely shrewd. He swerved the cruiser right across the highway and came to a skidding stop on the shoulder, the door open and his hand going for his pistol almost before the car stopped.

"He's got my rifle but it ain't loaded," Clem said excitedly. "But he's got a knife!"

The young trooper nodded, looking a little nervous himself, and he said, "Okay, Melvin, come on out, or I'll start shooting through the side of that flimsy rig!" And he advanced cautiously.

Melvin came out, but on the far side of the cart. The trooper was too close to see his legs and Clem was watching the trooper, but Duke was over there, and when the convict made his run forward to grab Clem, the dog, snarling as fiercely as any wolf, whirled toward him. The convict tripped on Duke's chain and Duke moved in and bit him three or four times on the right leg. Clem, meanwhile, bolted along the ditch with Pedro following, dragging Duke's chain. The convict and the young patrolman were left staring at each other. But the trooper had the pistol.

Clem got control of his nerves and walked back toward the patrolman.

"Stay where you are, Melvin, and put your hands behind your back."

"Lousy cops," Melvin growled, complying with the request.

The trooper handcuffed him. "Okay, get up, Melvin."

Melvin, Clem thought, a con named *Melvin?*

The man got his knees under him and struggled to his feet. "At least you coulda waited until I finished breakfast," he said, reminding Clem of the loss of food that had driven him to risk his life by signaling the trooper. He turned back to the cart and lifted the curtain to check. Why, the sono-fagun had barely touched the apple pie! Apparently he'd been too busy with a bologna sandwich. Relieved, Clem went back to watch the arrest.

"Lean against the side of the car," the trooper ordered.

"Now how the hell can I do that with my hands behind my back?"

"Put your forehead against the car and walk backward," the trooper said.

"Jesus!" the convict said. "I wish my lawyer was here to see this."

"All in good time, Melvin," the trooper said, amiable now that he had things under control. He shook Melvin down, finding no weapons, and said, "Stay there." And used his radio microphone. "Kaluski," he said. "Reporting in." A pause and crackling. "I got him," he said modestly, "but I'd just as soon not try bringing him in alone." More crackling. "Okay, I'll wait. Notify the roadblocks, huh? Roger . . . out." He hung the mike on his dashboard and looked at Clem in a friendly way. "Nice going, citizen. Where'd you pick him up, anyway?"

Clem gave him the details, while Melvin leaned uncomfortably on his forehead against the cruiser. "I'll be remembering *you*, Charley," he snarled.

"Oh, yeah?" Clem snarled back. "Boy, you think you can go around threatening people and eating all their food. Well, you're wrong."

"Was that what did it?" Melvin asked curiously. "I

thought I had you too scared to squeak. What did I do wrong?"

"Well, I thought you were eating up my apple pie," Clem told him.

"I shoulda kept my big mouth shut," Melvin said morosely.

"You wouldn't have got past the roadblock, anyway," the trooper said.

Something had been nudging Clem's mind, and he said, "You reckon there's a reward or anything for helping capture him?"

The trooper turned to the con first. "Okay, stand clear and I'll put you in the back seat." When that was done, he gave Clem a dubious look. "I hardly think so, Clem. He was only free a few hours, and it's not as if he was an important gangster or murderer."

"Whatta you mean, not important?" the con protested. "I contributed my bit to the crime statistics—and woulda done more if Charley there hadn't turned me in. I was going to hole up in his cart until dark, then steal me a fast car and knock off a liquor store or two, maybe shoot a few cops . . ."

The patrolman grinned. "My goodness, I'm certainly glad I caught you before any of that happened."

"*You* caught me?" the convict snorted. "Hell, the kid and his dog delivered me right to your doorstep. All you had to do was handcuff me—but on second thought, if you don't leak it around I was taken by a wet-eared kid, I won't press charges on your brutality."

The trooper laughed. "Humiliating, isn't it?"

"None of my friends would have any respect for me, and it wouldn't make you any hero, either."

"No reward, then, huh?" Clem asked, figuring why waste

155

his valuable time hanging around when he ought to be making tracks.

The trooper removed his hat and scratched his head. "Look at it this way, Clem. What you did today made up for what you were doing the other day, Saturday morning. Call it square, okay?"

Clem shrugged and grinned. "I guess so."

"Hey, Charley, you got it wrong," Melvin said. "There ain't no finder's fee on *me,* but there's gonna be a bounty on *you,* Charley. I got a couple torpedo pals due to get sprung in a few days, and it'll cost me a bundle, but I'm gonna give them the contract on you. They charge ten bucks per fracture, and I figure you'll be about an eighty, ninety-dollar job. They'll probably toss in a couple splintered ribs for free, 'cause they don't like stoolies, either."

Clem felt his scalp tighten, and his insides churned. He looked at the trooper worriedly.

Kaluski said reassuringly, "Empty threats, Clem. Small-time losers always run off at the mouth. He's just chipping enamel to keep from crying. Melvin doesn't *have* two pals, in *or* out of the pen, and besides, he hasn't got five bucks to his name." The trooper laughed. "That's only half a fracture, Clem."

Go ahead, laugh, Clem thought resentfully. You're not the one that has to worry about getting eight or nine bones broken. But he decided to put on a good front. "Who's scared of jailbirds?" he said. "I got a gun an' a durn good watchdog."

"Hey! That reminds me, officer! I want that dog's head sent to the lab immediately to see if he's rabid." The con gave Clem a triumphant look. "That's the law, right?"

The trooper winked at Clem. "Wrong, Melvin. According to the law, the dog has to be kept under observation for

156

a few days, and I'll be observing him regularly for the next week or so."

Clem had to grin, and felt a little easier in his mind. But not much. One thing sure, the con knew a lot of thugs and hoodlums. You had to bear that in mind.

All this time cars and trucks had been slowing down as they passed, the way cautious American drivers always slowed to pass a parked patrol car, and the people stared curiously. Now a big eastbound truck rumbled to a stop across the highway, and Clem recognized the driver. It was Shrimp.

"What's the trouble, Clem?" Shrimp hollered across the highway. "You exceedin' the speed limit again, buddy?" He twisted around and seemed to be reaching through the curtains of the bunk, as if shaking his partner awake. Or trying to. Without much success, it seemed. He opened the door and climbed down, carrying a net bag of oranges, and galloped across the highway. Looking at the highway patrolman, he said, "Clem in trouble?"

"On the contrary," the trooper said. "He just captured an escaped convict. More or less single-handed."

Shrimp looked curiously at the con and grinned at Clem in wonder. "Ol' Pete'll be sorry he didn't wanta wake up, when I tell him. Say, we brought you a present—California oranges."

Clem thanked him for the oranges and watched him gallop back across the highway and climb up into the truck, wave, and go roaring out of Clem's life again. Boy, if he could just go along sometime, instead of always standing by the roadside watching the truckers speed away. He sighed, and looked at trooper Kaluski.

"Well, do I need to stick around, or anything?"

The trooper shook his head. "If we need to clear up any

157

details we can catch up with you. Uh, say, Clem, I'm partial to navel oranges myself."

Clem opened the bag and gave him one. Then because of a vague feeling of sympathy and perhaps a faint hope of mollifying Melvin, he tossed an orange into the back seat of the cruiser. "Maybe they'll let you eat it later," he said gruffly.

"Naw, they'll steal it from me," the con growled. "But you mean well, Charley, so maybe I'll have my pals go easy on you—just break an arm and mark you up some."

Clem couldn't think of an answer. He started to go and then paused. "What's he in for?" he asked trooper Kaluski.

"Income tax evasion," Kaluski said, peeling his orange. "Gambling without a Federal permit. Assaulting an I.R.S. agent. And now attempted escape, which will nullify his prior good behavior record."

Clem nodded solemnly and headed for the cart, where he put away the oranges and gave the remains of Melvin's sandwich to Duke. Heading west again he saw the police and highway patrol cars beginning to converge on the capture scene. "From now on, boy," he said to Duke, "you better really sleep with one eye open at night."

Duke sort of nodded, like he didn't need anybody to tell him his business. Relax, old Duke would look after things. The reason he was so sleepy all day was because he stayed awake nights protecting people . . .

So that windy night, camping in another rest area, Clem was awakened by somebody rapping on the side of the cart and hollering, and Duke not so much as uttering a feeble bark.

"Man, you in there?"

Clem sat up with a jerk, scared and then abruptly relieved. "Hey, that you, Gaylord?"

"Yeah, baby. Just passing by and saw your stagecoach

parked here. Thought I'd see how you were makin' out."

Clem lit his candle. "Climb in," he said hospitably. "Hey, man, I figured you'd be in California by now." He unfastened the curtain and raised it, and crash-helmeted Gaylord Jackson grinned in at him.

"I had to make me some bread in Oklahoma City. That doctor hit me a lick, like I fretted he would—come to ten dollars. I got to get me some Blue Cross, or start mindin' my own business." He gave a mirthless laugh. "So I snatched a job washin' cars, but them cats socialize too much an' I didn't save so good. Carryin' my money don't make me lopsided. You still walkin', Clem?"

"Yeah, and my tennis shoes are about wore out," Clem said. "Hey, you want to get in? You hungry, Gaylord?"

"This cat's always hongry," Gaylord said, "but right now I'm sleepier than anything. Suit you if I spread my bed underneath here?"

"Heck, yes," Clem said, delighted to have company, even if those torpedoes weren't due to be sprung for a few days yet. "How about an orange and some cookies before you turn in?"

"Thank you kindly, Clem, that does sound good," Gaylord replied, accepting the bedtime snack gravely. "You go back to sleep now. We'll catch up on talking in the mornin'."

But they didn't, because when he woke up, the big Negro was clearly anxious to hit the road. He had a Sunday paper in his saddlebag to start the breakfast fire, and they found enough sticks to heat coffee water and fry some eggs. And they talked, of course, but not enough to suit Clem.

"You have been most gracious," Gaylord said, donning his crash helmet. "Maybe we meet again. That hog still needs a ring job or something, and I got a feelin' it ain't gonna run much longer without fixin'. So be lookin' when

159

you hit the towns; this cat liable to be 'most anywhere on up ahead."

Clem crossed his fingers and held his breath, and the motorcycle started and was gone, Gaylord waving a gloved hand in farewell.

Sighing, Clem started clearing up the breakfast mess and breaking camp. There was such a restless urgency about people on the road, an impatience to get going, to be moving. He often felt it himself, a need for more speed, an urge to run instead of walk. But he had to hold himself in for Pedro's sake. *He* could do more than ten or eleven miles a day, but the donkey couldn't, not pulling the cart. So they still had fifty-some days to go.

I better buy me some new sneakers in the next town, he thought as he wrapped his skillet in part of Gaylord's newspaper. When he started to put it into his utensil box, a headline caught his eye: TRUCKER DIES IN MISHAP. Tensely reading the news item, he was relieved to find it wasn't anybody he knew. It had happened Saturday, south of the city on a country road, when the heavily loaded truck swerved to miss a car on a bridge approach and jack-knifed into a ditch. There was only one man in the truck.

Maybe one of the trucks he'd signaled, trying to avoid the weight inspection, he thought. And wondered when somebody was going to claim the package he was hauling.

He led Pedro out of the rest area onto the highway shoulder and then back into the deep grass of the bar-ditch. He was getting weary of the constant wind. It didn't blow like this back in Conifer and, boy, it really shook him up to realize how far he'd come from home.

160

THIRTEEN

IT was midafternoon when he came down the long grade to the river, really too early to knock off for the day. But he was very hot, in spite of the wind, and Pedro was due a rest. Although by his standards it wasn't much of a river, a broad flat stretch of sand and willows with a narrow channel of rust-colored water wandering back and forth across the scoured riverbed, the map indicated it was the last stream of any size he would cross during the entire trip. And it had the further virtue of easy access. Car tracks ran down the sloping ditch past the end of the bridge and out onto the bare sand—where abruptly they sprayed off in all directions.

Clem led his small procession beside the balustered concrete span and into the shade underneath it just past the first massive pier, liking the sudden feeling of privacy. Because of the density of the bridge, cars and trucks passing right over his head made only a faint whining of tires and a fluttery swoosh of disturbed air.

"A little peace and quiet here," Clem remarked to his four-legged companions. "Just what the doctor ordered." Removing his hot, disreputable sneakers, he dug his bare feet into the cool sand and sighed. "Oh man, that feels nice," he told Duke, unsnapping the chain from his collar.

"Go work up a sweat an' take a bath. I guess we can kill an hour or two here without ruining our schedule."

Duke lifted a leg and anointed the base of the pier, staking his claim to the entire bridge, then flopped on his back and began rolling and squirming around in the sand. Clem unhitched Pedro, who immediately headed for the water. Clem braced the shafts with the sawhorse, discarded his hat and shirt, and followed. And after a long, indolent moment of indecision, Duke got up and tagged along.

To a hill-country boy the surrounding scenery was no great shakes, but it was very pleasant there beneath the bridge with the balmy sand underfoot and a diminished wind caressing his sunburned face, and all of a sudden he had no enthusiasm whatever for marching on into the hot afternoon. He might make three or four more miles before dusk, but what the heck. This was the best campsite he'd found in days, and if he went on he'd probably have to squat in the bar-ditch all night with the nerve-wracking traffic whizzing and roaring past. What if it was awful early to make camp? He didn't sign any contract to put in a full day *every* day. He was the boss, and if he wanted to knock off early, he didn't need anyone's permission. It's a democracy, so we'll vote on it, he thought with a grin, watching Pedro drinking at the edge of the channel. All in favor? "Me," he said. All opposed? Silence. "Okay, we stay," he said.

Down under the bridge he would be out of touch with the trucks for over twelve hours, and it would be just his lousy luck if his mail went whizzing past overhead—but there was always *something* to worry about, if a guy was the worrying kind. Which he was.

On the plus side, though, there was lots of driftwood. Firewood had become a big problem lately, and in the

162

morning he could load up some dead limbs to take along. He also might be able to catch a few fish.

After quenching his thirst, Pedro waded out in the water and stood there wigwagging his ears in an odd manner. Clem got the feeling he was remembering, or trying to remember, how he used to wade out in Royce Nolan's pond with the cows last summer.

Smiling, Clem took off his pants and waded gingerly into the cold water, which was about waist-deep. He swam, floated, bathed, and splashed luxuriously. After fifteen or twenty minutes he got out, shivering a little in the wind, and put on his pants, remembering how Della had lengthened them while readying for her own vacation trip to Kansas. He wondered about her, and Royce. And about Royce's cattle, which anybody could have rustled while he was gone. Burglars might have stripped the house, too. Boy, he thought disgustedly, you're a real worry-wart, you know it?

Pedro had wandered off to browse in a patch of willows, and Duke was ambling around with his nose almost on the sand, sniffing for game trails. Clem began to explore, too.

Presently he came to a half-buried log quietly rotting in a small delta of sandy muck. Reminded again of fishing, he wrestled it over to look for worms or beetles to use for bait, and found some of both. Knifing the top from a rusting beer can, he dropped the worms in and found a tall, slim willow sapling that he could use as a fishing pole.

Back at the cart he tied on a line with a small long-shank hook, split-shot sinkers, and a red-and-white bobber, and took time for a couple of oatmeal cookies. Then he followed the curving channel upstream so he could watch the westbound traffic for familiar-looking trucks. Even if they didn't have any packages for him, they made him feel less alone.

163

Fifty yards above the bridge he found an ideal fishing spot, a comfortable sand seat under a shady willow where the stream spilled into a deep pool flecked with yellow foam and shimmering with concentric silver sun rings where a soggy log reared out of the brick-colored water. Plunking a wriggling redworm into the eddying current, he lay back squinting up at the scattered afternoon clouds. He didn't expect much action at that hot, sunny hour. Any fool knew fish didn't bite worth a hoot on windy days, particularly not during the hot afternoon.

Suddenly the loose-held pole tried to jump out of his hands. He sat bolt upright clutching the shuddering pole tight and gaping at the taut line slicing the water with the bobber a dim blur below the surface. Heart thudding, he whipped the pole sharply upward and for a moment thought he'd snagged the submerged log. Must be a turtle, he thought disgustedly, feeling the heavy movement at the line's end. He arched his back for leverage and the weight shifted as the creature gave a little, lost the tug-of-war, and then came exploding out of the water so suddenly that Clem sprawled backward—and lay there in astonished elation, watching the shining wet blue-gray and white torpedo sail through the air above him and land flapping in the willow. Before he could recover from his stunned surprise, the fish came loose from the hook and plopped onto the sand, still struggling. Dropping the pole, he lunged full length under the tree to grab his prize and crawl a safe distance away from the water's edge.

It was a channel cat, longer than his forearm, a brawny charcoal-and-pearl beauty with an underslung, sharklike jaw and spots like big freckles. He guessed it would weigh close to three pounds, making it the biggest channel cat he'd ever caught. And what a surprise, coming out of a

164

rusty river like this. But if there was one, there must be others.

In the next half-hour he caught six more channel cats, and three bullheads, but none weighing much over a pound. Just good eating fish. Then abruptly they quit biting, or else he'd caught all there were. But he had enough for two or three great fish dinners. And it had been a thoroughly satisfying afternoon, something to remember out in the desert country where there would be no places to fish.

The sun was low in the west, and he was starting his supper fire when two men in a pickup came driving out onto the sand and parked nearby. Strangers always made Clem uneasy, so he pretended to ignore the men as they unloaded a bucket of minnows and started fishing with several casting rods apiece, one of the men going on up to Clem's channel-cat hole and the other trying his luck just above the bridge in Clem's swimming hole.

After about five minutes the nearest man walked a few paces toward the fire and said, "You been fishing, sport?" Clem nodded. "Do any good?" the man inquired conversationally. "Not too bad," Clem said, getting up from his squat and sauntering casually out under the bridge and displaying his catch. The man whistled and called to his friend, "Look at this, Lew!"

The other man, heavy-set and wearing coveralls with the sleeves cut out, walked halfway down the shoreline. "Not bad," he said. "Where'd you catch 'em?"

Clem grinned. "Up there where you're fishin'," he said, selecting four of the medium-sized channels and getting his knife out. He wished for some pliers, but managed to get them skinned. He saved the guts for bait in case he decided to set some lines overnight.

The two men hadn't caught anything by the time Clem started frying his supper. As he was ready to eat, the nearer

165

fisherman interrupted his restless pacing back and forth along the water's edge to call out, "What'll you take for the big one?"

"What'll you give?" Clem countered. Because he couldn't eat all of those fish for breakfast, and without ice he couldn't keep them from spoiling.

"Give you a dollar," the fisherman offered casually. Maybe a little too casually, because although Clem was tempted, he didn't jump to say yes. The man walked away, but when Clem was done eating, he wandered back again.

"I guess the fish had an early supper," he said wryly. He was tall and thin, with black hair and a heavy beard. "Only thing I've ever learned about fishing is if you've there when they happen to be in the mood you catch 'em. If they're *not* in the mood you could offer 'em turkey with cranberry sauce and they'd just spit in your eye."

Clem laughed.

The thwarted man said, "While I've got you in a good mood, I'll jack up my offer. Two bucks for the fish."

Because Clem liked the man and appreciated the company, he said, "Well, shoot, it didn't cost me anything and I had the fun of catching it, I guess I'll let you have it for a dollar. I got no ice to keep it from spoiling."

"I want it, and I'll tell you why," the man said. "I've got me a wife, a good woman but conceited as hell, every time I take her fishing she skunks me. I mean it, we go to Foss Lake and every time she keeps me busy stringing her bass or crappie, and the worst thing that can happen to a sensitive man is to be consistently out-angled by his wife. Women are poor winners, anyway, they have to gloat and rub your nose in it constantly. Last thing she said to me this afternoon was to bet five bucks I wouldn't catch enough fish for a meal. She said if I did, on top of the five dollars, she'd cook the fish for my supper when I get home."

166

Clem was touched. "Well, listen," he said, "you can have that baby for nothing."

"Friend, that's mighty generous," the man said, "but no soap. If I'm gonna be a liar and a cheat, I want it to hurt a little. Don't worry, I can afford it."

"Well," Clem said with a shrug, "I can use two dollars all right, I got to buy new sneakers. Mine about wore out from so much walking."

The man gazed at Clem's big bare feet and smiled. "I've got a better idea. I run a department store in town—you headed west?" Clem nodded and the man said, "I'll swap you the best pair of sneakers in my store for that splendid forktail. Then if my wife accuses me of buying it, as she usually does whenever I bring home a good one, I can deny it with an almost clear conscience. A deal?"

Clem was amazed. A really good pair of tennis shoes would run four or five bucks—if he had to buy his own, he couldn't *afford* the best—but this man was serious about trading for the channel cat. He said dazedly, "Sure, it's a deal." And out of gratitude for the unexpected windfall, he said he had hot water and instant coffee if the man would care for some. One thing led to another, and after they had introduced themselves—his name was Robert Fenwick— Clem explained about his journey, and Mr. Fenwick was quite impressed.

The other man joined them by the fire. "I'm disgusted," he growled, "and ready to take up horseshoe pitching." His name was Lew Meyers, and Mr. Fenwick filled him in on Clem's odyssey.

"Lew is a veterinary," he told Clem. "If your dog has mange, he'll sell you a dime's worth of salve for a buck."

"We call it summer eczema, and the salve is a buck and a quarter," the veterinary said good-naturedly, removing his round straw cap to reveal a thinning crew cut. He accepted a cup of coffee and began trying to outbid Mr. Fenwick on the fish. "Not only will I give you two bits more than the retail price of those sneakers, knowing full well this bandit gets about a sixty percent mark-up on everything," he said, "I will also throw in a thousand-mile check-up for your burro, including a chest X-ray . . ." Clem's grin wavered for a second, but Mr. Fenwick bridged the awkward moment, saying indignantly, "Sixty percent mark-up, nothing. Seventy-five, Lewis. At a mere sixty I'd go broke."

"Richest man in town," the vet told Clem. "And the tightest."

Clem hadn't done so much grinning since he didn't know when. One of the things a guy traveling alone missed—and Clem had been traveling alone a lot longer than seventeen days—was this sort of kidding around. It struck him that he liked adults better than people around his own age. They were more tolerant, accepting a guy the way he happened to be, and not always needing a laugh at somebody else's expense. It made Clem feel great to have these men treat him like an equal, a fellow fisherman they respected because he had the fish to prove his competence.

The men were talking about the best time to fish, and Bob Fenwick said, "You know we really should come back here tonight and try our luck."

"Right," Lew Meyers said. "We have a buffet supper and invite all the channel cats, since we've got all this perishable bait and our friend Clem to guard our trotlines. We set them now and come back around midnight, run them, and take home a tubful of big ones."

"He's a dreamer," Bob told Clem, grinning. "But expectation is half the fun of fishing, isn't it? Ordinarily we wouldn't set trotlines here and go off and leave them. A lot of wild

168

kids come out here at night to guzzle beer and hot-rod all over the riverbed—you probably noticed the tracks."

Clem nodded, with a tingle of uneasy foreboding.

"Sometimes these hooligans cut trotlines just for the heck of it, but with you camping here I don't think they'll bother us. Vandals are basically chicken."

They baited two long trotlines, and while Clem helped, the thought of an invasion of wild teenagers continued to make him uneasy. Vandals might be chicken, but he'd read about teenage gangs, and the possibility of being visited by one gave him the willies.

It was dark when his fishing partners finally departed, promising to return around midnight to run the lines—and bring him ice for his cooler and a pair of size ten sneakers. Mr. Fenwick took the big channel cat along for his supper, and Clem moved the rest of his fish to a shallow riffle where he thought they would be safe from turtles. He decided that if there weren't any fish on the trotlines at midnight, he would give Robert and Lew the rest of his afternoon catch.

Building up the fire, he called Pedro in from the darkness, giving him a cupped palm of salt to lick and then tying him between the sulky and the protecting pier. He sat by the fire with a lazy, contented Duke for a while, listening to the muted traffic noises overhead and a lone whippoorwill off across the river. Somehow he'd always thought of them as being native to the Ozark country and was surprised to find one this far west. But they did seem pretty scarce here. Back home there would be five or six of them calling back and forth all night, and this one was apparently just talking to itself, as alone as Clem but more lonesome, because Clem had friends coming back around midnight.

He thought about getting to New Mexico and finding the sanitarium. He tried to picture his mother's face when she saw him. But what if she got well enough to leave before he arrived and they told him, "Why, Mrs. Marlow checked out last week, she has already gone back home." Well, that would be great in one way and terrible in another—he'd just have to turn around and start walking back, that's all.

Or what if she didn't want him to stay out there? He'd never in the world make it back to Conifer before school started. Anyway, he might have cut himself off from the Nolans for good, now. And the welfare people would slap him into some kind of maximum-security foster home.

To shake off his gloomy mood he chained Duke on the pier side of the cart and settled down to greet his friends when they returned at midnight. It was a comforting thought to know they would be back.

But the others got there first.

Clem didn't know how long he'd slept or what time it was when the three carloads of hooting, caterwauling teenagers arrived. He had tied down the end curtains and raised the side curtains only enough to let in fresh air. Now he peered out through the narrow space at the three cars lined up in the middle of the riverbed. As he watched, they dimmed their lights; he heard yelling and singing and hysterical laughter. It occurred to him they hadn't seen the cart on their arrival because of the concealing pier—but they would see it when they came back.

He felt for the cold reassurance of his rifle, which he loaded at night and unloaded mornings. Out on the willow-grown sand flats one set of headlamps went on again and the sound of a car radio grew louder, delivering the twang-clang-twang beat of rock 'n' roll, and he gaped at the sight of the kids dancing in the glare. They were two hundred yards away and mostly hidden by the cars, but he got the definite impression one girl was wearing only a bikini. Maybe they were going to swim as soon as they worked up

170

a good sweat. Anyway, with girls along they probably wouldn't be as ornery, though on second thought they might want to show off in front of their chicks.

Clem sighed and shook his head; he wasn't kidding anybody, he was just as scared of the hot-rodding, wild-living members of his generation as any uptight adult. He thought about hitching up and moving the cart around to the other side of the pier so they wouldn't be as apt to see him when they were leaving, but he was just too darn tired. Besides, a guy had to consider his self-respect. There was no real reason to expect any trouble from a bunch of kids having a good time, what the heck. He even envied them.

Minutes passed, and nothing happened, and after a while he went back to sleep, more reassured at not being alone in the night than worried about the kids.

He didn't wake up again until they were racing past the cart yelling hideously, circling the pier like Comanches besieging a wagon train and screaming like Comanches. "Yow oww woww!" they squalled, roaring within a few feet of the cart. "Yeeow!" they yelled as they slewed their cars in the sand to circle the cart. Clem lay there tensely staring up at the top of his flimsy fort, wondering what to do. If he stuck his rifle out and blasted a few shots into the air, would they beat it? Or would they start shooting guns of their own? "Yeeoww!" they screamed again.

Clem did what any sensible person would have done in a similar situation. He waited, hoping they would get bored and go away. But they didn't go away. Finally they stopped in a semicircle with their lights bracketed on the cart. Clem lay rigidly with his heart thumping painfully in his chest, straining to hear whatever stealthy shenanigans they might be up to. After a while a car door opened and closed furtively. He waited to hear something from Duke, but the dog remained silent.

171

"Nobody home," a boy's voice said. "Must have gone fishing."

Okay, Duke, Clem prayed silently. Snarl.

"Anybody home there?" the voice bawled. "Hey!"

A girl's voice said, "Come on, Jerry, let's go."

"Just want to say hello, is all. Just being friendly."

"Okay, Jerry," another voice said uneasily, "let's go, man, nobody home."

They didn't sound too sinister, Clem decided. But that guy Jerry wasn't in any hurry to leave. It was a sticky situation; if they left, okay, but if they didn't, the longer he failed to show himself, the more they would think he was scared. Which he still was, but not as much as he had been at first. They were just people, not much older than himself. But maybe half-crocked, and you couldn't tell what a drunk was liable to do. He'd had enough experience with Royce Nolan to know alcohol could make a guy pretty mean.

"Hey!" Jerry bawled. "Hey!"

"Man, you are loaded, you know it?"

"Sober as a judge," said Jerry. "Don't worry about me."

Clem thought about crawling out of the cart on the side away from the cars and getting Duke, but remembering how Duke had behaved when the bully Carl had been beating him, he just didn't have a hell of a lot of confidence in Duke in a crisis.

"Hey," Jerry said suddenly, "look what's behind the wagon, a mule! Someone must be here!"

"Let's cut out, man, let's go find some action, Jerry."

If I showed myself now, Clem thought, I could pretend I was deaf, and who could yell at me then?

"Who wants to ride a donkey? Hey, people, let's ride that burro."

Let's *don't!* Clem thought angrily. Then he had a second thought. Anybody fooled with Pedro when he was just

172

halter-tied, they were liable to get the tar kicked out of them. And Jerry sounded like a guy that needed it.

"Come on, don't fool with the mule," somebody said, and that got a laugh.

"You think I can't ride that donkey? Listen, they ain't made the thing I can't ride yet. How much do you bet I can't ride him?"

Clem had to do something. Pedro might hurt that stupid kid, and then his parents could sue Clem or something. It was time to get out of the cart and confront them. He raised the curtain, and yawning like a man roused from sleep, grumbled, "Can't a guy get a little shut-eye around here?"

"Hey, lookit, folks, somebody's home! He must be hard of hearing. Are you hard of hearing?" Jerry was a short, mop-headed boy who stood weaving against the eye-hurting glare of the headlights, a loud-mouthed rooster of a boy wearing only hip-hanging Levis. No shirt or shoes. No brains, either.

"I wish I was," Clem said, wondering how many others were in the cars and what their mood might be. "What do you want?"

Jerry reeled around in a kind of chimpanzee crouch to address the unseen audience behind the blinding bank of headlights. "Hear that? He wants to know what we want. He's one of them tough guys, looking for trouble, it sounds like." Wheeling back to face Clem, he nearly lost his balance, and there was laughter in the cars, and Clem well knew the effect laughter could have on the guy who caused it. There was something dismayingly familiar about Jerry, and it took only a second for Clem to make the connection. Kirby Newman. This bawling character reminded him of Kirby Newman. "You looking for trouble?" Jerry challenged. "You want to fight?"

"I just want to sleep, okay?" Clem said. Maybe this kid

173

picked fights and then the others piled out of the cars and all ganged up on the target. Wistfully touching the cold steel barrel of the rifle beside him, he thought how a TV hero would handle the situation. Just calmly crawl out of the cart with his rifle and say, "Okay, when I count to ten, if you're still here I start shooting out headlamps, one . . . two . . . three . . ."

"Hey, you one of them real mean cats?"

"Heck, no," Clem denied. "I'm just tired and sleepy."

"Aw, cool it, Jerry," somebody said. "Leave the kid alone."

Clem appreciated his defender, but Jerry merely held up a hand, waving for silence. "Wait a minute. Just sit down and shut up. I want to find out if this guy is tough or chicken."

"Quit while you're ahead, Jerry," a sarcastic tenor advised from the gallery. "You're sloshed—you can barely stand, let alone fight."

Jerry waved them away again. "Answer me, buster, you tough or chicken?"

"Well," Clem said irritably, "I don't need to be neither one when I got a dog so mean I have to keep him chained. Not to mention my loaded rifle. So just lay off."

For a moment Jerry steadied himself, then lurched around to face the cars again. "Okay, men, let's go," Jerry said triumphantly. "Y'all heard him threatening us. Pile out and let's get him, show him what happens to snotty-nose kids who come around asking for trouble."

There was a moment of total silence, with Clem holding his breath, and then somebody inside one of the cars laughed derisively, and said, "What do you mean, let's get him, Jerry? You're the one he threatened, not us peace-loving types. You don't need no help. Show us how to do it, tiger."

174

Clem heard snickers and giggles in the other cars.

"Well, listen," Jerry said. "C'mon now, you guys with me, or not? He says he's got a gun."

"Don't worry, Jerry, he shoots you, we'll make sure we get you to a doctor."

And Clem thought in sudden revelation, They're not all on his side. And he also realized Jerry didn't want to fight by himself. So who's calling who chicken around here, anyway? We're *both* chicken. He even felt kind of sorry for big-mouthed Jerry, who apparently didn't command the respect and admiration of his friends. He'd talked himself into a corner, and now he had to put up or shut up—but he'd talked Clem into the same corner. And there seemed to be four or five girls in the audience, which made all the difference. A guy couldn't back away from a fight with girls watching, not if he had to live with them, like Jerry—not even if he'd never see them again, like Clem.

Oh, well, what the heck, ever since his fight with Kirby Newman he'd been looking forward to his next, in a way. Remembering the proud feeling he'd had, even though he'd lost, he felt a sudden surge of confidence, because the main thing he'd learned from Kirby was that getting whipped didn't hurt much and was no disgrace if a guy fought his best and refused to quit.

Putting on his shirt so he wouldn't look so scrawny, he lifted the back curtain and got out of the cart, stuffing in his shirt-tail and digging his bare toes into the sand. Going around the cart, limping a little because anybody's leg muscles would be sore after seventeen days of walking, he held an arm in front of his eyes to ward off the glare from the head-light. Leaning against the cart, he said, "How about dimming them lights?"

Presto! They dimmed their headlights, and he could see better. Well enough to note that his adversary though quite

175

heavy was not all that tall. Clem probably had the reach on him. I'll jab fast and try to stay as far away as possible, he thought, and he said gruffly, "Don't worry about me using a gun. Just so it's a fair fight, is all I ask."

"Curtain going up, folks, pass me the popcorn," some witty guy said, but the rest of the kids ignored him.

"What about your dog?" Jerry demanded.

"He's chained up," Clem said. "Don't worry about him."

"What makes you think I'm worrying?" Jerry blustered, putting his hands on his hips and trying to stand staight. "How old are you?" he asked, obviously trying to kill time. He must have realized he was pretty loaded.

"I'm fifteen," lied Clem. "What difference does that make?"

The effect on Jerry was amazing. "Fifteen!" he bawled. "Well, that changes everything. I'm eighteen. I can't fight a baby! Hey, you guys." He turned to the cars. "Any you fifteen-year-old kids want a job?"

After a moment of silence, during which Clem devoutly hoped the bout would be canceled for want of a local contender, a voice said, "Me. I'm fifteen, going on twenty-five. Guess I'm elected."

They all laughed, and a guy yelled, "Go get 'im, Dixie."

Clem grinned uncertainly as a car door opened and a girl ran out onto the illuminated sand. A rather small girl with short blonde hair, wearing an oversized sweatshirt, cut off just below her rib cage, and a bikini bottom. She was boyishly slim but still very sexy, and Clem began to feel very self-conscious.

"Okay, rumdumb," she said to Jerry, shuffling her bare small feet in the sand and doing a parody of a fighter shadow-boxing, "I'm taking over, stagger out of the way, go sit in the bleachers, sonny."

"You're kidding," Jerry protested. "Come on now, baby,

knock it off." He tried to grab her arm, and she gave him a sudden shove that sent him sprawling in the sand. "Hey, Dixie," he said, indignantly. "That's no way to treat your date, baby."

"Go drink some more beer and pass out," she said tersely. "You have had it. Pull in your horns."

A guy in one of the cars told the glowering Jerry to shut up and get in and finish his beer, it was Dixie's fight now. And Jerry vanished out of the headlights, leaving an appalled Clem blinking at the cute half-naked substitute. My lord! Who ever heard of fighting a girl? This must *really* be a tough crowd.

Dixie stalked to within six feet of Clem and stood with her hands on her hips. "Where you from?" she asked. He told her: Conifer. "Where's that?" she demanded. He told her: about twelve miles west of the Arkansas line. "What are you doing over *here?*"

He explained about being on his way to New Mexico, standing there with his hands shoved into his hip pockets and painfully aware of his unseen audience.

"You been riding in that cart all this ways?" she inquired.

"Walking," he said ruefully, and explained about *that*. He could see her face, although shadowed, and she wasn't what you'd call beautiful. A small nose and a wide mouth and twinkling eyes. "You mean to tell me you walked all that distance?"

"Most of it."

"Wow," she exclaimed softly. "Looks like you'd be tired by now."

He shrugged. "I am."

She just stared at him awhile, and somebody in the cars hollered, "What are you waiting on, Dixie?"

Turning her head, she shouted, "Don't rush me, will you, please?" She had a nice profile, Clem thought. And boy,

177

she was built from the sweatshirt down, and probably under it too. "What's your name?" she asked him, and he told her, Clement Marlow, Clem for short, and she said, "I'm Dixie Funkhouser, and if you laugh I'll slap your face."

Clem shrugged again. "I knew some Funkhousers back home."

"Okay," she said, getting tough again. "We shake hands first."

"Listen," he said, alarmed, "you ain't really *serious*."

"Boy, I might be saving your life," she told him gruffly. "Take my advice, go along with the gag, huh? Jerry chickened out, like everybody knew he would. See, they don't *care* how old you are. He just spooked because he's basically yellow. And he's pretending to be drunk to get out of fighting."

"You mean you want me to . . ." Clem said uncertainly.

"Take a dive," she hissed. "That'll satisfy them."

It won't satisfy me, though, he thought. He didn't quite trust her, anyway. She just wanted him to make her look good or something.

"Hey, come on, Dixie!" somebody yelled impatiently. "If you can't do it, let somebody else take a crack at him."

"See what I mean?" she said in a stage whisper, and then in a loud tough voice, "Okay, we shake first, buster." She stuck out her hand.

Well, hell. He didn't know what else to do, so he clasped hands with her, a little surprised at the strength of her grip. And she suddenly yanked, pulling him toward her and grabbing his wrist with her other hand, trying to throw him over her back in standard judo fashion. But she was short, and he was tall and long of arm, and they wound up with him draped awkwardly over her back, one arm instinctively wrapped around her bare stomach, legs stretched out with his toes dug into the sand like plowshares. She sagged to

178

her knees and there they were, him on his knees behind her, still hugging her bare waist.

"You dum-dum!" she hissed. "Roll off onto your back when I twist your arm." She began to twist his arm, and it hurt, so he reared up, lifting her off the sand with his encircling arm and holding her in front of him. She kicked at his shins with her heels, and he jerked his hand and wrist free, letting her go. At just that moment she kicked back and fell right on her face in the sand. He felt lousy about it, but what did she expect? She scrambled up and whirled and said, "Oh, you stupid jerk!" Reaching for his hair with her left hand, she swung on open-handed slap at his face with her right. Without even thinking, he grabbed both of her wrists, dismayed about the whole incredible business. The last thing he'd ever expected to do, even if he lived to be sixty years old, was fight a girl. But he wasn't going to just stand there and let her clobber him, either.

Dixie Funkhouser panted angrily and kicked at his shin with her right heel and whispered, "Turn *loose,* you idiot. You're going to get hurt!"

Clem didn't know what she meant. It didn't make sense. "I'll turn loose," he said, hearing a car door open, "if you promise to stop. I don't want to fight a girl, darn it."

"Too late," she sighed. "Don't say I didn't try, boy."

Then a shadow fell across Clem and an authoritative voice said, "Okay, Dixie, I'll take it from here." And suddenly Clem had an inkling of what she'd meant, and released her wrists. A hard fist caught him on the temple and the ground under his feet dissolved, leaving him spinning dizzily. He was dimly aware of slamming into the side of the cart and then lurching helplessly toward the bright lights. Dimly he heard Dixie saying "Don't, Frank," and then his forehead smashed into a fist and he revolved in a swirl of

179

lights and darkness, falling, falling, until he hit the soft cushioning sand.

He lay there feeling numb. In the distance he heard Dixie saying, "You big bully. Someday you'll pick on a guy your own size!"

"Come on, Dixie, let's go. Come on, Dix, he ain't hurt, just stunned. He'll be okay in a minute. Come on, Dixie, you going or not?"

"You're all a bunch of rotten bullies!"

"You going or not? Make up your mind, baby."

"You can't just drive away and leave him lying there."

"Ah, he ain't hurt. Come on, Dixie, let's cut out."

Somebody was licking his outflung hand, and he forced his heavy-lidded eyes open, hearing the motors throbbing, and rolled his head to look. It was Duke, straining anxiously at the end of the chain under the cart, barely able to reach Clem's limp hand with the end of his wet solicitous tongue. Oh, great, Clem thought. Thanks a lot, stupid. Where were you when I needed you? You could at least have growled.

"We're leaving, Dixie, you going or staying, make up your mind, baby."

"Go ahead. You're a big hero, Frank, jumping on a kid that walked all the way from Arkansas and was half your size. If you're the human race, I'm resigning."

Clem pulled his hand away from Duke's laving tongue. He tried to push himself up from the sand and fell back feebly, everything spinning again. She do it? he wondered, trying to remember what had happened. A girl? My lord! Trying again, he got his elbows braced under him and his head up out of the sand.

"You hit me?"

"Frank hit you," she said bitterly. "Our brave leader, about two hundred pounds of him. You dope, I told you— but I didn't know *he'd* be the one."

180

The motors raced impatiently; an angry voice shouted, "You staying with him, Dixie? We're leaving now, come on!"

Ignoring the cries, she said, "I'll help you up, okay?"

"Don't want to get up yet." Clem sighed.

"They'll leave me if I don't go now. Look, I'm sorry."

"Well, shoot," Clem said philosophically, "wasn't your fault, and it could have been worse. Bicycle chains an' stuff, maybe busted ribs, but I still don't get it. I mean, I wasn't botherin' anybody. So why did . . . ?" He was interrupted by a blaring horn, then all three cars took it up in a continuous honking din.

"I don't know why," Dixie shouted. "But I'm ashamed." She got to her feet, saying something else he couldn't hear, as she finally walked back to the cars.

There was brilliant emptiness where she'd been. A car door slammed angrily; then the motors roared away, tires spraying sand as they left the riverbed. Clem lay quietly in the sudden blackness waiting to see if they would come back across the bridge. He heard them faintly overhead, one after another. Going west, all right, and he had to go west tomorrow. He wouldn't even know them if he bumped into them again, except maybe Dixie.

Aside from his throbbing skull he felt okay, and he considered just spending the night where he was, but after a while he crawled to the cart and climbed wearily in. Next time I'll break out the damn rifle, he thought. You can't fool around with people like that.

When the friendly men came back at midnight to run the trotlines, he just couldn't wake up. Duke barked savagely, probably because they were friends. They tried to wake him, but though he heard their voices and mumbled incoherent answers, he just couldn't force himself back to consciousness.

181

"When he sleeps, he really sleeps," the veterinarian said. "Leave him be."

The next morning he still had trouble waking up, and it really wasn't worth the effort, because he had a king-sized headache and a swollen bruise on his forehead. He vaguely remembered that Mr. Fenwick and Mr. Meyers had been there. Sitting up, he saw the shoe box and opened it, feeling better when he saw the clean new tennis shoes—and two pairs of size eleven cotton socks that hadn't been part of the deal. There was also a block of ice in the cooler, and he chipped off a piece for his head. He wondered if they'd caught any fish, and remembered his own stringer in the riffle, but he didn't feel like cleaning any fish at the moment. Not with a skull fracture.

Boy, he thought, as he held the ice to his forehead, I got a rotten record so far—two fights and two defeats. But I bet I could of whipped old Jerry, though.

FOURTEEN

THURSDAY afternoon found him in the middle of nowhere with a severe storm coming on and no place to hide. Highway patrolman Kaluski had stopped to tell him that that area was under a tornado alert until ten o'clock and advised him to look for cover. There's an old shelter ahead a couple of miles, the trooper had said. "When you get there, you better hole up until the storm blows over, Clem."

If you get there, he should have said. No matter how urgently Clem wanted to hurry, he couldn't. The cart was so loaded with pop bottles he had to rest poor old Pedro about every half-hour, and he sure couldn't expect any *speed* out of him. They hadn't passed through a town since Monday, and the next one was still five or six miles away. He was low on water, nearly out of ice, and completely out of oatmeal cookies and bread. He was limping again, too, from the splendid new tennis shoes, and plenty nervous about that sinister yellow-black sierra of clouds all across the southwest. He yearned for a place to convert a load of heavy glass into a pocketful of light money, a place to buy supplies and ice and fill his waterbags.

All day, whenever he heard a truck coming from the east he had looked back hopefully, listening for the hiss of air-brakes, but they had all roared on past, some greeting him with their horns, but most of them just waving. He wasn't much of a novelty to them any more. And none of them stopped to deliver his mail, or doughnuts. And nobody asked for the package he'd been hauling since Saturday morning, either.

The booming, rolling thunder and jagged streaks of lightning kept coming closer, and the first drops of wind-driven rain hit around five o'clock, with wind gusts that shook the cart alarmingly, and he still hadn't found the shelter the trooper mentioned. The only cover of any kind was the grassy bank on the south side of the highway, so when there was a break in the thinning traffic, he hurried Pedro across the pavement, thinking how deserted and lonely a highway always seemed just before a storm. The bank was about as high as the cart was tall, so that he couldn't snuggle in close. At least it would help break the wind. He had to remove some of the bottles before he could get in the cart, and he had tossed about fifty out onto the ground and was fixing to crawl gratefully in out of the stinging cold rain flurries when the first hailstones began to rattle on the roof. With abrupt consternation he backed out and hurried around to unhitch Pedro and lead him close to the north side of the cart, where he would be partially protected. While tying the donkey close with the lead rope he had an idea, and loosened the side curtain, pulling it out over Pedro and anchoring it to the harness. Old Duke was already cowering under the cart, and that was a bad omen, because everybody knew dogs had a sixth sense about storms.

He got bruised by a number of the hailstones before he could scramble back into the cart, which represented shelter but not safety, and he had just settled down to wait when the bombardment became a steady ear-splitting roar, like a dozen dump trucks unloading gravel.

Pedro flinched as the big ice balls whacked the canvas

184

over his back, and Clem unrolled his bed and shoved the mattress between the canvas and the donkey's shaggy back while the stones banged the roof like gunshots going off just over his head. Wind gusts whipped over the bank and shook the cart, and he kept expecting it to blow over on Pedro, or rip apart. Duke was howling with fear, wanting to jump inside, but it sure as heck wasn't much better inside, and Clem huddled weak with fear and shivering from the sudden wintry cold. The noise grew so loud that Clem howled a little himself just to ease the pressure on his eardrums.

After what seemed an eternity the bombardment let up, subsiding to a dwindling rattle, and then the awful ice fall was over—for the *moment,* at least, but Clem waited tensely, figuring it might merely be a lull, like the eye of a hurricane, to be followed by an even more brutal assault. But the thunder had rolled on north and east, and the wind gusts rocking the cart were more sporadic. Even the rain was light. Finally he took a deep shuddering breath and lifted the back flap to look out, and was absolutely astounded.

The white hailstones covered the ground like snow! Clem got out and went crunching through the ice cubes. Nobody would believe it, he marveled, unless they saw it for themselves. He stared at the five battered cars parked along the shoulders on both sides of the highway, the drivers stunned by the malevolence of the storm.

All that ice, just going to waste, Clem thought, after a few minutes, and went to get a pan. Free ice, he thought, but that was before he noticed the pop bottles he'd left out. The ice wasn't free if you figured it cost him about three dozen bottles too chipped or cracked to turn in. Filling his ice chest cost him around seventy-two cents.

Traffic slowly resumed from east and west, moving cautiously on the ice-carpeted pavement, and as the cars with ruined windshields and pockmarked tops passed by, the people gaped at Clem scooping up hailstones to put in his cooler. Boy, if he lived to be one hundred he'd never see anything like this again. Which was okay with him. But now that it was over he was kind of glad he'd been in it.

When he had the cooler filled, he hitched up again and crossed the highway, although it occurred to him there was no reason why he shouldn't travel in the south-side bar-ditch if he wanted to. He just didn't want to. He liked to drive on the right side of the road, that's all. And he wanted to find that safe place trooper Kaluski mentioned before he camped for the night, because the hailstorm might have been only a forerunner of the main storm and it was still three or four hours until ten P.M., when the tornado alert would end.

Before he had gone a quarter of a mile, the hailstones ended. He walked out of winter into summer again. Probably the ice barrage had covered only a narrow strip across the countryside, he thought, and he'd just been lucky to have had the unforgettable experience of being right in the middle of it.

By the time he had covered another fourth of a mile, Gaylord Jackson arrived from the west in a borrowed car with three pounds of barbecued ribs, a loaf of bread, a quart of buttermilk, and assorted fried pies.

"I was worried about you, Clem," he said gravely.

"So was I," Clem grinned. "You should have been here— I mean, you ought to drive on east and look at the hail. I never saw anything like it in my life before."

"See you later, baby," Gaylord said, recrossing the highway to the parked sedan that Clem wished he'd asked about. Whose was it, where had Gaylord got it? He also wished he hadn't told Gaylord what a great sight the hail was. It might even have melted by now.

He walked on, slowly, figuring there was no point in just

186

waiting. Gaylord could catch up easy enough. And about three minutes later Gaylord came back west and parked on the shoulder, and two seconds later the highway patrol cruiser parked right behind him.

"Forward my mail to the county jail," Gaylord said across the top of the car. "This cat has sinned improperly and imprudently, baby."

Trooper Kaluski stalked forward and the gravity of the situation got through to Clem when his friend the trooper failed to so much as nod at him.

"He's a good friend of mine," Clem said. "Gaylord Jackson."

"Yes, sir," Gaylord said. "Clem and me are old *buddies,* if that help my case any, officer."

Trooper Kaluski halted at a safe distance, but at least he didn't tell the big Negro to turn around and put his hands on top of the car, or anything undignified and degrading like that. "You made a U-turn across the highway back there," he said sternly.

"It was my fault," Clem put in. "He just come out here to see if I was okay, ain't that right, Gaylord?"

Gaylord nodded. "But I made that U-turn, Clem."

"Yeah, but I told you to go look at the hail. So it's my fault."

Trooper Kaluski left his pistol holster flap fastened down, but he had the ticket book in his hand. "You knew a U-turn was illegal, sir?"

Sir, Clem thought. Watch out when anybody calls you *sir.*

"I wasn't positive," Gaylord said, "but I had a hunch it was."

Clem removed the lid from his cooler and got out the lemon-sized hailstone. "Look at this," he said, hurrying around the car to show it to both of them. "I think it bounced off my roof during the storm."

187

The trooper gazed at the hailstone with the respectful astonishment it deserved, and took it carefully between his fingertips. "I've heard of them this big, but I never saw one before, Clem." He looked at Gaylord. "You have an operator's permit?" Gaylord nodded. Kaluski looked at Clem. "I would like to take this home and freeze it. Did you especially want to keep it?"

"It would only melt," Clem said. "You can have it."

"Thank you," Kaluski said, and smiled. "No time to waste, I'd better rush it to the freezer before it shrinks." He frowned at Gaylord again. "You and Clem are buddies, you say?"

"He fixed a flat for me a way back near Tulsa," Clem volunteered.

"Then we worked us a wreck together, east of Oklahoma City," Gaylord said. "Bunch of fool kids."

The trooper widened his eyes. *"You're* the one! You two? Why did you disappear like that?"

Clem said, "He had a bad cut on his arm and had to go to the doctor." He added an afterthought. "It cost him ten bucks to have it sewed up." And indignantly: "That's what it cost him to save those kids' lives."

"I'm sure the insurance company would have paid for it if you'd put in a claim," the trooper said. "You should have done that."

Gaylord shrugged. "It was only money. And I was just passing by on my way to California." He grinned. "At this rate I won't make it."

Clem was surprised at how Gaylord could talk *white* when he wanted to. Shut your eyes and he sounded just like the trooper. Better, even, not having that old Oklahoma twang. So how come sometimes he sounded liked a red-necked Southerner, an uneducated cat, and sometimes he didn't?

188

"Yeah, well," Trooper Kaluski said thoughtfully. "Where are you now? I mean, how is it you're here, if you were headed for California?"

"I took a temporary job in Clintsburg," Gaylord said. "I was running low on funds and needed some repairs on my motorcycle."

The trooper nodded, peering through his glasses at the hailstone. "Say, I'd better get this thing frozen before it makes a liar out of everybody concerned," he said. "Good afternoon, gentlemen." He smiled and turned back to his cruiser. Then as he was opening the door he called out sternly, "But don't *do* it again, okay?"

Solemnly, Gaylord made a circle with thumb and middle finger, meaning okay, no more U-turns. Then when the highway patrol car had sped away toward the next town, Gaylord laughed with relief and broke out the food. "Like I was saying when the fuzz cut in, baby, I heard about the big storm coming, and I thought I better come check on you—but I thought you'd be further west than you are, man."

"My average fell off some," Clem confessed, and explained about knocking off early that day under the bridge. "I figured *you'd* be further west, too," he said. "Like at least out in Texas by now."

While they pitched into the barbecued ribs, Gaylord explained he'd got as far as Clintsburg, the second town from here, but his hog was coughing and sneezing pretty bad, and then he saw this soul brother mowing grass at a motel, the Oleander Inn, and more or less stopped just to pass the time of day, and during the conversation this man mentioned there was an opening on his staff now that summer was come. Dollar an hour. Assistant landscape engineer and pool cleaner, et cetera. So Gaylord had checked his hog into a nearby garage for rehabilitation and accepted em-

189

ployment. He was renting a room next door to his strawboss for a dollar a day and trying to economize on living expenses, but alas, he was just so fond of food.

"Whoever invented the pig," he said, brandishing a spicy brown rib, "ought to have a national holiday named after him, baby. I can't feel nothing but sad and sorry for all them *Muslin* cats that has to give up hog for their religion."

There he went, lapsing into dialect again, Clem noticed, a little bewildered. "Anyone that don't like this," he said of the barbecue, "is crazy, boy. This is great eating."

Gaylord gave a pleased chuckle. "Had a hunch you'd like it. Took a chance you'd find it toothsome, baby." And presently he said, "By my calculations you ought to be passing the Oleander Inn sometime Sunday, an' I'll be snipping the shrubbery until noon. The man say I can work half-days on the Sabbath, said he don't mind if God don't care." He grinned his friendly, carefree grin, and Clem marveled again at his big white even teeth—boy, he must be in the one-toothpaste group with the fewest cavities. "Anyway, you make it before noon Sunday, we'll have us another pile of hickory-barbecued pig ribs, right?" Gaylord said.

"Right," Clem said, grinning blissfully. "I'll be there, boy!"

Gaylord stopped nibbling a bone and eyed him morosely. "I'd consider it a favor, baby, do not *boy* me, huh? Us cats are terrible sensitive about that word. I know you ain't puttin' me down, but don't anyway, okay?"

"Sure," Clem shrugged, "but you're always calling me *baby*."

"Okay. No more boy, no more baby. Right?"

There was still bread and meat left when they finished. "Leave you a bedtime snack," Gaylord said. There were extra fried pies, too, a pineapple and a mince. "Make you

190

a light breakfast," Gaylord suggested, and said well, he'd better get the man's car back to him. And he departed. Boy, you really meet some *nice* people, Clem thought, giving Duke the bones.

Those bones were the last solid meal Duke would have for a long time.

During the night the storm returned and caught him in the open, camped in the exposed bar-ditch because the unexpected feast had kept him from going on to a better place. But it was just a lot of thunder and lightning and rain, nothing much to a guy who had survived an avalanche of ice cubes. He needed water, and set various pots, cups, washpan, and skillet on the roof to catch it in. It rained less than an inch but added up to more than a gallon of water. He could have coffee for breakfast if he'd had some way to heat water, only he didn't.

It was still wet and gloomy around ten o'clock Friday morning when the German automobile hit Duke about half a mile east of Feather. The gaunt gray cat got it first, from an eastbound truck that honked first at Clem, *blap-blap-blap,* and then at the cat and Duke. Old Duke froze on the centerline of the four-lane stretch while the yowling cat became a squashed mess under the big wheels. Then Duke compounded his awful mistake, whirling and bolting back toward the safety of the ditch. He didn't quite make it. The man in the Volkswagen tried to avoid the collision, swerving and hitting his brakes, but it was no use, and Clem was paralyzed by the nightmare squeal of rubber and ghastly bang of metal against flesh and bone, watching in horror and disbelief as his dog went spinning into the ditch screaming in an almost human voice.

The Volkswagen stopped on ahead and the man got out to examine his front right bumper and fender, looking back

191

coldly. "It was not my fault, young man." Then he got back in and drove on.

And he was right, it wasn't his fault. It wasn't even the cat's fault, although it had no legitimate business there in the wet growth of the bar-ditch. And it wasn't Duke's fault, either. It was Clem's fault for not keeping him chained, for being dumb enough to think a dog could learn to balance knowledge against instinct. Just because Duke had learned not to chase any of the infrequent rabbits they had jumped in the endless miles of bar-ditch, that didn't mean he wouldn't chase a damn cat. The rabbits had bounced over the bank into the fields, or rocketed along the ditch to the nearest culvert, but the damned gray cat had shot right out onto the highway. And Duke, triggered by ancient instincts, had erupted in hot pursuit before Clem even had time to yell.

Oh you dumb hound! Clem sobbed. I told you a million times! I told you and I told you, why didn't you listen to me, you stupid nut?

Duke was all unnaturally sprawled and twisted in the wet grass, trying foolishly to get up, looking back at his wounded hindquarters and howling piteously. The bumper, the fender, something had torn a gaping, almost bloodless, foot-long rip in Duke's shaggy right hip and thigh, laying the skin back to expose the raw red meat underneath, and his hind leg jutted out at a terribly wrong angle. Clem knelt over him weeping, feeling helpless and mumbling meaningless reassurances, "It's okay, boy, you're gonna be okay, boy, take it easy, ol' Duke boy." I have to get him to the vet, he thought. I have to get him into town. When he tried to pat Duke on the head, Duke barked and bit him painfully, and was sorry about it but reproachful, too. See what you let me do to myself—I'm only a dog, you're supposed to look out for me, it's all your fault.

192

"I have to pick you up," Clem said, weeping. "I have to do it, I'm sorry if it hurts." He slid his hands under the grotesquely sprawled body and Duke bit him again, crying with pain and needing to get his teeth into something, and Clem was handy. "I'm tryin' to *help* you!" Clem hollered, clamping Duke's head against his shoulder so he couldn't bite again.

Cradling the injured Duke in his arms, Clem turned to face the westbound cars, gazing at the drivers in wet-eyed misery. Help me, please, he thought. But he didn't holler or try to stop them. Nobody wanted to haul a bloody dog in their car, unless it was their own pet, and Clem had no real hope that somebody would stop. Help me, please, he mutely begged, but they drove on past, glancing sympathetically at the boy holding the big bloody dog but not wanting any part of the sadness and the untidiness. If it had been a hurt child, somebody would have felt compelled to help, but he wouldn't have wanted to. People simply preferred not to get involved with other people's tragedies. And no matter what Duke might be to Clem, another man's dog is just a dog. Too bad, sonny, but you can get another, mutts are a dime a dozen. Take better care of the next one, kid.

The cars kept whizzing heartlessly past, and Clem really couldn't blame them. After a few minutes he started walking, pressing Duke's head against his shoulder, wincing unhappily at the awful panting and crying and tooth-clicking suffering. "It's okay, boy," he kept saying, wishing he had something to give Duke to ease his pain. And not believing it was okay, or even *would* be okay, but clinging to a faint hope. Somewhere in the town of Feather was a veterinarian named Lew Meyers who might be able to help. "It'll be all right, boy," he said, hoping Duke would understand and feel a little better. He didn't even look back to see if Pedro was following or think how much simpler it

193

would be to haul Duke in the cart, although his arms began to cramp long before he reached the service station at the edge of town.

The attendant, not much older than Clem, asked what had happened. Clem said a car had hit Duke, and where did the veterinary live. "Hey, that's rough," the guy said sympathetically, but with an odd wariness in his manner. "Turn north just past the schoolground," he said. "You can't miss it, big house with a cement-block building behind it." And as Clem plodded on with dependable Pedro clup-clupping behind, he wondered if that guy might have been one of the unseen teenagers who had bedeviled him under the bridge. This was probably where they were from, some of them, anyway, but it didn't make any difference now.

He passed the long block of schoolyard, playgrounds with shade trees, grass that needed mowing, an old two-story brick building, and a new low brick building, both looking empty and deserted. Turning up the next street with Duke moaning in his tired arms, he saw the big house ahead, just past the intersection. Shade trees and blooming shrubs and flowers, and pale green cement-block building behind it. A sign in the yard read: MEYERS PET HOSPITAL.

"We made it, boy," he said, cutting across the unfenced yard. A woman in a pale green smock was talking on the phone in the office, and she took one look and said into the mouthpiece, "Hold on or hang up, Marge, we've got an emergency patient." Laying the phone down, she came around the tall counter and sucked in her breath. "Oh, my," she said.

"A car hit him," Clem said, and started weeping again, against his will and mostly from relief because now finally someone else would take over.

"Bring him in here," she said gently, leading Clem

194

through a door into a room with a plastic-topped table and glass-fronted cabinets full of bottles. "On the table, please," she said, and Duke bit Clem one final time when he put him down, but only a nip. The woman, shorter than Clem and sturdily built, with a pleasant face and short brown summer haircut, filled a hypodermic needle with something and said, "Now then, old fellow, let's alleviate the pain a bit, shall we? Hold his head, please."

She got the needle under Duke's furry hide and pressed it empty, and right away he began to relax. In about a minute he sighed and went limp and quiet. "The doctor will be back soon," the lady said. "Meanwhile I'll do what can be done. Just in case there is internal hemorrhaging, we'll give this old fellow an injection to stop it and some antibiotics to fight infection." She gave Clem a brief scrutiny. "I don't believe I've seen you around town before, have I?"

Clem shook his head, ashamed of his tear-streaked face, and asked if she was Mrs. Meyers. She was, so he told her about meeting her husband and Mr. Fenwick out on the river Tuesday evening. She didn't need any further information. She said Lew had told her about Clem's trip to New Mexico. "There's nothing more we can do for your dog now," she said, "but I'd better put something on your bites." While she was dabbing iodine on his hand and arm, she said all Lew could do at this stage was assess the extent of the injuries and sew up the torn skin. They would have to wait until the swelling subsided before anything could be done about splinting the broken bones.

When they left the treatment room, there was old Pedro anxiously pushing against the screened outer door, wondering where everybody had disappeared. Snuffling and wishing he had some Kleenex, Clem asked Mrs. Meyers if she reckoned anybody would care if he let his donkey eat grass over on the schoolyard. She said she couldn't imagine why

195

anybody would object, and there certainly wasn't any reason for him to hang around. As Clem went out he heard her dialing the phone, and then saying, "Marge?"

There was a highline pole in the corner of the schoolyard with a guywire slanting down, and when he had Pedro unhitched and unharnessed, with the halter on, Clem tied the long picket rope high on the cable so the donkey had about a thirty-foot circle of grass to work in.

"Take your time, boy," he said. "We won't be going anywhere for a while, it looks like." Removing his sneakers and rolling up his clammy pants legs, he got in the cart and stretched out on his bed. Miss that Sunday rib dinner with old Gaylord, I guess, he thought. No telling when we'll ever get to the next town. And he thought somberly, she didn't fool me with her calm voice. Internal bleeding! Broken bones can be fixed, but internal bleeding . . . especially in a dog . . .

Blue sky showed under the half-raised curtain, and he remembered the sun had broken through the clouds a couple of times during that awful walk to town. Sunshine would be welcome, but it wouldn't change anything. Nothing would change anything. Not even praying. He'd never been good at it, anyway.

Listening to the unfamiliar town sounds around him, he thought, I wouldn't mind living in a town. There were a dozen different kinds of birds singing and chirping and calling, wrens and sparrows, robins, bluejays, a mockingbird, and others he couldn't readily identify. He heard kids hollering and a television set or radio going over across the street, and the sound of slowed traffic on the highway a block away. Nearby in the street he made out the quiet but distinct sound of a bicycle. If he lived in a town with paved streets, he'd have a bicycle. I'd like having neighbors, he thought, and lots of friends. It wouldn't be lonesome in a

196

town, if you knew the people. But it was if you were just a stranger passing through.

The sound of a bicycle was clearer now, then it stopped and a voice said, "Anybody home in there? Hey, Marlow?"

Startled, Clem sat up and raised the curtain. It was the girl, the bikini girl from under the bridge, what's-her-name —*Dixie!* Dixie Funkhouser, for gosh sakes. He blinked at her in surprise, and she just stared at him expressionlessly. She was wearing hacked-off denim shorts and another bare-bellied, loose-fitting sweatshirt with the sleeves cut off at the elbows, socks and soiled sneakers, and a baseball cap on her head. But he would have known her anywhere.

"Well, you're still alive," she said, laying her bicycle on its side and coming toward the cart with a kind of hip-swinging cockiness. She looked very attractive with her short taffy-colored hair, button nose, wide mouth, and long-lashed eyes. With a build like hers it wouldn't have been fair to give her a beautiful face, too, Clem thought.

"This your hometown?" he said, just to say something.

"Born here, Slim," he said tersely, putting her elbow on the side of the cart and leaning in to examine its contents. "And almost bred here," she added in that kind of tough voice he remembered. He was a trifle shocked, but he had to laugh. Almost bred here. That was a good one. "Why are you parked here on the schoolground?" she demanded.

He stopped grinning. "My dog got hit by a car, a Volkswagen."

She stared at him with blue-eyed compassion. "Gee, I'm sorry, Slim. He's over at Meyers, huh? Is he hurt very bad?"

Clem sighed and nodded. "Pretty bad, I guess. Internal bleeding."

"That's a rotten shame," she sympathized. "A Volkswagen!" They were silent for a minute. Then with sudden

197

animation she said, "Hey, what are all the empty bottles for, Slim? Did you drink all that?"

He explained, embarrassed to have her know he was so poor he had to glean a living from the bar-ditches (and with a big doctor's bill hanging over him now, he suddenly realized), but she didn't seem to hold it against him. "Hey, neat," she said. "You could travel all over America picking up bottles for grocery money. Hey! There's a service station just down around the corner and I'm going that way—I could fill my bike basket and cash them in for you. I bet I could carry twenty easy, forty cents worth—and buy you something and bring it back here. I mean, I guess you need to stay around until you know how your pooch is gonna make out, and I'm bored silly from nothing to do. So I wouldn't mind hauling some of those bottles for you, Slim."

"Clem," he said, figuring she'd forgotten his true name.

She grinned, and was suddenly almost beautiful. "I like Slim better, okay? I'll get my bike and you start handing out dead Indians."

Well, he appreciated it, but if she was just doing it to make up for him getting slugged by her ratpack leader, forget it.

While he was passing bottles to her, she said, "Do you play tennis?"

"Nope," he said, wishing he did if she did.

"I'll bring a couple rackets and teach you this afternoon," she volunteered. Why? he wondered. She didn't owe him anything. Not tennis lessons, anyway. But shoot, if she wanted to—at least he had the right shoes for it. "What do you need that I can get with forty-six cents?" she asked when the basket was full.

"Well, milk," he said, because he'd been without milk since Wednesday morning and was really craving some. A quart cost around twenty-six cents. Subtracted from forty-

198

six that didn't leave much to buy anything else he needed, like a loaf of bread. "Get yourself some pop," he told her.

"Aw, we keep it in the fridge at home," she said, "but I don't care for it much." She got her bicycle turned around and prepared to mount up. "Hold the fort, Slim."

He watched her pedal carefully off across the grass, her trim legs pumping rhythmically. Sighing, he flopped back on his pallet and thought, How about that? Even if he'd expected to bump into her here, he never would have expected her to be so doggone friendly.

The next person who approached the cart was his old fishing buddy, Lew Meyers, who had walked over from the pet clinic to deliver his diagnosis. Compound leg fracture, broken hip and pelvis, contusions and lacerations—all of which were remediable. Then there were the indeterminate internal injuries. They'd just have to wait and see how serious it was.

Meaning Duke might die, Clem interpreted wretchedly.

"We won't repair the bone damage until tomorrow," the big grave-faced veterinarian said. "I'll give him a distemper shot tomorrow, too. Around an animal clinic, distemper is always a hazard. Has your dog had a rabies shot in the last year, Clem?"

Not that Clem knew of. No vaccinations or inoculations at all.

"We'll do that later, then. Assuming he gets past the critical phase—you understand, son? We'll know in a couple of days. Now, if he makes it, he'll need lots of care for some time, two weeks, maybe. I understand your situation, so I have to tell you your dog won't be able to travel for approximately two weeks, even if you turn your cart into an ambulance. I don't know what a two-week delay will do to your schedule, but that's about the best I can promise you, Clem.

If you feel you have to go on, and don't expect to be coming back this way . . ."

Clem interrupted anxiously. "I'll wait. I don't have to be anywhere at any certain time, I can stick around okay."

The vet's smile seemed to indicate approval. "I was only going to suggest that, pedigree or no pedigree, a dog like yours would have no trouble finding a good home around here. He's the type of high-class mongrel people take an instant liking to. But if you're staying . . ."

Clem was shocked that anyone would even suggest such a thing. Let somebody else have old Duke? Man, you must be outa your mind, he silently informed the vet. Then it struck him that maybe Lew Meyers didn't think he could pay for Duke's hospitalization—and suddenly he wasn't too sure about it himself. "I guess I'll need to find me a job around here," he said. "Mowing lawns or something." And he blurted anxiously, "Listen, all I got is fifty-some dollars, but I can earn some more . . ."

"Hey, relax, pardner," the vet told him. "Even if you weren't an old fishing companion, the total cost wouldn't wipe out your nest egg, Clem—and naturally I knock off a little here and there for friends. At most, I'll only nick you for half of your savings."

Clem sighed. "That's a relief," he said.

"I thought it would be," the vet smiled. "Meanwhile, if you're going to be around town, maybe we can work in a fishing trip or two."

"Hey, terrific!" Clem said, and then they were interrupted by Dixie Funkhouser.

"Hi," she said tolerantly to the veterinary, then ignored him. "I decided," she informed Clem, "to make another trip so you'd have eighty-eight cents to blow on groceries. Then I thought what the heck, I'll haul the whole darn lot before I start shopping."

The vet said, "I'll see you later, Clem."

"What did he *say?*" she asked when Lew Meyers was gone. Relaying bottles, Clem told her—all he could do was wait and hope. Nodding, she said brusquely, "Be thinking of stuff you need." When she left with the second load, Clem was struck by the convenience of all this, and for a cynical second he was suspicious. Maybe she was fixing to take him for some easy money. Then he was ashamed.

There were three loads totaling sixty-three bottles (less than he'd figured, but don't forget the ones the hailstorm ruined) and coming to a buck twenty-six. When she returned the last time, she brought milk, bread, oleo, ten pounds of potatoes, and some pressed ham and mayonnaise and cheese he hadn't ordered. "This stuff is on me," she said. "So you'll have to invite me to lunch, Slim."

Well, man, what could he lose? She got in the cart and they ate sandwiches and milk, and he was alternately pleased and embarrassed. One thing for sure, she really took his mind off his troubles, sitting there crossways with her gorgeous legs stretched out, asking him questions about everything. Did he build the cart? What was in the boxes? How long would it take him to get to where he was going? Where did he get such a screwy idea in the first place? What's in that package in the corner there, Slim?

He told her about the damn package the guy had paid him to look after. Every day that nobody called for it, he got more and more curious about what was inside, was more and more tempted to unwrap it and find out.

"Listen," she said once, "if you want to take a bath you can use our bathroom, Slim. Pop wouldn't mind. He won't even be *home* until six."

Clem was embarrassed. My lord, did he smell? That was a heck of a feeling, being cooped up in close quarters with a clean, fragrant girl and figuring he probably smelled bad.

"You can use our washer-dryer to do your laundry, too," she said casually. "Better still, I'll take it on home when I go and throw it in. Nothing to it, just pour in detergent and push a button." She gave him that lovely crinkly smile, and he was astonished. He'd never known any girls very well, but surely Dixie wasn't like any other in the world. "Are you going to park here tonight, Slim?"

"Unless somebody tells me I can't," he said.

"They won't, but if they do, you can park in our yard."

There seemed to be no limit to her hospitality, but he had to stay near the animal clinic. And where there was grass for Pedro.

Dixie wiped her fingers on her sweatshirt. "Bundle up your dirty clothes and I'll be on my way," she said. Then as she was leaving she turned around and remarked, "No sense in you having to fix your own supper, I'll bring you some—hey, do you like green onions, Slim?" Clem said he liked any color onions. Crinkling her small nose at him, she said, "We have oodles of onions and radishes in our garden." And she rode off on her bike, going east to the next corner and then north out of sight. Clem continued to stare at the spot where she'd disappeared. She was one heck of a nice person any way you looked at it. The more he saw of her, the more beautiful she seemed.

Still in a daze, he led Pedro over to the veterinary's place and watered him from a tub under a hydrant. While the donkey drank, he stuck his head in the office door to see if there was any news about Duke. Mrs. Meyers was on the phone again, but she gave him a grimace of sympathy and shook her head. But at least old Duke was still alive. And the sun was shining down on a green, flowerful world.

When Pedro finished drinking, he filled the small tub again and peeled off his shirt and washed himself, wishing

202

he'd thought to bring soap along. Wishing also that he had a nice clean shirt to put on.

Tying Pedro to the guywire again, he got back in the cart and stretched out on his bed and had a nap, his first daytime snooze since the journey began. Dozing, he thought how strange it was—if Duke hadn't got hit by the Volkswagen they would have gone right on through Feather without stopping, without seeing Dixie Funkhouser again, never knowing what a great person she was. He wasn't *glad* Duke got hit, for gosh sakes. But he was glad it had only been a Volkswagen.

He was awake again, still pleasantly numb and yawny, when Dixie came back around three o'clock, but she had a couple of rackets and a tennis ball, and he felt obligated to play. Especially after she delivered two pairs of dungarees and two unusually white T-shirts, all neatly pressed and folded.

"My gosh, you didn't need to iron this stuff," he protested.

"Who irons?" she shrugged. "I whizzed them through the mangle, it only takes a minute. You ready for a tennis lesson, Slim?"

Not ready, but willing, he put on his sneakers and followed her around the school buildings to the empty concrete tennis court. They lobbed awhile, and she ran his legs off, which he didn't need, and then she was patiently inducting him into the mysteries of the serve when suddenly but very belatedly he thought, Oh, hell, it's Friday!

He should have parked at the south end of the schoolyard by the highway, where Ken would see the cart. Too damn late now. Ken would be halfway to Tulsa. Wondering what happened to Clem, probably.

"Let's face it, Slim, you're not very *coordinated*, you know it?"

"I got a lot of growin' to do yet," he said defensively.

"Sure, I know that," she said amiably. "Girls develop faster physically. At fifteen any boy is still kind of clumsy, I guess."

Yeah, fifteen, Clem thought wryly, remembering that was how old he was supposed to be. "We hit our peak at around seventeen," he told her, gruffly.

She nodded, bouncing the tennis ball on the concrete. "Lots of girls seventeen are already married and have babies." She lifted her gaze to him and grinned. "But most of them didn't plan it that way, I guess. They were just stupid." She bounced the ball some more, gazing off across the shaggy schoolgrounds. "I'm already physically developed, except I hope I grow a few inches taller. And don't get any bigger *otherwise,* for gosh sakes." She eyed him appraisingly. "If you keep growing you'll really be tall. You want to play any more?"

"It's too hot for all this exercise," he said, and she laughed and said:

"You're not ready for the Davis Cup matches yet, but I guess you could learn to play a *fair* game of tennis."

But who with? he wondered. He couldn't recall even seeing any tennis courts around Conifer. "Basketball's my game," he told her modestly, and he had good reason to be modest. What he really meant was he hoped to *become* a good basketball player eventually, being tall and all.

They sat on the schoolhouse steps watching neighborhood kids playing on the swings and slides, and he couldn't think of much to say. He had never been alone with a girl before the way he had with Dixie today, and it taxed his mind considerably. But one thing kept scratching at a corner of his mind, and presently he said, "Old what's-his-name, your gang leader. What's he do? He work or anything?"

"Frank?" she said. "He just loafs around the poolhall,

204

I guess." Clem felt her eyes on him. "Why?" she asked, and he shrugged.

"I just wondered."

"What would you do if you met him again, Slim?"

"I wouldn't even know it was him. I never saw 'im that night."

"If you're lucky, you never will see him," she said grimly.

He bought that. "You reckon they might bother me?" he asked. "They'd recognize my cart, I guess. Some of them have probably seen it already."

"I don't think they'd do anything much here in town." She frowned, her eyes just two tangles of long lashes. "You could park in our yard, only that might antagonize the rats, especially Jerry. He thinks he's got a claim on me." She stood up abruptly. "Seeing me here with you would make the jerk jealous, too. Anyway, I've got to bake a ham and peel spuds and fix Pop's supper."

Baked ham, he thought. She'd said she would bring him some supper. If he had to fix his own, he would probably just boil some potatoes and eat them with oleo. Even before Duke got hurt he'd realized he couldn't afford meat very often. Man oh man, baked ham!

Walking back to her bicycle he said, "You do the cookin', huh?" She nodded absently. "How come?" he asked. "Your mother work or something?"

She kicked at the grass, head down. "Nobody works where Mama is, if you believe the preacher. She died when I was thirteen. No brothers or sisters, so I'm the head cook now."

Clem was stricken with remorse, figuring he'd brought up a taboo subject.

"I'm not complaining," Dixie said. "I know plenty of girls who can't boil water or sew on a button. Brother, will *they* make lousy wives." She gave him her special smile. "I don't like to brag, but let's face it, Slim, I'll make some old boy a pretty good wife."

Clem didn't doubt it for a second. In about ten or twelve years he would like to find a girl just like her to marry. Possibly sooner.

"I'll come back after dark," she said, mounting her bike. "Keep the racket and ball to practice with. Against the schoolhouse wall."

"Okay," he said dutifully, and this time he didn't watch her out of sight, knowing it would make him feel depressed. He practiced serving against the schoolhouse awhile but his heart wasn't in it. He fretted some about missing Ken, and about missing the Sunday rib date with Gaylord Jackson. And losing two whole weeks waiting for a dumb cat-chaser to get well—if he *got* well. No iffing, Duke *would* heal up. He just had to. And he wondered what Dixie's mother had died of, remembering that Candy Labra's mother died of TB—but that was before they had all these great miracle drugs.

A car stopped in the street and a tall man in a coat and tie and summer hat got out. For a tense minute Clem thought it was somebody coming to tell him to get the heck off the schoolyard with that donkey. But it was only Mr. Fenwick.

"Just stopped by to say hello, Clem," he said affably. "Lew told me where you were—sorry to hear about your dog. Lew is talking about the three of us hitting the river some afternoon with a can of fat redworms, and I'm all for it. Incidentally, that old forktail I swapped you out of was prime eating, buddy. I even let my conceited wife have a few bites."

Clem laughed, remembering about Mr. Fenwick's skeptical wife. "I wish I'd woke up that night," he said. "Did you do any good?"

206

"The trotlines?" Bob Fenwick said. "Nope. No keepers, Clem. I think you were right, channel cats bite best in the afternoon now."

They chatted a few minutes longer, and Mr. Fenwick said if Clem was going to be around town awhile, come see him at the store. Clem said he would, but it turned out he didn't. The merchant also extended a supper invitation for next Tuesday night, but that didn't pan out, either. Still it was great to know he had friends in Feather, and after old Bob drove on, he thought again that it would be nice to live in a town and have some permanent grown-up buddies like Lew and Bob—and a girlfriend like Dixie.

FIFTEEN

Aт sundown when he went to check on Duke, the vet remained noncommittal. Holding his own, he reported. Passing blood, but that was to be expected. However, there was as yet no evident edema.

"I'll do everything I know how to do, son," Lew Meyers said, gripping Clem's shoulder gently. "And I know how to do quite a lot."

Drawing a quavery breath, Clem nodded and went back to the schoolyard. To use up time and to preserve some grass near the cart for later, he took Pedro into the middle of the schoolgrounds to graze on a particularly lush green patch. Old Pedro would really benefit from a few days of just resting and eating, and the layover would also be appreciated by Clem's feet.

He hoped the local school board wouldn't mind a little donkey manure here and there. It was great fertilizer, in case they didn't know.

Dixie brought the jumbo ham sandwiches with the meat sliced almost as thick as the bread, with lettuce and mayonnaise and pickle, plus green onions and radishes, and a big Thermos of coffee with sugar and cream. It was dark, but the streetlamp on the corner furnished enough light to eat by. The sandwiches were individually wrapped, and he saved one for later, thinking he would enjoy it more after she went home because he wouldn't be so self-conscious. She watched him eat the first one like he was her favorite program, and he didn't chew and swallow so well with an audience.

She said the Thermos was her pop's, he filled it with coffee when he left mornings. His name was George and he was a flow superintendent for an oil company, going around to producing leases and checking to be sure they weren't pumping more or less than their daily allowables. Her pop had a geology degree, and that's what she wanted to be, a geologist. Not in the petroleum end of it, but just a rockhound, probably a teacher.

"Are you going to college, Slim?"

Clem swallowed before he was ready. "If I can. I sure hope so."

"There's a junior college here," Dixie said. "I can get the first two years for practically nothing, living at home and all. Then I'll go to O.U., because they've got a real good geology department."

"I guess I'll take art," Clem said. "Commercial art."

"Wow!" she said softly. "You mean you can really draw?"

Clem shrugged deprecatingly, but then he decided it was no time for modesty. "I draw pretty good," he said. "And it's what I like."

"You're really different, Slim," she told him. "Cool. I mean, all the boys I know around here are—" she shrugged "—oh, slobs, jerks, you know, just out for kicks. No ambition or anything. You know what really impresses me about you, Slim?"

Chewing, he tried to think what there might be about him that would impress her, but he couldn't come up with anything. "My appetite?"

"I'm serious," she said, laughing. "I mean, it really

amazes me. I'll bet not one boy in a million would do what you're doing, you know it?"

Well, that lent itself. "You mean going to New Mexico?"

"I mean the *way* you're going. The average teenage guy wouldn't walk ten miles to see his mother, or anybody else. But look at you."

Looking at himself, Clem found a tendency to let the misunderstanding slip by, but he overcame it. "Well, I didn't *know* I was going to walk," he pointed out. "I thought I was gonna get to *ride*. Turned out my donkey thought different, that's all."

"Yes, but you didn't turn around and call it off, you kept going."

Okay, if she wanted to admire him, he didn't aim to stop her. It hadn't ever occurred to him there was anything heroic about traveling his way, like a turtle with fallen arches. He knew he could have been there and back already hitchhiking, but that wasn't the point.

Clem finished the sandwich warmed by her obvious approval. Sure his trip was unusual—but how many guys happened to own a donkey cart? Look at it from that angle awhile. Also, how many guys hadn't seen their mother in over two years? But Dixie was right. Hardly anybody ever *walked* to New Mexico any more.

"That was larrupin' good eating," he said. "I'm saving the other one for latter, so I can look forward to it awhile, okay?"

She nodded, her smile hazy in the shadowy light of the streetlamp. "Tomorrow I'll fry a chicken," she promised. "Let's take a walk, huh?"

Just what I need, Clem thought wryly. But she only meant walk around to the steps of the old grade-school building, away from the light. Someone might blunder along and see

210

her and go blab to Jerry—not that it was any of *his* damn business, but he was unreasonably jealous.

Jealous of who, for heaven sakes? Clem thought, leaning back on his elbows and watching the car lights go back and forth down there on the highway. The sounds of a town sure differed from the country.

"Nice night," Dixie remarked, and he said, "Yup."

"You're not very gabby, are you?" she commented.

"Nope," he said.

She chuckled. "That's who you remind me of, Jimmy Stewart."

Gary Cooper, she probably meant. *He* was the yup-and-nope man.

She sighed. "What are you thinking about, Slim?"

"Nothing," Clem grinned. "My mind is an open blank." Then for a second he heard that sound again and identified it: the high, thin, pitiful crying of a dog. It's old Duke! he thought with a sickening lurch of fear. The sound died away, and although he strained tensely to hear, it wasn't repeated. Maybe I ought to go see about him, he fretted. Maybe his shot wore off and he's hurting and wondering where I'm at.

"Just a blank, huh?" Dixie said.

"Well, I was wondering about my dog, I guess."

"Oh, boy," she said sarcastically, "I'm real flattered, Slim."

Embarrassed, he said, "I heard a dog howling, was why."

After a silence she said, "I just thought you *might* possibly be thinking about *me*. I must be losing my glamour."

"I was thinkin' about you," Clem said, trying to mend fences. "Like what a swell person you are. How to thank you for being so nice to me and all. I'm stupid about things like that, sayin' how I feel. But, anyway, you're terrific."

She laughed. "Let's face it, you're absolutely right."

211

So that eased the pressure there for a while, and he relaxed and thought if that was Duke crying, Lew would do something about it, give him another shot to ease the pain. But the silence continued, and he began to wish Dixie would talk.

She merely sighed and sat with her elbows on her knees and her chin on her fists, gazing at the night. And sighed again, and finally said resignedly, "You really are different. Boy, are you different!"

"How do you mean?" he inquired, puzzled by her tone.

"Any other boy I know," she said, "if we were here on the steps in the dark like this, he would at least have *tried* to kiss me by now."

Clem was startled. Kiss her? My lord! Suddenly he could hear the thumping of his heart against his ribs. In a way he'd thought about kissing her. But he sure hadn't figured *she'd* thought about it, or would consider such a thing.

In a voice that shook a little, he said, "Heck, I figured you'd get sore an' belt me. Besides, I thought you went steady."

"Nobody owns me," she said. "I'm a free agent, Slim."

"Yeah, well. I just didn't," Clem said lamely, "I mean, well . . ."

"Why would I belt you? What's so wrong with kissing?"

Nothing wrong with kissing. Nothing wrong with flying, either, if a guy had some pilot training. But Clem simply had never kissed a girl, or been kissed by one. "Personally, I've got nothing against it," he muttered, and she said practically everybody did it all the time. "Yeah, I guess there's a lot of it going around," he said.

"Always has been, always will be." She shrugged. "But I guess if a girl happens to be repulsive . . ."

"You're the most unrepulsive girl I ever knew," Clem responded.

212

"Well!" she said. "That's something! Thank you."

But they just kept on sitting there on the steps. She gave an uncertain laugh, followed by an increasingly strained, silent waiting. He knew in general what to do, but he just didn't trust his ability to bring it off. He couldn't make the first move. He was paralyzed. Petrified.

Dixie sighed again and started getting up. "Okay, I can take a hint," she said grimly.

"Well, jeez!" Clem said despairingly. "Listen, take tennis, for instance. I didn't even know how to hold the dang racket. And I stumbled all over the durn court. Well, this is the same deal."

She gazed down at him, her face in shadow. "Muscular coordination hasn't got a thing to do with kissing," she said. "Anyway, you never played tennis befo—!" Suddenly she sat down again. "My gosh! Slim, do you mean to sit there and tell me you never kissed a girl before?"

Humiliated, Clem said, "I mean to sit here and tell you I never kissed a girl *yet!* What's so strange about that?"

She giggled. "Well, it must be some kind of *record,* that's all."

"Maybe I never seen a girl before I *wanted* to kiss, you ever try looking at it that way?" he demanded, stung by her amusement.

She tried to muffle a laugh and failed. "I'm sorry, Slim, I wasn't laughing at you, just the way you sounded. What you said was sweet, if you meant it. About wanting to kiss me, I mean. Do you?"

"Well, sure," he growled. "Just don't expect any miracles, is all."

"Why, you're a miracle. Don't worry, there's nothing tough about kissing." She moved over closer and waited solicitously for him to start. So he did.

As it turned out, Clement Marlow was a latent smoocher

213

with an inherent knack for kissing. It also turned out that Dixie was obviously fond of green onions, but shoot, so was he—it only made her seem more human. Anyway, the important thing was, kissing proved to be pretty terrific stuff. No wonder people spent so much time thinking about it, talking about it, and doing it.

He walked her home, three blocks north of the school, stopping several times en route to see if he still remembered how to do it, and then spending quite a bit of time saying good night.

During one of the terminal clinches she sighed. "Marlow, where have you been all my life?" Over around Conifer, he thought drunkenly, except the first year when I wasn't even born yet. Reminded of that chronological disparity, he realized that nothing could come of all this. Even if he wasn't going to New Mexico, if, say, he had just moved to Feather permanently, she would inevitably find out that he had lied about his age, and that would end it, because no teenage girl wanted to be called a baby-sitter. So he'd better try to think of her as just a nice friendly older woman tutoring him in the mechanics of osculation. Although, man, at the rate he was progressing, he might be teaching her before he left town.

"Have you ever been in love, Clem?" Dixie asked.

Clem? he thought. What happened to Slim? "Well, yeah," he said, remembering Candy Labra, the fire-dancer. "Once, I guess—for about thirty miles."

"I guess I'd better go in," she said finally.

Clem walked back to the schoolyard, his feet scarcely touching the sidewalk. But when he got there, he abruptly crashed to earth, because while he'd been away someone had dumped his sulky on its side.

At first furious, he simmered down when he checked and found no real damage had been done. After one brief attempt to lift it himself, Clem harnessed Pedro and hitched him to the top wheel and let him pull the cart back upright.

With the curtains down he lit a candle and checked the stuff that had been banged around and spilled. Nothing was ruined, but the package he was keeping for the trucker's unknown friend had got pretty wet from melted ice when the cooler overturned, and he pondered gravely whether he ought to check to see if whatever was in the package needed drying.

Carefully picking the knots out of the string with the point of a knife blade, he cut through the masking tape holding the edge of brown wrapping paper in place, unwrapped a shoebox that was also taped securely, hesitated momentarily, gave in to his curiosity, and reached for the knife again. Under the lid was a thin layer of cotton. Under that were a lot of small bottles bedded in more cotton. Dry cotton. Okay, it hadn't got wet. And in the bottle he opened were pills. A whole mess of little white pills.

A birthday present for some guy's wife, the trucker had said. Some present, boy! What was she, sick or something? Maybe they were baby-prevention pills, Clem thought, but he had a depressing suspicion that they weren't for some guy's wife at all. What if they were some kind of *dope?* Try that on your four-string banjo, boy!

Removing one pill, he put the bottle back and temporarily rewrapped the package. Tomorrow he would get some tape and try to fix it back just like it was, so nobody would know it had been opened. And he would see if Lew Meyers knew what kind of pill it was . . .

In the morning he awakened to a chorus of cheerful birdsongs and the mournful anguished crying of a dog. Reminded and suddenly very worried, he dressed in a hurry and legged it over there. The sun was up, and the vet seemed to expect Clem's early call.

215

"Thought you'd be materializing about now," he said, smiling. But he had pretty gloomy news. Edema. A definite hematoma. He would have to drain Duke's intestinal cavity and wash it with saline solution, but not to worry, it was a fairly simple operation he'd performed any number of times.

"Was that him I heard howling last night?" Clem asked worriedly, and Lew Meyers said not necessarily, there were six other dogs in the cages and most of them hollered once in a while. The poor little fellows just wanted to go home. "Would you like to go back and say hello to Duke?" he asked, and Clem sighed and nodded.

They went through a door into a utility room with a big deep double sink and mops and buckets and disinfectant, and cases of horse meat in big cans, and then through another door into a long room with cages along both sides of an aisle. Duke was lying in the front cage on the left, and he didn't look good. But when Clem spoke to him he tried to wag his tail and made noises in his throat like he was trying to talk. Pleading noises that made Clem's eyeballs suddenly hot. The other dogs started barking and whining, wanted to be let out of the cages, and they were all so active and healthy that Clem hated them and didn't want to stay any longer. Turning abruptly, he started to leave.

"I'll let you know how it goes, son," the vet said understandingly, and Clem nodded and kept going, blinking hard.

SIXTEEN

A SHINY red Mustang was parked by the schoolyard and a man in gray slacks and a loud flower-patterned sport shirt was standing between Clem and his breakfast. Even skinnier than Clem and not much taller, he wore sunglasses and was bald in front and kind of pale. His black hair stood up in a wavy crest, fluttering in the breeze. "A good morning to you," he intoned sonorously. "I take it you are the owner of the donkey cart?"

Clem nodded warily.

"Permit me to introduce myself. Robinson Elsworth Abernathy, principal of this magnificent seat of learning."

"I'm Clem Marlow," Clem said, figuring the principal was going to tell him he couldn't camp there any more.

"Marlowe with an *e,* or without?"

Clem spelled it for him, wondering what difference it made.

"Then possibly not kin to Christopher Marlowe, although the terminal *e* could have been dropped somewhere along the line of descent."

Clem shook his head. He never heard of Christopher. No kin.

Mr. Abernathy tugged an earlobe as if to stimulate his mental processes. "English dramatist and poet, about 1560 to 1590. Rather disreputable genius, as I recall."

217

The educator peered through his sunglasses. "Are you sure you weren't in my English Lit class last season?" he demanded. "Never mind, it isn't relevant. I direct your attention to this sprawling academic complex. Note how excessively it runs to unshorn grass. No doubt a happy circumstance in your donkey's narrow frame of reference, but to my mind a minor calamity, since the regular custodian languishes at home with what promises to become a chronic debility."

If he thought he was confusing his listener, he was wrong. Clem followed his reasoning. The school janitor was sick. Or maybe, judging from the principal's sardonic tone, only pretending to be sick. "Goldbricking?" Clem asked, and the principal smiled approvingly.

"That is my diagnosis," he said, "and having taught school these many years, I consider myself an authority on that syndrome. But unless I am able to contrive a happier arrangement with the funds so grudgingly allocated by the board of education, I shall be obliged to mow the area myself. Most reluctantly, I might add. But so many people consider it an insult to work for a dollar an hour."

Clem nodded sympathetically.

"So now," Mr. Abernathy said, "when I should be enjoying my well-earned rest, I find myself in a pickle. Unless the cavalry comes charging to my rescue, I'm the patsy. Not only will it blister my scholarly hands and lame my dormant muscles and subject my pallid epidermis to possible second-degree sunburn, but I fear it may tarnish my authoritarian charisma. Who ever heard of Simon Legree cutting grass? I'll an object of ridicule."

"You mean you hafta mow the schoolyard yourself?" Clem guessed.

The principal nodded. "That onerous, Herculean task I must begin without further dawdle *unless* I can locate a

218

surrogate disposed to work for the insulting stipend of a dollar an hour." He peered at Clem. "Did you say something, Marlow?"

"A dollar an hour wouldn't insult *me*," Clem said eagerly.

"You're hired," said the principal. "To tell the truth, Lew Meyers assured me you'd be amenable to persuasion. By the way, he is a member of the school board, so naturally I was joking about their being penurious, even though they certainly are." He gave a pained smile. "How soon can you begin the project?"

"Soon as I grab a bite to eat," Clem told him, thinking, Jeez, it'll take all day, at least, maybe I'll earn nine or ten bucks!

Mr. Abernathy said he would go get the power mower gassed and ready, and Clem was about to bite into the ham sandwich he'd forgotten to eat last night when Dixie came riding through the sunny morning with a quart fruit jar two-thirds full of creamed and sugared and still piping-hot coffee. She gave him a slightly shy smile. He grinned back pretty casually, no longer self-conscious around her. Thanks for the coffee. How you feeling? Okay, how are *you* feeling? Terrific.

When he told her about the job, she was all for rushing home to get her dad's lawnmower and help him. Lord, no! he said. He was getting paid by the hour; the longer it took him the better. So presently she said, well, she would bring him a sandwich and some iced tea later, and she went back home.

The first thing he did was move the cart down by the highway, getting between the shafts himself rather than taking the time and trouble of harnessing and unharnessing Pedro. It seemed to him the cart pulled a lot easier than old Pedro made out. Parking it where it was bound to be

219

seen by any westbound truckers with mail and doughnuts to deliver, he led Pedro into the middle of the schoolyard and tied him to a jungle gym.

When he went to get the mower, Mr. Abernathy said, "We'll call it eight o'clock. Keep your own time. Should anyone inquire, I shall be out at the golf links with niblick and mashie, flailing ineptly at a Scotch kumquat." Holding his wristwatch up and staring at it fixedly, as if it were a stopwatch, he suddenly swung his other hand downward and said, "Go!" Then he turned and walked lazily toward his bright-red Mustang.

Clem grinned after the principal, thinking, Boy, if there were more teachers like him, school would be fun.

The power mower threw to the left, meaning he would have to go around the schoolyard clockwise. It started instantly and cut a smooth thirty-inch swath as fast as he cared to push it, which wasn't very fast, of course, if a guy was getting paid by the hour. There was the safety factor, too. He had to go slow in order to see anything ahead in the shaggy grass which the whirring blades might throw dangerously across the street and injure someone.

It was going to be a long, hot, lucrative day, and he'd be too busy to worry much, and for all that he was grateful.

It wasn't ten o'clock yet when Sam Sorrenti stopped. Clem was halfway along the south side of the schoolground when he saw the big eastbound blue-and-silver GMC pulling to a stop across the road. In the days since he'd met the tough New Jersey trucker, Clem had thought about him frequently and wondered if they would meet again. Now he was pretty thrilled as Sam Sorrenti strode across the highway stretching the kinks out of his muscular arms and shoulders. Clem switched off the power mower and trotted to meet him.

"Where were you Tuesday?" Sam demanded. "I looked for you all along this stretch, but you'd pulled the vanishing act, pal."

Clem explained about camping early, out under the river bridge. The swarthy trucker nodded, then observed that the bridge was less than twenty miles from here, and shouldn't Clem be about a day on west of Feather by now? So Clem explained Duke, too.

Sam Sorrenti expressed sympathy, then whistled reflectively. "Two weeks," he murmured, rubbing his blue chin and shaking his head. "The deeper into summer it gets, the hotter and drier it is out there, Clem. How far could you travel in two weeks if you weren't stalled here?"

"Oh, about a hundred and fifty miles, I guess," Clem said.

Sam stared off across the schoolyard. "It's still two hundred to Amarillo from here," he said. "A two-week delay and it will be August before you pass Amarillo, pal. Uh-*unh!* I don't think so. You better keep moving, Clem."

That worried Clem, but what could he do? "I *got* to wait," he said.

"Yeah, well, look—how big is a dog? How much trouble is a dog to haul? Listen, pal, we'll see your dog catches up when he's well enough to travel. One of us truckers will give him a lift. He can hold down the idiot seat, be the co-pilot." He grinned reassuringly. "I'll start spreading the word when I stop for lunch. Maybe one of *our* rigs will be through here . . ." He thought for a couple of seconds. "Be one a week from Tuesday, another in about seventeen days. In case someone else doesn't give your dog a lift, I'll have our drivers check when they hit town, okay?"

"Well, gee, sure," Clem said, feeling both very relieved and very depressed. He hadn't thought of the possibility that someone could bring Duke on west when he was recovered. "I have to stick around a couple days to be sure

221

he's going to make it," he said. And suddenly realized how much he would miss Dixie and Bob and Lew. Sighing, he said, "I could start Monday or Tuesday, I guess. I ought to know the score by then."

Sam Sorrenti smiled approvingly. "Well, it's still a long haul to Newark, too. Hey, listen, you like grapefruit, pal?" When Clem nodded, he loped across the highway and returned juggling three big yellow globes in each hand. And suddenly, for no particular reason, Clem remembered the mysterious package. He'd been so upset at the clinic he'd forgotten to ask Lew Meyers about the pill, and now he got it out of his pocket. Sam dumped the citrus into the cart and took the pill. Did he know what it was? Yes, by God, he thought maybe he did. He touched it to his tongue for a moment and widened his dark eyes.

"Where'd you get it, Clem?" he asked quietly, so Clem told him. "That lousy sonofabitch!" the trucker said disgustedly. "Using an innocent kid for a drop." He pushed back his cap and rubbed his chin. "What you're hauling," he sighed, "is a small fortune in bennies, pal. Pep pills. Bootleg amphetamine. Bought in Mexico for a few pennies each and worth up to fifty cents apiece in this country. A number of truckers and people who travel a lot use 'em, and so do college students, and I guess high-school kids lookin' for kicks. They're illegal—you need a doctor's prescription to buy them."

Fifty cents apiece! Clem was thinking. And maybe a couple hundred in each of those bottles, and thirty or more bottles! Wow! "I guess," he said nervously, "I better get rid of 'em, you reckon?"

Being human and imperfect, Sam Sorrenti hesitated a moment. Then he sighed noisily and shook his head. "I don't think so, pal. When the man says give him the package you better be able to produce it. And act like you haven't

222

the foggiest idea what's in it. And you shouldn't tell any-body else about the pills, either."

Clem nodded, feeling uneasy, wishing he wasn't involved. "Who you reckon will ask me for 'em, some gangster?"

Sam Sorrenti shrugged. "Some poor service station opera-tor having a rough time competing, or a greedy cafe owner catering to truckers. They rationalize, Clem. It may be illegal, but it isn't necessarily immoral. Some truck driver trying to make a round trip to Phoenix without any sleep might stay alive and in business a while longer because he spent five bucks on bennies. And the guy who sold him the pills turned a quick two-dollar-and-a-half profit. The thing to remember, buddy, is that anybody earning an illegal profit is running scared, and a scared pusher is a dangerous guy. So tape that package back like you found it and forget you ever looked inside, okay?"

Clem nodded, wishing he hadn't looked inside.

"Well, I gotta roll it," Sam Sorrenti said. "Take it easy, pal." He started away, but then he turned around. "One thing for sure," he said, "you don't lead a dull life, Clem."

Grinning lamely, Clem thought, You can say *that* again, boy!

The truck was hardly out of sight when Dixie arrived on her bike with a tinkling Mason jar full of sweetened iced tea and a thick cold ham sandwich. "I hope you're not getting sick of ham," she said with a smile. He decided not to tell her he wasn't staying two weeks. It might make her sad. Or worse yet, she might not care. Because it made him self-conscious to eat with somebody watching him, he asked her if she would go find out about Duke. She nodded and took off on her bicycle.

A few minutes later she was back. "Listen," she said, "instead of me bringing you some fried chicken, why don't

223

you eat supper at our house, Slim?" Today it was Slim again. He started to think of excuses, because in his mind her father was seven feet tall and weighed about two-sixty and had the kind of cold X-ray eyes that could look at a guy and tell if he'd been kissing Dixie or not. But as if reading his mind she added, "Pop will be leaving early for the weekend. I'll tell him I'm not hungry, and we'll eat after he leaves.

"Oh, and one other thing, Slim. I've got a date—one I made a week ago, a two couples deal I can't get out of easily. I mean it wouldn't just be Jerry sore, but the other couple, too."

Clem concealed his disappointment. "Well, okay," he said casually. "I need my sleep if I'm going to get an early start."

"An early start where?"

"If I get all this mowed today, I'll probably head on out in the morning," he said, figuring he probably wouldn't finish it today. "I made arrangements to have my dog hauled on to wherever I'm at when he's well enough to travel." It struck him that she hadn't reported on how Duke was making out. "Listen," he said tensely, "what'd the vet say?"

"He said he'll talk to you later—he had to go alter some bull calves."

That seemed ominous. He didn't want to think about it much. Or about her having a Saturday night date with Jerry. "Well, I better get back to work," he said stiffly, not looking at her. "Thank you kindly for the refreshments. I probably won't get all this finished before dark, so I guess you better give me a rain check on the fried chicken. Maybe next time I'm passing through town . . . on my way back to Conifer . . ."

"I'll leave the tea," Dixie said, getting up and brushing grass clippings from the seat of her shorts. "I'm keeping you

224

from your work—you better get back to mowing, Slim."

Dissatisfied with the whole scene, he started the big Lawnboy and mowed on to the corner before he looked back. And by then she was gone. Okay, what the heck. A guy with nearly six hundred miles still to go couldn't afford to get involved with dames he met along the wayside. Kiss 'em and leave 'em. All her kindness had just been making up for Frank's clobbering him under the bridge. So call it even, now.

All the same he halfway expected her to show up around noon with some lunch and was disappointed when she didn't. And not because of the grub.

But Robinson Elsworth Abernathy showed up at noon, looking like a slightly sunburned Saturday golfer relieved it was over for the week. "Have you had lunch yet?" he inquired, and for some contrary reason Clem said he had. "Yessir, I already ate."

The principal winced. "You just earned an F in English," he said. "This greasy paper sack contains two cheeseburgers drowned in mustard, onions, and pickle relish, some French fries, plus a leaky container that cost the board of education twenty cents and consists of two cents' worth of root beer, a penny's worth of crushed ice, and seventeen cents worth of something we refer to euphemistically as Yankee ingenuity. I would starve before I'd subject my duodenal ulcer to such fare, and I'm happy for your sake you've *ate*, Marlow. But I'd deem it a favor if you'd drop this gastronomic booby trap into the nearest garbage can." He looked at the mowed part of the schoolyard. "Offhand I'd say you're performing your duties commendably. Keep up the good work, and remember, labor is rest from the sorrows that greet us." Thrusting the bag into Clem's unresisting hands, he started away.

Clem stood there looking after the red Mustang, and

225

then he sat down cross-legged and ate the maligned food, which might not be high-toned enough for a college graduate with an ulcer but was a rare and savory treat to a lanky fourteen-year-old. He aimed to save some for later, but it tasted so great he couldn't stop.

About an hour later he was just across the intersection when Lew Meyers returned from drastically altering the destiny of a group of male calves. Getting out of the pickup, Lew gazed toward Clem for a moment, then walked over to the schoolyard. Clem switched off the mower and waited.

"Well, dammit, I wish I could tell you everything's fine, Clem, but it's too soon to be optimistic. I drained a considerable quantity of bloody fluid from Duke's abdomen and put a drain tube in him. I set and splinted the broken leg—the pelvis will look after itself." The veterinary scrubbed his hand through his thin crewcut and expelled his breath noisily. "So it's like before, Clem, we just have to wait and see. Okay?"

Clem sighed resignedly. "Okay, I guess."

"You have any lunch yet?"

Rubbing his tight belly, Clem managed a grin. "Boy, I'll say!"

"Listen, if you want to take a shower when you knock off, come on over, Clem. It's in the basement, in case I'm not around—use the outside door and help yourself to towels and soap." He smiled and left.

Plodding behind the mower again, Clem thought if old Lew couldn't pull Duke through, probably nobody could. Except God—who might be too busy sparrow-watching to worry about one dog.

When the sun began to cool, he saw that he couldn't possibly finish the job before dark. And there sure weren't any headlights on the mower, so he'd have to put in a couple hours in the morning even if working on Sunday was a sin.

226

It was long past suppertime, and Dixie hadn't delivered any Southern-fried chicken. In the back of his mind he'd sort of expected her to come, and hoped she would. Even without the chicken. She didn't have to give him anything. In fact, he was more jealous than hungry. What kind of girl could kiss a guy for hours on Friday night and then go out with her steady boyfriend on Saturday night like nothing had happened?

The sun was a red globe balanced on the far rim of the prairie when Mr. Abernathy showed up. After complimenting Clem on the splendid job of grass-cutting, he produced a pen and envelope and began figuring up the damages, as he put it.

"Take me a couple hours tomorrow to finish," Clem apologized guiltily, "but I'll throw that in free for good measure."

The principal eyed him sternly. "That's un-American, my boy, and anti-labor—only a scab would toil on the Sabbath for anything less than time and a half. Let's see, you began, for all practical purposes, at eight A.M. and it is now virtually eight P.M.—a twelve-hour day! That's a teacher's shift. Thirty minutes off for lunch, I presume?"

Clem nodded. "I went to the bathroom a couple of times, too."

"Such things are covered by the contract. Eleven and a half strenuous hours—and I'm belatedly informed that the minimum wage is a buck-twenty."

Clem was surprised, but too tired to think.

"Correct me if I'm wrong, Marlow. We owe you twelve dollars for the first ten hours, two-seventy for the extra ninety minutes, and three-sixty for two hours you'll put in tomorrow. If my calculations are accurate, we owe you eighteen-thirty. Is that right?"

Clem gaped at him incredulously. "Eighteen *dollars?*"

"And thirty cents. For which I herewith shall inscribe you a warrant, as is the custom. Present it to the school board in session or any member thereof—in this case, Lew Meyers—and he will honor it with money or accept it against any outstanding debts you may owe him. Does all this meet with your approval?"

"Well, I sure ain't complainin'."

The principal winced. "Please, I'm not one of your avant-garde semasiologists who hold that ain't is quaint."

Clem grinned sheepishly.

"Well, Marlow, since you'll be using the mower tomorrow, there's no point in locking it in the storeroom tonight. Keep it by your conveyance, along with the petrol can, and guard it with your very life. I assume you'll be in residence tonight?"

"The way I feel, I'll be goin' to bed early," Clem said wearily.

When the principal had gone, Clem transferred Pedro to a lush patch of grass saved especially for that purpose, in the approximate center of the schoolyard. Then he moved the cart there, and the Lawnboy and gas can. Well, she's probably with Jerry now, he thought bitterly. In a car at a drive-in movie, smooching and guzzling beer—Busch Bavarian, like the empties they left under the bridge.

After a leisurely shower in Lew Meyers's basement, he put on a pair of the denims Dixie had mangled for him, feeling cleaner than he'd felt for quite a spell. When he went up the steps and out into the yard, Lew was waiting. "Clem," he said gravely, "I know you'd like some good news to sleep on. Will you settle for some cautious optimism?" Clem said he would—what choice did he have? "The prognosis as of this moment looks good."

That didn't seem very reassuring, but Clem pretended to be cheered up. Going back to the cart, he couldn't analyze

228

how much of his melancholy was about old Duke and how much was because of Dixie. And if a good part wasn't about his whole trip and his mother's illness.

Too tired to bother with supper, he settled for a grape-fruit and some milk. Fastening down the end curtains, he left the side canvas up enough to let in fresh air, and stretched out on his bed in just his pants, yawning and wiggling his tired toes. It was a warm night, not sweaty warm, just pleasant, a great night for sleeping. Well, shoot, he reflected philosophically, I would have been too sleepy to fool around with her tonight, anyway. And as he drifted off he worried a little about somebody turning the cart over again with him in it. Better not mess around with me, boy . . .

Several hours later he woke in panic when somebody stumbled over the Lawnboy. He lay still, unable to move, thinking they were out there in the shadowy night slinking up on him, fixing to turn the cart over. A cold worm crawled up inside his backbone and squirmed coiling around his hair roots, causing electric tingles in his tight scalp. He wanted to yell so they would beat it, but he couldn't breathe properly.

And then just outside, a yard from his face, she whispered, "Clem? Are you asleep? Hey, Slim!"

"What?" he said, tremendously relieved.

She gave a soft laugh. "Hey, wake up!"

"Unh!" he said, sitting up. "Is that you, Dixie?"

"How many women were you expecting, boy?"

"Hey, what time is it, anyway?"

"It's late, past midnight. Can I come in? I brought you some chicken. I mean if you're not mad."

"Who, me?" he said, sitting up. "Mad?" He unfastened the side curtain and raised it. "Can you climb in? Step up on the wheel."

229

She came piling in on top of him, giggling under her breath. When they got untangled, he lowered the canvas again, thinking, My lord! Who else would bring a guy fried chicken this time of night?

"You hungry?" she asked in a tone of voice that subtly cued him for a negative answer. "Naw," he said. "I never eat between sleep." She giggled. "Stick of Juicy Fruit?" "Sure," he said. He felt her squirming around, bumping him as she got rid of the chicken, and he lay back down because he was too tired to sit up.

"I had a rotten time," she said softly. "I missed you, Slim. I kept wondering what you were doing."

"Sleeping," Clem assured her. "I put in a twelve-hour day. Earned eighteen dollars and thirty cents."

"Wow," she murmured, tracing his left collarbone with a fingertip. "Anyway, I finally busted up with Jerry. Listen, did someone tip your cart over Friday night?" Clem said "Uh-huh," and she sighed. "It was him, the jerk. He was *bragging* about it, for Pete's sake. How adolescent can you get?"

Clem was busy with the gum.

"Funny," she said, "if you hadn't happened along, I guess I would have gone on running around with that bunch of kids and feeling kind of flattered because they let a girl my age join the gang—but to tell the truth, I was getting pretty disillusioned with them. At first I thought they were really something, but I guess if you're halfway intelligent you soon find out they're not much at all. But it sort of hastens the process to meet somebody who *is* something, Clem."

"Like who?" he asked, amazed.

"Well," she said, laying her soft hand on the curve of his neck, "a boy who would work twelve hours mowing a schoolyard, for example. Or a boy who would walk all the way to New Mexico to see his mother. I can't get over that,

230

Clem." Suddenly she clamped his chin in her strong fingers and stopped his chewing. "Listen, will you write to me? Even if it's just picture postcards? Then when you're settled, I'll write to you, Clem. People can stay friends all their lives just writing letters, even if they never see each other again— even if they marry other people and have families and live clear across the world from each other, they can be friends."

"Well, why not?" he said. "I never knew anybody I'd rather be friends with, that's for sure." He put his arms gently around her.

"It's funny," Dixie murmured. "I know girls that do wild things just to spite their mothers, you know? And boys, too, I guess. Not for fun or because they really want to especially, but just to get even with their mothers. So my mother has been dead a couple of years, and it doesn't much really matter what I do, you know?"

Clem nodded, stifling a shivery compulsion to yawn.

"So when I'm tempted to do something I know I shouldn't, it's like Mom is *there,* watching, not stopping me, but not wanting me to do it. So I don't. I mean, I haven't yet."

Clem nodded again. "Like me," he said. "All year I studied hard trying to make all A's and B's, just so I could send my report cards to my mom. If she'd been there, I probably wouldn't have tried so hard."

"Yeah, it's about the same thing," she agreed.

They kissed, and it was very sweet and relaxing, very peaceful in the quiet night.

And suddenly it was broad daylight. One of them had pulled the thin blanket up—and they were cuddled snugly together, Clem on his back with his arm under Dixie's head, her face on his bony shoulder, her hair tickling his cheek. It was a rare and lovely way to wake up, he thought, breathing carefully so as not to disturb her, listening to the birds

231

singing and Pedro snorting the way he always did in the morning.

Dixie sighed and stirred. "Must have dozed off for a minute," she said, yawning. Then her eyes widened and she lifted her head and looked around at the clearly visible interior of the cart. "Oh my lord, it's broad daylight!" she gasped. "Sunday morning!"

"A day of rest," Clem said, because he wasn't thinking too well.

"A day of *scandal!*" she moaned. "Sixteen people are probably looking at this cart right this minute, Clem! What are they going to say when they see Dixie crawl out and go slinking across the wide open spaces of the schoolyard? I didn't much mind having all the women in town thinking I was a *tomboy*, but holy mackerel!"

"Well, I'll just have to stay hidden in here all day, I guess. Keep the curtains down until dark, and hope nobody comes and looks inside. Oh, boy! It could get to be a long day."

A bulb lit up in Clem's mind. Stay in the cart, curtains down, okay. But not necessarily all day. "Hey, relax," he said. "This thing's got *wheels* on it, and I pay a full-time donkey to pull the durn thing. I'll smuggle you home with no publicity."

"You're a genius," she said with relief. "Sneak me home right under their cold wet noses. Know what I'll do when we get there? I'll cook you the biggest breakfast you ever ate in your whole wicked life."

She came close. He'd eaten more in the old days, on winter mornings, but for a summer breakfast it was impressive. First she sat him down in the cheery living room and got the Sunday funny paper for him to read. Then she brought him a glass of tomato juice. He worried a little about her father coming home, but she'd assured him he

232

wouldn't, and even if he did, he wouldn't care. Clem couldn't keep his mind on the funnies for listening to her whistling in the kitchen, frying bacon, boiling oatmeal, making coffee. And the whole meal was just the way he liked it. Oatmeal with cream and sugar, bacon and eggs, and buttery toast with strawberry jam, strong coffee with pure cream, and a dish of fresh berries with cream to tamp it all down.

While he slowly and blissfully packed it away, she nibbled at her own food and watched him with admiring approval. "Everything okay?" she kept asking. "Terrific," he sighed.

When he was through eating, Dixie laughed abruptly and said, "Well, anyway, now you can say you slept with a girl, Slim."

Clem grinned, embarrassed because it didn't seem proper to kid about stuff like that on Sunday.

"I guess I ought to feel ashamed, but I don't," she said. "If I had it to do again, I'd do it again. I'm glad it was you, Clem."

"I'm glad it was me, too," he said sincerely.

Looking up at him she said, "Do you have to leave today?"

"I got fifty-some days of walking to do yet."

"I know," she said. "And naturally you're anxious to get there, I don't blame you. Listen, I'll visit your dog so he won't be lonely. Every day, if you want me to, Clem."

"I'd appreciate it," he said. "And I'll write you, I promise. And someday I'll be comin' back through here . . . *we* will." Suddenly a demoralizing confusion swept over him—he'd never really given any thought to the return trip. His mother couldn't *walk* back to eastern Oklahoma, but he couldn't leave Pedro and the cart in New Mexico, and they probably wouldn't be able to afford a trucking fee. He sighed, thinking, I might even have to sell Pedro and the cart to get money for bus tickets. Then he thought, Duke couldn't ride

233

a bus, what about him? I never thought about all that. He hadn't ever really thought his way beyond the simple goal of seeing his mother again, except to vaguely figure he'd have to find a job and a place to live and go to school out there next fall.

"When I *do* come back through here," he said with a confidence he didn't feel, "I'll stop off long enough to take a few more lessons. I mean tennis lessons."

She laughed.

When they were saying goodbye at the door, she said, "I don't know what's so great about you, Clem, but you turn me on more than any boy I ever knew."

She couldn't have said anything that would have pleased him more. As he rode the cart along the quiet Sunday streets of Feather he got the feeling he would never be ill at ease around girls again. He knew exactly what to do. Up to a certain point, anyway.

SEVENTEEN

Even with the late start, he made good time Sunday, mainly because he didn't stop for pop bottles, feeling financially secure—Lew Meyers said twenty dollars would take care of Duke's hospital bill. There were few trucks, but lots of Sunday drivers who stared and smiled and waved but thankfully didn't stop him to satisfy whatever curiosity he aroused. The days were longer now, too, and he kept going until sundown, when he finally ate the rest of Dixie's chicken.

They were in sight of Clintsburg on Monday afternoon when Ken Whittle overtook them and stopped to deliver a sack of oatmeal cookies and pay his customary brief visit. "You get the doughnut shipment all right?" he inquired, and Clem shook his head in dismay. "What doughnut shipment?" Last Wednesday, Ken said. Barney Cobb in a Hershel's Hatchery truck on his way to Mexico with a load of baby chicks. Clem sighed. He'd had a premonition he was missing out on something when he was under that dang bridge—but he'd give up a sack of doughnuts anytime to meet someone like Dixie. Out of a growing curiosity Clem asked if Jasper Hicks was with Ken, and Ken moved his unlit cigar around in his teeth and said old Jasper's ulcer was bothering him and he was sacked in, and Clem thought, He's *always* sacked in. Well, how's it going, pal? Fine, Clem

235

said, how is your mother? "We drove over Saturday and had supper with her," Ken said, fidgeting. "Strawberry short-cake—she froze a crate of 'em, and made preserves out of another crate she bought, and said tell you she'll send you some pretty soon. Well, I better get on the road."

Hello Clem, goodbye Clem. Same old story.

The highway didn't go through downtown Clintsburg, which was a big relief, and presently Clem saw the promi-nent sign that said OLEANDER INN MOTEL, and he started thinking about enjoying another mess of barbecued spareribs with Gaylord Jackson. The only Negro he'd ever known, just like Dixie was the only girl he'd ever really known. And come right down to it, there were only two kinds of people, good ones and bad ones, and that's what he had in common with Gaylord and Dixie—all *three* of them were what you'd call good people. Nice folks.

He'd been hoping he'd see Gaylord around the motel pruning a hedge or something, but he wasn't, and Clem hated to go driving in there with his rig and ask. There was still a lot of travel time left in the day, and he was debating about just going on past when a stocky older Negro suddenly rose up out of some ornamental shrubbery and hailed him. Clem tied the donkey to a fireplug and went across the divided four-lane highway.

"You must be Mister Marlow," the Negro said.

"Yessir," Clem said. "Is Gaylord Jackson around?"

The man shook his grizzled head, glancing uneasily over his shoulder. "Mister Jackson ain't heah," he said, and everything about him was cautious. He eyed Clem over the low hedge. "You miss him by an hour, maybe. How you doin'?"

"Okay," Clem said. "You expect him back pretty soon?"

"Can't rightly say," the Negro said and took another

236

careful look around. "I dunno, maybe he's in trouble with the law."

Clem raised his eyebrows. "What did he do wrong?"

"I dunno," the man said, as if he'd just as soon not discuss it any further. "Policeman said something about a missing wristwatch. From a wreck that happen way on ovah east somewhere." His glance narrowed on Clem, in a meaningful way. "Maybe you be wise to keep goin' along."

A wristwatch and a wreck. Clem didn't get the connection, but if the police had detained Gaylord over the wreck, it seemed as if Clem ought to be there, too, helping remember the details. Where that night was concerned, Clem had a photographic memory—and he didn't recall any wristwatches. Hey, maybe those grateful people in Latham wanted to give Gaylord a watch as a reward for all he did that night!

"Where did they take him?" he asked, and the Negro said the County Courthouse, two blocks south. Sheriff's office, most likely. "You goin' to get mixed up with it?"

"Sure," Clem said. "If they want to know all about that wreck, two memories are better than one. Besides, we're supposed to eat some barbecued ribs for supper, me and Gaylord. My turn to buy."

"Could be young Jackson ain't goin' to eat no ribs for a spell. Not if something's missin' an' the law got a black suspect handy—least that's been my experience of how white folks' law works." His voice had soured, and his manner was no longer so friendly.

Nuts with that kind of talk, Clem thought, being the son of a late deputy sheriff. The law was tough on *all* poor, uninfluential people, no matter *what* color they were, his dad used to say. It took a lot of geetus to hire a good slippery lawyer, his dad used to say.

In the interests of speed he left Pedro hitched to the fireplug and loped back to the last intersection, then south two blocks to a big glass-and-brick building set back on a broad green lawn. Inside the front doors a wide cool hallway stretched through the building, and about halfway along a sign said *Sheriff's Department*. He wished he had a nickel for every time he'd been in the sheriff's offices in Conifer, but this wasn't the same, this was strange country.

The door was open, and he went right on in like he'd voted for this guy all his life. There was a tall counter across the room like a dividing wall, with a couple of desks and chairs and filing cabinets, and two closed doors leading into other rooms. Four men were behind the counter, two of them unknowns. Gaylord was sitting in a swivel chair tilted back reading a *True Crimes* magazine, and highway patrolman Kaluski was leaning on the counter talking to two capable-looking men in cowboy hats with familiar badges on their gray shirts. They were ignoring Gaylord, and he was ignoring them. But everybody looked curiously at Clem, and for a second there he almost lost his cool, but he'd matured a lot in the last weeks.

He gave trooper Kaluski a brief nod and leaned on the counter and said, "Hello, Gaylord, what are you doing here?" Then he said, "Hi, Mr. Kaluski," but didn't ask what *he* was doing there.

"Who, me, man?" Gaylord said. "I was invited by these friendly gentlemen to have a little what they call dialogue, baby. The subject of this routine inquiry is, did I happen to notice if I stole a wristwatch off'n one them white boys while we was pullin' 'em outa their badly depreciated vehicle on the night of April the sixteenth." He shook his head. "I knew so *well* not to mix up in other folk's troubles. My pappy always tol' me, Son, he say to me, mine yo' *own* business, don't do nuthin' *to* nobody, or *fo'* nobody, an' don' let *nobody* do nuthin' to or fo' *you,* an' maybe you

238

be able to stay outa trouble in this troublesome world."

Clem blinked at him. "You mean you're under arrest?"

"Well, I ain't what you'd call free to get up an' go, man," Gaylord said. "We all settin' around waitin' to see do I get sent back fo' trial or jus' run outa town."

"Now, wait a minute, mister," one of the officers said. "No call for you to get smart." He eyed Clem. "Who's this feller, anyway?"

Trooper Kaluski told him. Clem was the other witness. The two of them had undoubtedly saved some of those kids from burning to death—a woman who finally stopped to help said the car started burning shortly after her arrival.

"All right," said the sheriff, scratching his neck, "now let me make something clear. We got a formal request from the sheriff over there to pick this man up, if possible, an' by God that's our only connection with it. If they tell us to hold him until they can come after him with a warrant, I might not like it, but I'd be obliged to do it. Although personally I don't see how they can make any case against him." Suddenly he growled, "It ain't no wonder to me the way people hurry on past highway accidents, because this is about the kind of thanks they generally get."

"Well, listen," Clem said, uncertainly, "Gaylord's not the only one that handled those hurt kids—there was me, and that woman, and don't forget the ambulance drivers. There were lots of people milling around there."

The trooper and the sheriff and his deputy all nodded like they knew too well how crowds formed around tragedies.

"How did the law over there know where to find Gaylord?" Clem asked abruptly. "He never left a forwarding address."

"I'll have to take the blame for that, Clem," the highway patrolman said, almost apologetically. "Saturday afternoon I saw Sergeant Walters at headquarters and told him I'd located his missing accident witnesses, if he still cared. He thought some about having you fellas make depositions for the record, if you actually saw it happen."

Clem shook his head. "We just heard it, was all."

"I know," Kaluski nodded. "Jackson told us all about it. The sorry thing, Clem, is that when Walters told the sheriff over there he'd found out who you fellas were, and where you were, it turned out that a wristwatch was missing from one of the dead kids and his influential pappy was doing some tall howling about it. Not only was it very expensive, it was a graduation present to the boy and has considerable sentimental value. You know how it is."

Clem suddenly knew how it was. "Sure, I get it—they figure while we were dragging kids out of that car we were taking time to roll them."

The trooper shrugged and spread his hands. "Look at it from the father's point of view—he's offered a hundred dollars reward for the return of the watch. And the way you fellas so modestly avoided publicity and dropped out of the picture . . ."

"I didn't drop out of the picture," Clem told him. "I been on the highway every day in plain sight."

"Anyway, nobody's accusing anybody of anything so far," the sheriff said. "That way I understand it, the dead boy's family has got a lot of clout in those parts and the sheriff there would purely appreciate it if we'd locate, uh, Jackson here and just detain him until they could decide what they aim to do. He's supposed to be calling back on it any minute now, and I'll lay you three to one they'll say forget it and sorry to bother you. Whatever happened to that watch, they got no real case against you fellas, or anybody else."

Clem leaned on the counter frowning at Kaluski. "You passed me on the highway a while ago, and you knew who

240

I was—I guess you didn't know me and Gaylord was wanted then, huh?"

"I knew," the trooper said sheepishly. "The sheriff here had called me on the radio. Well, what the heck, you were coming this way . . ." He grinned faintly. "Right into the trap, you might say. Fact of the matter, Clem, your friend Jackson urged us to leave you out of it, and I readily agreed. It was my big mouth that caused all the trouble, and I didn't want to cause you any more delays."

In a way, that was a load off his mind, but in another way, it made him feel angry and a little guilty. He looked at Gaylord sitting back there trying to act calm and unconcerned but betraying a certain resignation, and he wondered if the law over in Latham would have had Gaylord picked up if he wasn't a Negro. Clem also wondered if Gaylord wasn't wondering the same thing.

"Well, if they take him back, they ought to take me, too," he said shakily. "We're partners when it comes to rollin' dead kids we drag out of wrecked cars, ain't that right, Gaylord?"

"Hey," Gaylord said, "you know you're kidding, and I know you're kidding, but these here gentlemen maybe don't appreciate that kind of humor. You go on along, Clem. Don't worry none about me. I'm not in no particular hurry to get somewhere like you—and man, the rate you're movin', you can't afford no detours. Like the sheriff says, they can't make much of a case against me, all they can do is delay me a few days—an' lose me my job I was plannin' to hang onto a couple weeks to save me some bread. You can still log some more miles today, so stop messin' around an' get at it."

Clem shook his head stubbornly. "It's my turn to buy us a pile of barbecued ribs, remember? Anyway, listen, two of those dead kids we never even went near, the ones that got

241

thrown out when that car first hit. The only corpse we handled had to be the one pinned underneath. Remember? You tried to lift the car an' I tried to drag him out, first by grabbin' his wrists—and *he* sure wasn't wearing any darn watch. Then we finally both dragged him out by the *ankles* so you never even touched his arms. And I'll testify about that in court, if necessary."

Gaylord shook his head. "No, man, you don't understand. It would just be your word and my word, and that ain't proof. Who's going to believe us? Nothin' we *say* going to make any difference. So you back off now, Clem. Go on an' see yo' mama, hear."

"Well, I'll stick around and see what happens," Clem said.

"I'll tell you one damn thing," the sheriff declared irritably, "if I don't hear from that old boy over there pretty soon now, I'm not going to detain anyone. I'm fixin' to turn this man loose, Kaluski. I don't like the position this puts us in, like we're harassin' this fella or something. We don't have no discrimination around here, everyone gets along fine, no race problems or any of that stuff."

Gaylord suddenly smiled. "I notice that since I been here. The darkies keep their place real good."

"Now don't go gettin' insolent, fella," the sheriff growled.

Clem wished to heck Gaylord wouldn't antagonize the law like that. You shouldn't wise off at policemen or county laws, because they didn't like smart guys, especially smart Negroes. Wanting to change the subject, Clem remembered that package in his cart that he was tired of having to worry about. Despite Sam Sorrenti's advice, he just wanted to get *rid* of it, and the logical thing would be to turn it over to the authorities.

So he was just getting ready to tell Trooper Kaluski about how he'd got saddled with the pills when one of the inner doors opened and a man stuck his head out and said the

242

sheriff in Latham was calling back. While they waited, Clem saw a couple of drops of sweat on Gaylord's forehead.

They could hear the sheriff in the other room, but all he was saying was yeah, and uh-huh, and okay, and you bet, and finally goodbye. When he came back, his weatherbeaten face was solemn.

"Well, people, it just goes to prove something or other," he said. "Turns out that kid hocked his goddam wristwatch for money to buy the booze. One of the other kids finally blurted out the truth. So they're just awful sorry to have caused all this unnecessary unpleasantness, and I'm supposed to apologize to you on their behalf, Jackson, and tell you how much they *regret* everything. Go ahead, spit, or tell me what I can do with their apologies."

Gaylord sighed loudly. "I just feel relieved, is all."

"Well, this might help a little," the sheriff went on. "That hundred bucks the kid's old man was offering for the return of the watch—that meant so much to everybody except his kid, apparently—now he wants to give it to you two as a token of the town's gratitude. Fifty bucks apiece." He lifted his bushy eyebrows and grinned. "Ought to pay for your lost time, fella."

Gaylord was staring at him incredulously, and suddenly he leaned forward and started slapping his thighs, snorting with laughter—then he really let go, stomping the floor and slapping his legs and laughing like a fool. "Oh, man," he said, and shook his head in wonder. "Dig that white daddy —if he can't put somebody in the jailhouse, he do the next bes' thing an' lay some bread on 'em! Hooweee!" He laughed some more, and it was infectious, causing the rest of them to grin and chuckle, seeing the joke of it. Finally Gaylord got control of himself and said, "We s'pose to go over there to collect it?"

243

"We can pay you here, and they'll reimburse us later," the sheriff said, and that kind of set Gaylord off again.

"Re-im-burse," he chuckled. "That is *so* wild!" Then he sobered abruptly and shook his head. "You tell them nice generous folks Mr. G. Jackson thanks them, but he can't use that kind of money. Fifty dollars is a lot of cash, but I wasn't doin' what I done fo' wages, that was free. Not for sale or hire. No way."

"Well, shoot, that goes for me, too," Clem said stoutly, feeling obliged to follow Gaylord's example, even if his heart wasn't entirely in it. "It wouldn't feel right, taking pay for something like that," he declared.

Trooper Kaluski looked at him dubiously. "It's not tainted money, Clem, and it might come in real handy before you get to your mama's."

"I can make expenses just picking up pop bottles," Clem said. "Well, can we go now?"

Kaluski nodded. "I'll drive you two wherever you want to go."

Gaylord laughed. "Thank you, I appreciate it, but I had my ride in a fuzz buggy for today. I feel like walkin'." Giving Clem an owlish stare, he said: "Going my way— on foot?"

"Only way I ever travel." Clem grinned and followed him out into the hot afternoon. "I'm parked across from where you work."

"Where I used to work," Gaylord said grimly. "After the way the fuzz checked with the boss man before roustin' me, I got a feelin' they have my severance pay waiting. Nice motel managers don't mess around with transients that have any kind of doin's with the fuzz."

He was walking too fast for Clem, as if anxious to find out where he stood with the motel manager. Really too early to eat barbecued ribs, anyway, Clem thought. Probably not much after four, judging from the sun—he could still knock off a few miles before time to make camp, and probably should.

"Thing about it is, I like this job," the big Negro said glumly. "Outdoors work, trimmin' an' mowin'. Fact is, I enjoy 'most any job I don't have to be around people— yessuh, yessuh, hey you *boy*—I don't mean only white people hey-boyin', some of the worst in my experience been stuck-up blacks." He sighed as they turned along the highway toward the Oleander Inn. "It sure was nice bein' a landscape engineer while it last, anyway."

Clem kept tagging along, unable to decide whether to cut on across to his cart and wait, or follow Gaylord, or split the difference and just hang around the driveway entrance.

"It could have been all summer," Gaylord said mournfully, pausing by the entrance, looking around at all the hedges and shrubs and watered green grass. "I could have stayed all summer—an' didn't know till right now that that was what I was plannin' to do."

He started on toward the motel office, and for some reason Clem continued to follow him. Just to see if he was out of a job, maybe. Still wanting to buy a pile of ribs and share them with Gaylord.

A stocky white man in slacks and a colorful sports shirt came out of the motel office and watched Gaylord in a poker-faced sort of way, but then he smiled as Gaylord halted. It was a puzzled, searching smile, Clem thought, like the man was maybe looking at Gaylord for the first time.

"Well, boss, you fixin' to say hello, or goodbye?" Gaylord asked the man—so he must be the manager.

"Tell you the simple truth," the manager said, "a few minutes ago I was thinking about laying off some of the help, Jackson. But then the sheriff called me and explained the mix-up, said instead of being a shady character, you're a hero, and those grateful people over in Latham were only trying to track you down so they could give you the Carnegie Medal or something. A *cash* reward—which you turned down, so maybe you don't *need* your job here, eh?"

"I was aimin' to need it all summer, boss," Gaylord said. "I don't mind takin' money for work, but that other . . ." He shook his head. He turned to Clem and introduced him, and the manager smiled and said the sheriff had mentioned Clem, "And how are you, young man?"

"Okay, sir," Clem said self-consciously.

"Well, Jackson," the manager said, "since you're a hero, I won't dock you for the hour you missed, but it's still quite a while till five o'clock, so get back to work."

"Right," Gaylord said cheerfully, and turned to Clem. "Listen, man, you keep travelin', an' when I knock off I'll buy some hickory-smoked ribs an' catch up with you on up the highway."

"It's my turn to furnish the grub," Clem protested.

"Never mind, man," Gaylord said, moving so Clem had to follow him. "My pride cost you fifty dollars, and I got me a good job, so the food's on me."

Clem shrugged and quit following. "Okay," he said, and went on out across the highway. And when he was about two hundred yards west of the Oleander Inn Motel, the highway patrol cruiser slid to a stop on the shoulder and Trooper Kaluski wanted to know if Gaylord was all right.

"I guess he's all set for the summer," Clem said.

Mr. Kaluski nodded, getting out and coming around the cruiser. "Now listen, Clem," he said scoldingly, "that man's pride was hurt, and I don't blame him for refusing the money. But the man who offered it, he's hurt a lot deeper than his pride. He lost a son who just graduated from high

246

school, and he lost his head about the wristwatch, I'll grant you—but think how he'll feel when his effort to make amends is slapped right back into his teeth. The money isn't important to him, and maybe like you said, you don't really need it. Your Negro friend doesn't need it if he's got a job, but let's you and me level with each other, Clem. I know all about your dog getting hurt, and the vet's bill, and you could have other emergency expenses before you get to the end of your trip.

"Now, I can't see where your racial pride's been bruised, so don't be stupid, Clem. Why make things worse for that grieving father?" Trooper Kaluski reached into his shirt pocket. "I got the money from the sheriff, five crisp, clean twenty-dollar bills, and if you don't take it, buddy, I may write you up a ticket for not having a registration tag on your vehicle, or a mule-skinner's license, or the required lights and reflectors . . . Take the dough! Use it if you need it, or save it if you don't. That man will never miss it—in fact, he'll deduct it from his income tax, so just consider this a gift from your old Uncle Sam."

Clem didn't require that much persuading, but he felt funny accepting the whole hundred dollars. Maybe at supper, when they were digging into those delicious ribs, he could talk Gaylord into accepting his rightful half. "Well," said Clem, accepting the money, "I sure wouldn't want to hurt anybody's feelings. I'll hide this fortune in my footlocker and keep it for insurance, like."

"Good thinking," Trooper Kaluski said. "See you later, Clem."

"Oh, hey, wait!" Clem shouted, remembering the package. He got it out of the cart and told the whole story, except for a few minor details like how he'd opened it and knew it contained illegal drugs. But Kaluski was a smart man; he was clearly suspicious from the start.

247

"All right, now, let's run over your story again," he said. "On that morning when you were giving eastbound trucks the high sign, one of them stopped and the driver paid you two dollars to keep this package until an unknown 'friend' asked for it. Describe the truck, and the driver, if you can remember."

Clem remembered pretty well and saw the trooper agreeing with him and nodding to himself.

"Sounds like the truck that jackknifed on a county road that morning, trying to slow down for a narrow bridge— hit the side and went into the creek, pinning the driver in the cab. Under water." He rubbed his collarbone thoughtfully. "He was probably overweight and taking an unfamiliar detour to avoid the scales." The trooper balanced the package on spread fingers. "Wanted to get rid of this just in case, and then didn't have a chance to notify the guy who was supposed to get it from you, Clem." He plucked at his lower lip, staring at the package. "Sure am curious about what's in it."

"Well, I'm tired of being responsible for it," Clem said, fighting his natural tendency to blab everything he knew. Kaluski said he'd take it off Clem's hands, and in case the owner ever did ask for it, just tell him to contact the patrol. He got in the cruiser and made a U-turn (Why not? Who could give him a ticket?) and headed east in a hurry, no doubt figuring he'd already wasted too much time around Clintsburg.

Clem pulled his hat down over his eyes and headed into the late afternoon sun thinking, Every step I take is like dipping a bucketful of water out of a big lake I have to empty—and, baby, I mean a *big!* It sure felt strange to have over a hundred bucks in his pocket—doggone it, now he'd have to start worrying about hijackers and hold-up men.

248

"Clem, throw down your strongbox, we know you're carryin' a shipment of treasury rugs . . ."

But at least he was no longer in danger of being swooped down on by the FBI. Boy, it was a relief to get rid of those bennies.

He was watching ahead for a shady place to stop, figuring it must be around five-thirty, when a car pulled off on the shoulder beside the cart, bleeping its horn cautiously as if the driver didn't want to cause anybody's burro to stampede. Clem looked around, figuring it was Gaylord—and nearly fell down with stunned surprise.

"Della Nolan?" he said incredulously. He turned back and took a couple of steps, and Della blinked at him through the windshield of the familiar green Pontiac, and then she put her head on her crossed arms on the steering wheel, like she was tired, or trying to think, or maybe crying. He began to feel alarmed. She couldn't make him turn back, not after he'd come this far. She sure couldn't *take* him back! Unless she made him sell Pedro and the cart, which was out of the question.

She kept leaning on the steering wheel with her face hidden, and he approached the car warily. The windows were up on account of the air-conditioning, so he opened the door and she turned her head enough to stare at him with one glistening eye.

"What are you doin' here?" he asked in a shaky voice.

"What are *you* doin' here?" she replied, and lifted her wet face from her crossed arms. "You a rotten kid," she said, and started crying noisily, hiding her face again. "You really know h-how to h-hurt a guy! You s-selfish, thoughtless . . ." Then she just bawled, with her shoulders heaving, and he stood there holding the door open, feeling helpless and distressed.

249

"Well, hey," he said worriedly. "Aw, come on, now. Listen . . ."

"Oh, Clemmie, whu-why didn't you tu-tell me you wuh-wanted . . . ?" She raised her head and wiped at her eyes. "No! I should have known without being told, but all I ever thought about was *me!* Instead of running off to Kansas, I could have taken you to see her . . ." She broke down again, and he felt a little less worried. "I'll be okay in a minute," she said, and snapped on the radio, and music came pouring forth. Too loud—or anyway, loud enough.

"Little Green Apples," the tail end of it. Then the announcer said the weather in Amarillo was eighty-five degrees and sunny. Forecast: more of the same but with scattered showers moving into the area tomorrow night or Wednesday morning. Then there was a fast-talking commercial, and Clem looked back east thinking about Gaylord and wondering why Della had come looking for him. Oh, lord! he thought with a sudden squeeze of fear, don't let it be terrible news! He cleared his throat, but was afraid to ask, and another top pop platter began spinning in Amarillo.

"How did you know where to find me?" he said gruffly.

"Your friend Mrs. Whittle, how else?" she said, sniffing and wiping her wet cheeks. She reached over and turned the screechy hollering singer's volume down irritably. "Didn't you think I'd be worried enough about you to ask if she'd heard from you?"

He shrugged, thinking Well, heck, Mrs. Whittle couldn't lie if Della *asked* her, but he was kind of surprised Della *had* asked her.

"She sent a box of cookies an' stuff," Della said, hiccuping. "There's some mail, too." She nodded toward the back seat. "I suppose you're wonderin' if I drove three hundred miles just to call you a rotten kid." Her smile was quivery, but genuine—she wouldn't smile like that if it was bad news,

250

would she? "Well," she said, "I just happen to be on my way to New Mexico to visit a second cousin of mine in a sanitarium, an' I thought you might want to go along for the ride, maybe."

That really shook him. See his mother *tomorrow* instead of nearly six weeks from now! Oh, wow! Oh! Good old Della, boy! She was really a great person! Only, he couldn't just go off and leave Pedro hitched to a fencepost . . .

But Della was way ahead of him there. "The only problem is what to do with your donkey and cart," she said, "and I thought about that on the drive over here, Clemmie." She turned to look back toward town. "Listen, hon, I passed a little farmhouse back there a couple hundred yards, and I don't see anything on west. Turn around and we'll go see if they'll let us leave your wagon and mule there a few days. Naturally, we'll offer to pay them something, unless they try to swindle us," she said. "I mean, how much is a little grass worth?"

"Well, they'd have to water him," he pointed out.

"Hey, buster, you're really lookin' good," she told him. "All brown an' healthy, an' older, even. You know?"

He grinned self-consciously. It was the hat, mostly, but come to think about it, he felt older.

"Well, look, I'll drive on back and haggle with them," she said. "Hurry it up, handsome." Smiling through her streaked make-up, she made a U-turn across the highway, causing a couple of oncoming automobiles to honk disapprovingly. Clem grinned with excitement and thought, All my friends break the U-turn laws like that, including Trooper Kaluski.

He loped back east and Pedro trotted after, and when they turned into the neat grassy farmyard Della had made all the arrangements. Shucks, the elderly man said, no bother at all, young lady. He'd just turn that desert night-

251

ingale into the barn lot and Clem could park the rig back yonder somewhere. When Clem explained the vital importance of leaving the cart in plain view of the trucks passing by, so people wouldn't be worrying about what had happened to him, the old man said why sure, just don't block the driveway, son.

Clem parked it where eastbound trucks could see it in plenty of time to stop, in case Barney Cobb in the hatchery truck wanted to leave that sack of doughnuts on his way back from Mexico.

As he got some clothes out of the footlocker he asked Della how long they would be out there, and she said, "Hon, I'm only going to stay long enough to say hello to your mama—I've got to get on back home, for reasons I'll explain later. But don't worry, I'll give you enough money to stay a few days and buy a bus ticket back to this town. I wish I could let you stay a month."

No, he thought, he couldn't stay that long, anyway— he had to come back here and get Pedro and the cart, and old Duke, and head on west again in time to start school. He would explain all that to his mother. Just think! Tomorrow he'd be seeing her! Would she recognize him? He'd changed a lot in over two years.

He remembered to ask the farmer to tell Gaylord what had happened. When he came back, they'd take another crack at the smoked ribs.

As soon as they were whizzing west with the air-conditioning like a refreshing breeze, Della said, "All right, talk, hon. Tell me everything that's happened."

Well, hell, he wasn't about to describe everything that had happened, but he told her about meeting Gaylord and the various truck drivers, about the wreck and about the escaped convict, but not about the package of smuggled bennies. He censored the episode with the little girl in the pond, and minimized the business under the bridge, except for catching all the fish. Never mind about getting clobbered by an invisible guy with a wallop like a mule's kick. Frank what's-his-name.

Then there was Dixie Funkhouser, and he toned *that* down. Clem Marlow didn't go blabbing it around if he slept with a nice girl—at least, not to a woman.

When he told Della about old Duke's dumb accident, she let out a big sigh and nodded. "I noticed he was missing," she said, "but I was afraid to bring it up—I sorta guessed something must have happened to him." She acted very sympathetic.

He neglected to mention the hundred-dollar windfall, figuring he was going to need that dough if he ever moved to New Mexico permanently. He felt a little bit chintzy about it, but only a little bit.

Della said enviously that it sounded as if he'd been having some great adventures, something to tell his grandchildren about some day. But Clem figured they probably wouldn't believe it—sonofagun, now that he'd recalled all the stuff that had happened in a little over a month on the road, he hardly believed it himself.

EIGHTEEN

They stopped for supper in Shamrock, Texas, and Della told him to eat hearty, although she was on a diet herself. She said he didn't need to lose any weight; in fact, she was afraid his mother would think the Nolans had been starving him all winter.

Clem had a jumbo cheeseburger with French fries, a bowl of chili, and a glass of milk, plus apple pie à la mode and a cup of coffee, and Della watched him enviously. He ate faster than usual because he was so eager to be whizzing across the Texas panhandle.

But then when they were speeding west again at sixty-five miles an hour through rolling grassland with no houses or service stations to break the monotony, he was over-whelmed at the thought of making this part of the trip on foot. If Della hadn't turned up, would he have reached New Mexico with Pedro and the cart? He wouldn't even think about that now, but only about how soon he'd be seeing his mother, and how swell Della was.

He was leaning back in blissful luxury, listening to the radio, when Della said, "Clemmie, the reason I'm going to just say hello to Lora and come on back is that I've made up my mind to leave Royce."

Rolling his head on the back of the seat, he blinked at

254

her, not knowing what to say. Congratulations? Or . . . that's tough! Or what?

"I've had enough," she said. "I mean to be gone when Royce gets out of jail. I'm going to sell the cattle and some of the furniture, and see a lawyer about a divorce. Then I want to head west. Denver first, then down to Santa Fe— I've got friends both places—then on out to California. My brother lives in Fresno, maybe I'll settle there. I can find a job anywhere, I'm not worried about that." She gave him a sidelong look. "All I'm worried about is you, hon."

"Well, shoot," he said, "don't worry about me, if that's all."

"The point is, I don't know where you'll stay when you get back, all I know is it won't be with us." She glanced at him again.

He just shrugged nonchalantly. What the heck, he could stay in New Mexico, hadn't she figured that out yet? But, man, it was a darn good thing he'd got this great idea when he did, instead of hanging around until the Nolans split and left him at the mercy of the welfare people.

"Look, Clemmie, I don't think you ought to tell your mama I'm busting up with Royce. It would just upset her."

"Okay, I won't mention it," Clem promised, but he crossed his fingers, because that would be the clincher, boy. If he didn't have any place to go back to, his mother couldn't very well argue about his plan to come live in New Mexico until she was well again. But for some reason he still didn't want to let Della in on his plan to stay out there —being a woman she might start thinking up all the logical reasons why he *shouldn't,* even if it wasn't exactly any of her business any more. He could think of plenty reasons himself, but the heck with it, his mind was made up.

"Are you mad at me, hon?" Della asked. "Do you blame me?"

255

"Well, shoot, no!"

"I'm young yet," she said vehemently, as if arguing with herself. "I can still have a good life, even kids, a family. I can make a whole new start in California. Or somewhere."

Clem suddenly felt sorry for her, because she didn't sound as if she believed it; in fact, she sounded kind of hopeless. But at least she could see a lot of new country.

The sun went down behind the blue-black skyline of Amarillo before they got there, and it was full night when they left the last lights behind. Clem was yawning, because it was his usual bedtime. With Daylight Saving Time it didn't get dark until around nine any more.

"Listen, that yawning is contagious," said Della. "You crawl over in the back seat and flake out—as Royce would say. Damn him, anyway, I guess he's going to haunt me for a long time." She shook her head as if to shake Nolan from her mind. "Don't worry about me, I'll stop for coffee presently and take some don't-snooze tablets. Will it bother you if I turn the radio up louder?"

"Heck, no," he said, because it didn't matter whether it would or not—just so she kept herding that little old Pontiac toward Carrizozo, New Mexico. He was probably too churned up to sleep, anyway, and besides there wasn't room on the back seat for his lanky frame unless he jackknifed it in what would soon become an uncomfortable position. He felt for his mother's birthday card in his pocket, remembering what she had written on it:

I can't believe you're really fourteen, Clem dear, and that the last time I saw you you were not yet twelve! I'll bet you've grown so much I'd scarcely recognize you. I wish I had a recent photo of you—don't they take school pictures anymore? I'd like to show everybody here what a handsome son I have.

256

He thought about the school pictures. They cost a couple bucks, and besides he wasn't photogenic and would have just acted nutty with the other kids around. Anyway, it simply hadn't occurred to him he ought to send her a picture so she'd know what he looked like. Well, shoot, she'd see for herself tomorrow—and he sure hoped she wouldn't be too disappointed.

Folks, meet my handsome son from Oklahoma . . .

When he woke up with aching knees it was velvety-gray daybreak and the car was parked off the highway, with Della snoring on the front seat. Badly needing to use a restroom and stretch his sore cramped legs, he got out stealthily so as not to disturb her. He didn't even shut the door, although a couple of big noisy diesel trucks were going by, tires whining loudly. Stretching in the pre-dawn gloom, he saw the purple mountain looming against the eastern sky, and suddenly thought, Boy, this is the *West!* This has got to be New Mexico!

When he got back to the car, Della was awake and they drove into Tucumcari, where they stopped for gas and breakfast. After Tucumcari, Clem expected to see mountains all around, but they fell away behind them and it was just rolling hills that soon seemed monotonous, just miles and miles of fenced rangeland, with no country stores or service stations—and no water. When he brought Pedro and Duke on out here, he'd have to camp in the bar-ditches at night, with no wood for cookfires, for days on end; he'd need three or four more canvas waterbags, at least. A knot of worry grew in his stomach, because he just hadn't realized the West would be like this—somehow he'd thought there would be tourist attractions every few miles.

"Well," Della yawned, "how do you like New Mayhico?"

"Okay," he sighed. There wasn't much grass along the

257

highway; he'd have to stop when they came to places where Pedro could graze awhile.

"We ought to be there by two o'clock, according to my arithmetic," Della informed him cheerfully, but that was in the car. She was thinking in terms of miles a minute, and he'd be lucky to do ten miles a day in this kind of country. It was so depressing that he forced himself to quit even thinking about it and tried to imagine what the reunion would be like—and suddenly he got all nervous and flutter-gutted about *that*.

Well, shoot, he'd just grin at her and say—oh, something casual like, "Hey, lady, I came to take you back to Oklahoma—I got the extradition papers . . ." Well, no, that sounded silly. "Hello, Mom, I happened to be in New Mexico and I just thought I'd drop in and say hi." No, doggonnit. I'll just say—well, I'll give her a grin and say, "Hello, Mom . . . it's great to see you—wonderful to see you again . . ."

He got the map from the seat and Della said, "We stay on Fifty-four all the way, hon." Clem said he was just check-ing. In the lower right-hand corner it said "How to read your map of New Mexico," and under that were Highway Markers, Road Classifications, Mileages, Special Features, and Population Symbols. According to the last, any town marked with a plain circle had a population of less than two hundred and fifty people. Checking where they were now, he saw there were three such towns in about a sixty-mile stretch, so maybe it wouldn't be as bad coming through here as he'd figured. That first stretch had been twenty-one miles, this one was twelve, the next would be ten, then fifteen on to a city of over two thousand. Boy, according to this map there were quite a few of those dinky little towns, close enough to the highway so maybe he could camp at the edge of them. At least the water and ice prob-

258

lem would be solved. But then he saw that on that last stretch to Carrizozo there were forty-three miles without any towns at all! And mostly mountains, it looked like!

Shook up, he folded the map and watched the low hills roll astern, listening to Della humming along with the Mexican music from the radio. As they passed through one of the towns, Della said, "These houses look pretty Mexican, don't they, hon?"

He said he'd noticed that, too. Thinking, They don't like to be called Mexicans any more, though—Spanish-Americans, I'll have to remember that.

"I know it's colorful an' picturesque an' all," Della remarked, "but I wouldn't much want to live around here. Too hot."

"Well, maybe it's nice in the winter," he said optimistically.

"All I know, hon, is that I'm happier and happier I decided to make this safari and save you a long hike—my God! Think of anyone havin' to cross this desert on foot!"

Yeah, my *God!* he said to himself, thinking of just that. Right now, though, the deeper into New Mexico he got, the more he felt the tight pull and drag of two invisible wires, one stretching on ahead to his mother, the other tightening behind him, its far end anchored to a tree full of redbirds and robins on a shady clear creek east of Conifer.

At long last the highway began to climb and twist and there were scrubby trees like cedars or spruce. They were in the mountains. The map said this was the Cibola National Forest, but the real timber was probably higher up in the hazy blue ranges to the west. Boy, he could enjoy the scenery now, if he didn't keep thinking of having to look at it again in August on foot.

When they descended to sun-scorched lowlands again, some real desert now with cactus and yucca, the still mountains loomed close on the left, and it was less than fifty miles to Carrizozo.

"First thing we'll do when we get there, hon," Della said with a weary yawn, "we'll go shopping and buy you a classy sport shirt and some white Levis—and some sandals, too. Huaraches, they call 'em out here, I think."

He was pleased and touched. She must have been reading his mind. He'd been thinking how he looked in his old lengthened denims and tennis shoes. But he felt obliged to protest a little. "Well, hey, listen, it's costing you enough already."

"It isn't really my money, hon, it'll be coming out of the dependent's check from your daddy's Social Security, so it's really your money. We were supposed to feed and clothe you with it, and that's all I'm doing, isn't it?"

Well, he wasn't about to give her any flack. After all, he hadn't been any financial burden to the Nolans during the last half of June, or July, and she'd be getting another check in a few days. About fifty-three dollars, he thought it was. Gosh, if he could get that much every month and earn a few bucks washing dishes or something, he could make out okay out here . . .

A sign at the edge of Carrizozo said Pop. 1,623, El. 5,247, which put the town pretty high up in the mountains. Della found a clothing store in what seemed to be a genuine adobe building and decided to be extravagant, buying *two* shirts and *two* pairs of Levis, and two pairs of colorful socks to go with the Mexican sandals.

"Let's face it," she said, "you need a whole new wardrobe for school next fall. After I get home, as soon as the July and August checks come, I'll endorse them and have Mrs. Whittle hold them for you. Then when you get back you can buy some winter shirts an' a windbreaker an' like that, okay?"

"Okay," he said, thinking he could write to Mrs. Whittle and she would have Ken deliver the checks to him, along with a batch of doughnuts or something, somewhere along that old endless highway. In this desert country a guy probably wouldn't need as much clothing . . .

Returning to the stuffy closed car with the packages, he started worrying about changing into some of the new clothes before going to the sanitarium. But Della had everything under control. There was a motel just before you got to the turn-off to the sanitarium, which was on a rise about a quarter of a mile east of the highway and looked kind of like a small college campus from a distance. Della pulled in and stopped at the office.

"We'll rent a room now an' clean up before we go on over," she said, getting out. "Mercy, will a shower feel good!"

When he was all dressed, with his rather shaggy hair neatly combed, he looked in the mirror and thought, Not too bad—you throw about twenty pounds of meat on there and you'd have something an average mother wouldn't be ashamed of. Anyway, his dad had been tall and lanky, so maybe she'd figure it was just natural for him to be gawky. But well-dressed, boy. He couldn't remember when he'd felt this presentable.

NINETEEN

I̲т was pleasantly cool in the lobby, with comfortable chairs. Della leaned back and closed her eyes. She was tired and sleepy on account of him, and he hadn't really thanked her properly yet. He wanted to, but so far he just hadn't been able to think of the right words. Boy, she was okay.

"Listen, hon," she said with her eyes shut, "you let me say hello first, I'll only stay a few minutes. Then I'll go on back to the motel and sleep a few hours—you won't mind walking back over there when they run you out of here, will you?"

"Shoot, no," he said. "I'm used to walking, Dell."

She opened one eye and smiled at him. "I guess you are, at that. Anyway, sweetie, you let me snooze until about ten o'clock, then I'll head for home. I asked the motel manager to call the bus station in town and find out how much a ticket back to Clintsburg will cost, and I'll give you the money. Then tomorrow he'll transfer you to a cheaper room, and I'll pay a couple days rent on that and give you some eating money, okay?"

Feeling kind of crummy, he said okay. Doggonnit, he'd need all the money he had just to be sure of getting out here again. Someday he'd make it up to Della, and if she was going to sell all of Royce's cattle—which she had paid for in the first place, according to a fuss he'd overheard last winter—she would have lots of money, maybe a couple thousand bucks.

Thinking about the hot desert outside this cool building, it occurred to him that sand and lava and mountains and skimpy desert plants was all the scenery his mother had seen for over two years. No wonder all her postcards had looked the same.

A young suntanned man, in Bermuda shorts and a sport shirt even more colorful than Clem's, was coming briskly across the room.

"You're the Marlows?" he asked, and Clem had a sudden attack of stage fright. After a second he stood up saying, "I am, and this is Mrs. Nolan, our cousin."

The man nodded at Della. "I'm Dr. Duncan." He stared at Clem with not very friendly intentness.

"Well, it's about time you came to see your mother," the doctor said. "Where the dickens have you been for the past two years, anyway, fella?"

It caught Clem off balance, and suddenly his confused emotions overwhelmed him. The breath caught in his constricted chest and throat, and he gave a ragged, gulping sigh, feeling his face go stiff, squeezing his eyelids shut against the tears. He slumped into the chair and leaned forward, hiding his face from the doctor.

"I didn't know . . . she w-was goin' to b-be here . . . this long," he said through clenched teeth. "I live . . . I l-live . . ." He gestured vaguely, gasping for air. "Oklahoma," he managed to say. "In the eastern part. I didn't think . . . I didn't know sh-she'd be . . ."

"Aw, hey, fella!" Dr. Duncan said, embarrassed. "I wasn't really criticizing you, son. I was only . . ." He sighed.

And Della said in a flat, weary voice, "For your information, Mister, Clemmie was walking out here to see his

263

mother. It's only about eight hundred darn miles, and he wanted to see his mother bad enough to *walk* that far." She sounded a little emotional herself.

"Walk?" the doctor said. "You mean hitchhike?"

"I mean walk!" she said. "With a little dinky burro an' a two-wheel cart to haul his stuff in, an' his dog. But he had to walk."

"I rode through the towns," Clem said, gaining control of his tears. "On paved streets I rode the cart."

"You wanta know where I found him?" Della asked furiously. "You wanta know how far he had already walked, Mister?"

The doctor nodded.

"He was three hundred miles from home, that's all. We live seventeen miles from the Arkansas line, an' he was clear out in western Oklahoma limpin' along the damn highway. So don't you stand there and imply he doesn't love his mother!"

The doctor held up his hands in rueful surrender. "I didn't mean that and it certainly isn't true. I was tactless, and I apologize."

"Well," Della said forgivingly, maybe because he was, after all, a personable young man, "we're both pretty tired, and I shouldn't have been so touchy, I guess."

"Tell you what," the doctor said, "let's all have a cold Coke and start over." He went after the soda as if glad to escape.

"Are you all right, hon?" Della asked, and of all the times she had asked him that, it was the first time it ever sounded like she really wanted to know. Clem shrugged and nodded.

"I'm okay," he muttered. "Sorry I acted like a baby."

"Listen, sweetie," she told him earnestly, "don't you ever be ashamed of showing honest emotion. Maybe if more men could shed a tear now an' then, this old world wouldn't be so loused up."

Well, okay, he thought. But do it in private, for gosh sakes, don't make a spectacle of yourself.

"We both got upset," Della said, laughing a little. "You think I should apologize to young Dr. Kildare?"

Clem said to forget it, and Dr. Duncan returned with three frosty Cokes and pulled a chair around facing Clem, and said, "Tell me about where you live. I'm from New Jersey, myself. This your first trip to desert country? What do you think of it, so far?"

A trifle confused, Clem said yes, this was the first time he'd even actually realized there was country like this in the U.S.A., and where he lived there were all kinds of trees and plants and rivers and creeks and it was called the foot-hills of the Ozarks, and you had some cold weather and snowstorms in winter, but boy, from about April until November it was great. And to tell the honest truth, he didn't care too much for this desert country.

"I've heard a lot about that region," the doctor said. "All those lakes—Tankiller, Bull Shoals, Grand Lake, Texhoma. Lots of great fishing, right?"

Clem nodded, thinking, Why is he stalling around like this? Something must be wrong, or the doctor wouldn't be wasting his time in conversation.

Della cut straight to the point and said, "Could I go in for a few minutes first? I need to go on to the motel and grab some shuteye, but Clemmie can stay as long as he wants—or as long as you'll let him. I'll have to start on back tonight, for any number of reasons, but he'll take the bus in a few days."

The doctor nodded. "Okay by me, if it's all right with Clem."

Clem nodded. Boy, from now on, anything Della wanted

265

was okay with him. Besides, now that he was actually here, he felt a strange reluctance to see his mother. She might be so changed . . .

A nurse came into the lobby and nodded to Dr. Duncan, and he said, "Well, I guess she's finished primping. You can go on in."

So Della left them, and Clem felt very self-conscious.

"If you were a married man," the other told him with a grin, "you'd understand the delay, Clem. She wanted to get prettied up."

And Clem finally said it, anxiously. "How *is* she, sir?"

The doctor swished his Coke around and frowned. "Son, we have a stock answer for that, as you may know. We usually say a patient is doing as well as can be expected. But I've already made one mistake with you, and I won't try for two. I know you didn't come eight hundred miles just to be kidded." He measured the fluid content of the bottle with a professional eye and lowered it a swallow's worth. "Frankly, Clem, she hasn't been doing too well this past year."

Clem felt like he was turning to stone, and it was all he could do to speak. "Well," he said, clearing his throat, "I thought . . ." He'd *known* something was wrong, after all this time! "I thought there was all these new like miracle drugs nowadays . . ."

The doctor nodded with a wry smile. "Yes, we have them, Clem. And sometimes they actually work miracles. But maybe the latest up-to-the-minute medical discovery is the frequently baffling fact that medical treatment alone is often not enough, and a great deal depends on the patient's emotional attitude, his will, or lack of will, to get well. Now, I've only been here a year, but they tell me your mother responded to treatment and her prognosis was very good for quite a while. Then it leveled off. She didn't get worse,

266

but she didn't get better, either. And I have a hunch in her case the biggest problem was the fact that she was so lonely."

He nodded glumly. "She kind of gave up because she was homesick and discouraged," he said.

"Your visit may be just the tonic she needs," the doctor said, slapping Clem on the knee. "I'd say you're just what the doctor would have ordered. Listen, son, you tell her you'll come back again—say during the Christmas vacation, so she'll have that to look forward to. And you write to her a couple times a month, telling her you expect her home reasonably soon. You know, you *could* hitchhike out at Christmas, and I guarantee you'll be well fed and housed while you're here."

I won't need to hitchhike, I'll *be* here Christmas, Clem thought, but for some reason he didn't feel like informing Dr. Duncan of his plans. He might not approve.

"I want to emphasize the importance of writing her often," the doctor said, getting out a cigarette. "You want one?" he asked, holding out the pack.

Shaking his head, Clem thought, He thinks I'm *that* old!

"Good for you," Dr. Duncan told him. "Acquiring the habit is easy, kicking it very difficult. But like I said, pal, you keep those cards and letters coming. That's an order."

He chatted on about smoking for a while, and then Della came out. "Your mom's anxiously waitin' for you, hon. I told her how thoughtful an' sweet you were about cleanin' up the kitchen every evening an' all that." She gave him a meaningful look. "Remember now, don't upset her."

Nodding, Clem got to his feet feeling pretty weak-kneed, like he had to stand up in front of the class and recite a poem.

"Listen, hon, let me sleep until about ten, okay? You can watch TV—or if you get sleepy, just have the manager call me. Remind me to give you some money—or maybe I'd

267

better leave it out for you when I get over there." She sighed and waved her hands helplessly. "I don't even know what I'm sayin', Clemmie. See you later." She headed for the door, but turned back again. "You don't mind walkin' over?" she asked, then shrugged. "I already asked you, didn't I?"

"Come along, pal," Dr. Duncan said, taking Clem in tow.

It was a bright, pleasant room with booths at either end that were closed by glass partitions. Clem suddenly felt terribly let down. He'd figured at worst they'd only be separated by a table, and he'd hoped in the back of his mind that he might get to touch her, even if only to sort of shake hands. He hadn't expected to get to hug her or kiss her or anything like that, but gee whiz, he sure would like to *touch* her again.

There were microphones to speak through and she was standing up with her hands touching the glass and looking through it in a half-smiling, eager way, and he would have known her anywhere. She was thinner, and her auburn hair was streaked with gray, and there was a kind of fragility to her eager smile. But her eyes were the same, dark and beautiful.

For a long, shy moment they just stared, his mother smiling and Clem grinning foolishly, and then she said, "Oh, Clem, is it really you?" in that husky voice he'd missed so terribly. "Oh, my, just look at how you've grown! Somehow I expected you to look just the same, isn't that silly? You're so *tall,* and lanky—just like your daddy! And so *handsome!*"

He grinned self-consciously with a fist-sized lump in his throat—he'd imagined this reunion a thousand times, trying to plan what he'd say to her, and now all he could say was "Hello, Mom." That damn glass partition didn't help matters any. Finally he blurted, "How are you?"

"Oh, ever so much better, now that you've come to see

me," she said, and he remembered the last time he'd heard that pleasant low voice was when she was leaving to come out here—her last words had been: *Now you mind your grandmother and behave yourself or I'll be forced to come back here and whack your backside, young man.* That was a century ago, and boy, he'd wished hundreds of times she'd come back and really whale the tar out of him, if that's what it would take. Once a day, even—and twice on Sundays.

She seemed at a loss for words, too. Then she reached into the pocket of her robe and said, "I look at this real often, darling." She held up his final report card, which he'd sent at the end of school. "I show it to everybody and brag about what a smart son I have." Then with mock severity, "But what's your excuse for spoiling all those lovely A's with a C-plus in penmanship?"

Smiling at her, he confessed his own bafflement about his writing. You'd think a guy with a talent for drawing would write neatly, but it didn't work out that way. "What I think it is," he said, grinning, "I got a batch of bad pencils."

"Same old Clem," she said. "You always did come up with original alibis. Maybe your penmanship would improve if you wrote more letters, son. Know what I mean?"

He nodded, thinking, They're not feeding her the right stuff, she's too slim. Then he thought, Look who's talking. She's probably worrying about me being so skinny.

They just looked at each other a little longer, then she said, "How do you like New Mexico?"

"Terrific," he said. "Or do you want me to be honest about it?"

She smiled. "Great place to visit, but I wouldn't want to try raising potatoes and corn here. Oh, Clem, how I miss the trees, and the changing seasons back home. Sometimes I'd give a million dollars just to spend a few hours back

269

there in the blessed woods, sitting on a stump looking at the oaks and hickories."

Swallowing a lump, he said, "Next spring's bound to be great, and we'll *be* there, huh? Both of us. You'll be all well by then, Dr. Duncan said, and we'll go back . . ." He stopped, a little flustered. Not so much because he'd given away his plans, but because it struck him that school wouldn't be out yet here.

She was giving him a curious, soberly searching look. "Did you say *we'll* go back, son?"

So he told her, in a torrent of words that tripped over each other. "I'm coming out here to stay until you're well, me and Duke and Pedro, we're already practically halfway here, they've got great schools out here, and I can find some kind of part-time job in Carrizozo and come see you practically every day . . ."

"Oh, no, darling," she said. "You can't do that!"

Well, he'd expected her to not be grabbed by the idea right at first. But he'd expected to argue her into it without too much trouble, only now no matter what he said, she just wouldn't listen.

"It just isn't practical or feasible, darling. Oh, I would love to see you every day. And if we were rich people—but all we have, Clem darling, is the Social Security money and the rent money from our place, not enough . . ."

She stopped because of his expression. "Hey, you mean we still own our old place, Mom? You mean we still got a home?"

"Oh, Clem, didn't you know that?" she asked him. "Of course we still have our home, only it's rented to strangers now. We get sixty dollars a month, and they pay the taxes— but you know how renters treat a place." She sighed. "We'll probably have to do a lot of repairing and cleaning up when we move back in—but in the meantime, if you came out

270

here, it would create so many problems, darling. You're under age and would probably have to live in a foster home, with strangers—I've always taken some consolation from just knowing you were living with relatives."

Relatives, he thought. Like Royce. Friends? Name a couple. Well, Mrs. Whittle. And maybe Molly Hicks. Of course, back east of Conifer in their own neighborhood, he had old friends. "Well, shoot," he said without much conviction, "I could find me some kind of job out here, Mom. Washin' dishes or something. I could rent a room . . ."

She shook her head. "No matter how tall you are, darling, you're still only fourteen, and there are laws—besides, I don't want you working, I want my smart son concentrating on his studies, making big fat A's."

He shrugged, feeling in spite of himself a certain guilty relief. "I guess it was a pretty dumb idea."

"It was a very sweet and touching idea," she said, "but it wasn't practical. Darling, you'd be so homesick out here, believe me, I know—and there'd be no point in *both* of us feeling miserable and uprooted, now would there? Although I miss you like the very dickens, it pleases and reassures me to think of you back home waiting for me—and I promise you it won't be much longer. I really and truly believe I'll be home in time to share next spring with you. You'll see, I'll be telling our tenants to move out the first of the year and we'll move back in and plant a big garden. Oh, how I yearn to watch things grow again, and store food for the winter. We'll have a cow and chickens and pigs, and I'll fatten you up, old boy, just wait and see if I don't."

They smiled at each other happily, and he thought how terrific it would be, going back to the old neighborhood, fishing and hunting and swimming.

"You see," she chided, "you didn't really want to stay out here."

271

"No, but I aimed to, Mom."

"I know and I bless you for it, even if I can't allow you to," she said. "If one of us has to be here, the other one has to be there. Holding down the fort."

It was easy to agree with her now. Della might even change her mind and not leave old Royce—women *did* change their minds a lot, didn't they? Shoot, even if she went through with it, a guy could stand some court-appointed foster home for a few months, even a year, if necessary. Anyway, he wasn't about to tell his mother he wouldn't have anywhere to live now. Wait until he found out where he would be, then he could pretend in letters that it was a real break for him . . .

A tall nurse came into view on his mother's side of the glass and smiled through it at him. "I hate to break this up, but too much happiness all at once is bad for the metabolism or something. You come back at ten o'clock in the morning, and you can talk longer, maybe a couple hours."

"We've settled the big issues," his mother said with a twinkly smile. "Tomorrow we can just gossip. Darling, I'm so glad you came, you've made me very happy, Clem . . ."

"Me, too," he said. "Only I should have come sooner, Mom."

His mother gave him a little wave, and he watched her walk away, kind of slow like she wasn't too strong, or didn't have much energy, anyway. But she looked back and grinned and gave him a big happy wink . . .

He wasn't in any great hurry to head for the motel, so when he went back to the cool lobby, he got a Coke out of the machine and sat down, beginning to have a kind of pleasantly rubber-jointed reaction. Boy, he just couldn't believe he was really here and had really seen his mother again. It was almost as if those two long, lonely years were erased, as if they hadn't happened. All that sad, worrying

272

time and awful distance had been bridged now. And she hadn't looked half as bad as he'd feared; in fact, she looked great, except for being thin, and that didn't really mean anything. Look at him, and he was strong as a horse.

After a while he got up and walked on back to the motel. When he reached the Pontiac, he suddenly remembered Mrs. Whittle's box. He sure wouldn't mind a couple of doughnuts or cookies to hold him until dinner. Cutting the string and splitting the masking tape, he opened the box eagerly, and there on top of some waxed paper was a pale-green envelope, and under the waxed paper were doughnuts and cookies both. Chocolate chip cookies, practically his favorites. Stuffing one in his mouth, he opened the letter and began reading, and after a few lines he jumped in the air, nearly spilling everything.

"Dear Clem," Mrs. Whittle had written in a tidy long-hand that made him a little envious, "Mrs. Nolan has told me of her decision, so I will try to be simple and direct. Don't worry about where you will live when you come back, for I want you to stay with me. I've grown very fond of you and your menagerie and find myself missing all three of you and feeling quite lonely. Besides, I need someone to help me 'run the ranch,' and I yearn for someone to cook for. Ken's trucker friends stop by frequently for coffee and pie, but I get terribly frustrated at mealtimes with nobody here to appreciate my chicken and roasts. Eating alone is no fun at all.

"It happens that the county judge is an old classmate and family friend and I'm sure there will be no difficulty about getting official permission for you to stay with me, and you need not feel in the least obliged or beholden, as I'm sure you will more than earn your board and room—and so will your four-legged friends. Especially Duke, as I am having

273

a dickens of a time with rabbits and woodchucks raiding my garden. They eat the carrot tops and the peanut vines and cabbages, and later on that old woodchuck will be after my tomatoes. Pedro will earn his keep, too, since I have grand plans for a rock garden and nothing to haul rocks in until you return.

"You must tell your mother all about me and our long friendship. Let her read this letter. Now that Mrs. Nolan is giving you a lift and you won't need to hike all that incredible distance and back, I should judge you'll be coming home in August—in time for us to start hauling rocks, and wood for the fireplace.

"Meanwhile, drop me a card with your mother's address and I will write to her. For her immediate information you might tell her I'm sixty-seven but still hale and hearty, and I will see to it that you study industriously and write to her at least once a week." It was signed, "Affectionately, Ellen Whittle."

Clem read it through again to be sure it said what he thought it said, then he flopped off the bench onto the grass and grinned dazedly up at the cloudless sky. If I'm dreaming, don't wake me up! he thought. Wow. WOW! WAHOOOO!

Usually he didn't much approve of divorce, but he sure hoped Della wouldn't go back to Royce. Even if she did renege, surely she would let him live with the best cook in eastern Oklahoma. Man oh man, live in that neat house with a fireplace, television, all those books, all that great food . . .

About Friday he'd say goodbye to his mother and grab a bus for Clintsburg and try to argue Gaylord into taking his rightful half of the reward money. Then he'd aim old Pedro for Feather, and by the time he got there, the schoolgrounds ought to need mowing again, and if Duke wasn't ready to travel yet—or, heck, even if he was—he might hang around a couple of days and let Dixie Funkhouser give him some more tennis lessons. Any stuff like that he could learn this summer would be a great help when school started in September. A couple of months of Mrs. Whittle's cooking ought to fleshen him up some, but even if it didn't, he was all permanently done with clowning—and besides, with new clothes he wouldn't feel so self-conscious. But if people like old Kirby Newman wanted to kid him, okay, what the heck, he could take it. Up to a certain point. But if they wanted trouble, he would buy that, too. People like little Molly Hicks wouldn't poke fun at him, and maybe after knowing a cool girl like Dixie, he'd be able to talk to Molly.

All the truck drivers would be surprised to see him heading back east, and some of them were bound to stop and ask, "Hey, Clem, ain't you goin' the wrong way?" And he'd just shrug and say, "I already *been* to New Mexico, now I'm on the return trip." He could make a joke about how he discovered a new shortcut.

Heading for the motel coffee shop for some milk to go with the cookies, he decided to look for a picture postcard to send Mrs. Whittle, whose letter would sure take a load off Della's mind, probably. Sonofagun! It was sure as heck a load off *his* mind!

One thing about it, next fall when the teacher had them write themes about what they'd done this summer, he oughta be able to think of *something* to write about.